OBSESSED

WILD MOUNTAIN SCOTS, #1

JOLIE VINES

Editing by Emmy Ellis at Studio ENP

Proofreading by Zoe Ashwood

Cover design by Elle Thorpe at Images For Authors

Cover model photography by and copyright of Regina Wamba www.reginawamba.com

Cover model: Steven Christensen

❀ Created with Vellum

PRAISE FOR JOLIE'S SCOTS

A selection of five-star reviews:

- If you loved Jolie's *Marry the Scot* series, buckle up, because this new generation are **hotter, edgier and sexier** – Elle Thorpe, author of the *Dirty Cowboy* series
- Highly recommended for anyone looking for **a modern-day Highlander to swoon over** – Viper, Goodreads reviewer
- I swear, every time I pick up a Jolie Vines book, I think: this is him, my favorite hero, **no one will be able to top him.** And then I read the next book and the process begins again - Chikapo9, Goodreads reviewer
- Jolie Vines has fast become a **one-click author** for me - J. Saman, bestselling author
- I loved this book! It had all that I would expect with **hot Scots and rambling castles** – Paula, Goodreads reviewer

To those who put their lives on the line to aid lost souls

BLURB

He's the leader of the mountain rescue service. She might just need saving.

Lochie
For too long, I've been alone. Just me and my daughter. Keeping her safe is everything, so taking a job in the remote Scottish Highlands suits us fine.

I shouldn't need anything more.

Yet I'm beyond distracted by a lass.

Smart, beautiful, and living right next door, Cait McRae makes it clear she's not interested.

Every sly glance tells another story.

It's all I can do not to throw her over my shoulder and take her home.

Cait might claim she only wants to explore the physical, but I know she's wrong.

She's mine.

If the people pursuing us both don't destroy what we've found.

Cait

I always knew I was different. No one ever caught my eye.

Until a huge, scowling man moves in next door. He's the new head of the mountain rescue service, and a single dad to a sweet little girl.

Turns out, I'm a late bloomer, as all I can think about is Lochie.

But someone else wants me.

A series of strange events point to one conclusion. **I have a stalker, and the danger I'm in is only just starting.**

--

The *Wild Mountain Scots* series follows on from the *Wild Scots* series with more of your favourite McRaes. Meet the **brooding, tough, protective men of the mountain rescue** and the beautiful women who tame their hearts.

READER NOTE

Dear reader,

Thank you for picking up *Obsessed*, the first in my series about the men of the mountain rescue. Get ready to swoon!

In case you didn't know, the series comes hot on the heels of the *Wild Scots* books—five of Cait's cousins have already had their romances.

If you've read those, have you met their daddies? The *Marry the Scot* series features the fathers of the *Wild Scots* and *Wild Mountain Scots* crew.

All the stories are standalone, and each has its own happily ever after.

Be sure to check out Obsessed's delicious audiobook too!

Enjoy my hot Scots.

Love, Jolie x

THE McRAE & FITZROY FAMILIES

Marry the Scot - Series 1
Wild Scots - Series 2
Wild Mountain Scots - Series 3

Julie's Scots

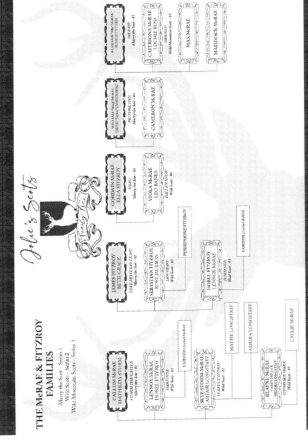

1

*L*ochinvar

From a short distance away, the white piece of paper under my car's windscreen wiper fluttered in the breeze, innocuous even as it tore through my peace of mind.

The folded note bore my name—my old name—written in a bold pen.

We'd been found.

My heart pounded, and panic washed through me. A day of travel lay behind us. Weeks of planning this journey now wasted. We'd have to get back on the road and leave Scotland again. I dug my fingers into my hair, stifling a howl of frustration.

All the preparation. All the careful arrangements. Ruined.

With rigid, locked muscles, I glanced around the car park, squinting at the people hustling in and out of the service station. Someone was watching us. We had to go.

"Da? You're crushing my hand." Isla tugged her fingers from mine. "When we get to the cottage, I want to put my unicorn duvet on my new bed, then I'm going to line up all my books on the shelf. There will be a bookshelf, won't there?"

I answered through gritted teeth, "Sorry, sweetheart. We cannae go."

My tiny daughter's expression dropped. "No! Ye promised."

I'd promised more than that, though she'd never know exactly how much. Gripping her hand once more, I strode the distance to the car, alert for attack.

Isla wailed, dragging her feet.

"Remember what I told ye?" I asked her. "We need to stay safe."

"I know. That's why I'm Isla Ross now, and not our other name. That's why we came here. Da, please don't change your mind."

We reached my newly purchased off-roader, and I snatched the paper from the windscreen. "This is why. Someone has followed us and put this here. We have to leave. Right now."

Under her mop of blonde curls, Isla's eyes widened. "No, Da—"

"I know you're disappointed, but we have each other and that's all we need. I'll do anything and everything to protect ye."

Tears filled her eyes, and I clamped down more on my urge to yell. This wasn't fair, not on the six-year-old who needed a stable home. Not on me, a man exhausted by worry.

We had nowhere else to go.

"I wrote the note!" Isla burst out.

I halted my spiralling thoughts. "What?"

"It's mine. I put it under there for you to find when we

came back from the bathroom. I'm sorry." She burst into a flood of tears and threw her arms around my waist.

Fear receded, and I stared at the piece of paper, crumpled in my hand. *L. MacNeill,* it read. I flipped it open, and inside was a red heart, drawn in crayon.

I love you, daddy. From Isla, was scrawled underneath.

Oh fuck. Oh fucking God.

I'd officially aged a year in sixty seconds.

"Sorry," Isla blubbed.

I crouched and wrapped her in a hug. It took a long minute before I could speak. "Christ, sweetheart. Naw, it's me who's sorry. I jumped to a conclusion."

"I wrote it when we were driving, using the new pens Auntie Blair gave me. I thought you'd like it. My letters are so neat."

"They are. Perfectly so." I hushed her, stroking over her yellow hair, so different to my dark-as-night own.

I needed to calm the hell down.

No one knew where we were. Even my sister didn't have our new address. Isla was still safe. We could continue.

With another hug, I strapped my lass back into her car seat and kissed her forehead, then drove us on.

The last forty minutes took us deep into the Highlands of Scotland, to a remote estate where I had a new job and we'd settle in a new home. For a while, we could hide and be happy.

Yet the echo of my alarm still infected me.

I drove, edging over the speed limit, needing to escape the sense of danger.

Finally there, I pulled up outside our cottage—one of two that backed onto a thick pine forest and a good distance from any other property. Isla sat forward, peering out.

"What's that woman doing to her door? Is she painting

words on it? That's naughty. I can see a 'B', then an 'I' and a 'T'. Oh, but the paint is running."

I stared, too. Our neighbour, a woman I'd yet to speak to but who my boss had assured me would help with childcare if my job called me out late, was gazing at her front door, not noticing us.

Then I saw the painted slur.

There was no chance she'd done this herself.

My anger spiked again because I'd had it with threats, worry, and stress. With driving four hundred miles and thinking I'd have to drive us back.

Whatever the fuck was going on here had one pissed-off Scotsman to contend with.

2

Cait

The red paint dripped like blood, and I gazed at my cottage door, my gut tight.

Of all the emotions I could stir in another person, obsession scared me the most. This had all the hallmarks of a spurned lover. Except that was hardly the case.

As a pre-teen, I'd been followed by boys who asked me out, caught on my apparently perfect face. Likewise, teenaged me gained admirers in droves.

Until they got to know me better. Then, they gave up.

No amount of good looks could replace the fact that I had nothing to offer them. Or them to me. Zero, zip, nada sexy feelings. It hadn't happened for me once, not for any boy, man, or woman. It had become common knowledge that Cait McRae just wasn't interested.

I still feared the attention. The infatuation my birth mother had had for my father that led to the disastrous first few months of my life.

At twenty-three, I'd hoped the days of random crushes were past me.

The events of the recent few months and now the word splattered on the entrance to my home told another story.

Bitch, it read.

Well, thanks very much, weirdo.

Gravel crunched behind me, and I twisted around. Two people exited a car. A man and a little girl.

My new neighbours, I assumed, and my heart sank. Why the ever-loving heck did they need to arrive right at this moment?

"Back in the car," the man barked at his daughter.

She did as ordered, and he stalked over to me.

"What the hell is this?" He glared at the door as if the slur was aimed at him, not me.

Lochinvar. That was his name. My uncle had recruited him as the new head of the mountain rescue. He looked the part, too. Dark hair, a close-cut beard, and dangerously intelligent almost-black eyes.

He was huge, too. A mountain of a man. Wide shoulders stretched his t-shirt, sizable muscles plain.

Instinctively, I took a step back. "This is my place. I'm Cait. I just arrived home and found it."

His gaze swept over me. "Ye havenae been inside?"

"Not yet."

"Unlock the door."

I bristled at the order but still obeyed. I'd seen enough horror movies to know that the woman should never enter the creepy house alone.

Except this wasn't a creepy house. It was my home, my lovely cottage that I'd decorated and furnished. My refuge from a busy life. The place where I intended to raise a family.

Besides, I wasn't on my own in this scenario.

The lock gave way, and I pushed inside, the stranger

right behind me. His heavy hand landed on my shoulder, and he restrained me, sweeping the living room with a fierce focus.

I flipped on the light against the evening's gloom and peered around. Nothing was out of place. Envelopes sat in a pile on my desk under the window, right where I'd left them. On the stone floor by the edge of the rug, my boots lined up undisturbed, and my sofa blanket draped at a jaunty angle, as I'd arranged it before work this morning. To the left, a clear line of sight into the kitchen gave the all-clear that way.

"I don't think anyone's been inside," I breathed.

Lochinvar grunted then strode in the opposite direction to the closed door of my bedroom.

"Wait!" I squeaked, leaping after him.

While the rest of my tiny four-roomed single-storey home was neat, my bedroom was the opposite. Next to my bed, a patio door led to a small paved space out the back, bracketed from the forest by a low wall, and I often used the space to dry my laundry on an airer. Last night, I'd arrived home late after dinner with my family and grabbed the airer inside, and this morning, I'd dumped the lot onto my quilt.

Lingerie. All of it.

Fancy lacy bras. Thongs with gauzy panels and embroidered flowers.

My new neighbour stuck his head inside. "Holy fuck," he muttered. "Someone's been in here. The dirty bastard's been in your drawers."

Hot, I squeezed past his huge frame and whipped the blanket over to conceal my underwear. "Nope. This is my doing. I left it like that."

Two dark eyebrows rose, then Lochinvar continued on

to the last closed door—the en suite. "Clear," he remarked and stalked back into the living room.

I closed my eyes for a second and tried to see a pattern in the recent minor disturbances. My stolen coat. My work emails opened before I'd read them. I had no idea who was behind it.

I'd also told very few people about it, too, and intended to keep it that way.

Where I lived, on a remote estate in Scotland, I was surrounded by family, which was both wonderful and slightly smothering. My parents and twin brothers respected my space, but if they heard about this...

A voice came from outside the cottage. "...paint on the door. Some arsehole up to no good. I need your police contact so we can get someone here."

Oh, flipping hell.

I rushed out, my hand up. "Please don't. I can handle this."

Lochinvar glowered, his eyebrows forming a solid line. He stuck his finger into his ear and turned away, listening to the conversation I could only assume he was having with my uncle, the man who'd hired him.

There was no chance Da wouldn't be here in twenty minutes.

"Aye. Grand. I'll do that." Lochinvar hung up and twisted back. "What's the problem? This needs reporting."

Annoyance rose at the presumption I couldn't handle this myself. "Did you seriously just tell my family? Do ye know what you've done? The whole estate will find out in minutes. How about minding your own business?"

He reared back. Then his eyes narrowed. "Do ye know who did this?"

I fought the urge to grind my teeth. "No, but I'm more

than capable of working it out on my own. I've been managing just fine for months."

I caught myself too late, and Lochinvar homed in on that sliver of information.

"This has happened before," he deduced.

"I didn't say that, and don't ye dare repeat it to my uncle, Da, or any other family member who comes steaming over."

My chest heaved, and I stared him down. Likewise, the stranger glared back, hands on his hips, and breathing hard.

We locked gazes.

Why the hell was he so angry? I was the one who'd been attacked.

The car door popping open claimed both our attentions.

"Da?" came a small voice. "Is it safe?"

Lochinvar broke eye contact with me and swivelled to go fetch his daughter: a sweet little darling with blonde curls and big eyes. I wanted to meet her, too—part of his coming to work here was the agreement that we'd help with looking after his child if he had rescue call-outs overnight. I'd volunteered for that, more than happy to have a little one to care for before I had my own family.

Except right now, I was so hopping mad with her father, I couldn't stand it.

I stomped inside and changed into old clothes then grabbed a bucket of soapy water and a scrubbing brush. Maybe if I was lucky, I could get rid of the evidence before anyone else saw it.

3

*L*ochinvar

At the gates of the wee village school, Isla turned her anxious gaze on me, the grey-and-green uniform we'd rustled up at late notice too big for her tiny frame. For the past couple of days, I'd made every effort to settle her in, and she was handling the changes well.

Like me, she coped.

"Tell me your name," I asked.

"Isla Ross," she said, no hesitation over what we'd practiced. "Will ye be picking me up?"

"I want to. For my first day, I hope I willnae be out on the hill. See ye this afternoon." I stooped and wrapped her in a tight hug, then sent her to scamper inside with the friendly teacher we'd met yesterday.

Ongoing, I'd rely on the school staff and locals to help with Isla's care if I had a call-out, but from what had happened after our arrival, I wasn't so confident with the original plan.

It bothered me that my neighbour hadn't wanted to tackle the fucker who'd painted abuse on her door. I guessed it was a boyfriend she'd fallen out with, which only made it worse. If she didn't stand up to him, he'd only do worse next time.

No way did I want that impacting my daughter if she happened to be in the house.

Annoyed, I got my arse into my car and stepped on the accelerator.

The road circled the loch, autumn winds churning up the grey waters.

It was a pretty place, the Cairngorms National Park, and reminded me of where I'd done the best part of my growing up—in Torridon, far to the north-west. I'd visited to climb the mountains but never lived or worked here. A remote and wild place, its charms were in the isolated, small communities, and the fact Isla and I could hide here while I still earned enough to live on.

It felt like home.

I'd researched the place carefully before I committed, but there were limits to what a man in my circumstances could do.

I passed a castle, then drove out to higher ground and onto a moor. A large aircraft hangar loomed in the distance. My workplace.

A man waited in the car park. He hailed me as I climbed out.

"Lochinvar Ross?"

"It is. Glad to meet ye, Mr McRae." So far, we'd only spoken on the phone. I strode over and shook his hand, taking in his blue jumpsuit and ready smile.

"Gordain, please. Come inside and I'll give ye the tour."

Inside the hangar, with its huge sets of doors opened to the concrete expanse outside, we passed a row of helicopters with busy crew and a class underway with an instructor at a whiteboard. The scent of oil and fuel hung in the air, redolent of the military base I'd left.

Gordain gestured at the throng. "Flight school and heli hire this side. Rescue service operates over here."

We continued on to a segmented part of the wide space. My gaze shot instantly to the gleaming helis, different to the for-hire ones. The first, the S-92, was a common sight for me, but the second was less so. I gravitated to the Sea King and patted her underbelly.

"I didnae expect to see one of these," I said.

"I've held on to her. Probably for sentimental reasons."

I switched my gaze back to Gordain. "Ex-military?"

"Aye, I was a pilot in the RAF. Ye served in the search and rescue career that I wanted."

He gestured to what must be the operations office, and I followed him in, lifting my chin to the offer of coffee.

Gordain poured us both a steaming mug, and we sat at a conference table. Around us, maps lined the walls. Incident boards waited on stands. The door to an equipment store lay ajar with high-visibility red jumpsuits on locker doors.

The tools of my trade.

I itched to get started.

Gordain indicated to the notes left up on one of the boards. "We had a call last night. Six hours to get a lad off the hill. Twenty-year-old on one of those challenges."

I snorted in dislike, knowing exactly what he meant. People came into the mountains to test themselves but also for bragging rights disguised as charity fundraising. Climbing the biggest mountains in the country on a time limit. Or worse, speeding between England then Wales to climb their highest peaks, too.

"No idiot should climb a mountain under a time constraint. They're asking for trouble."

"Aye, he was well-equipped at least, but the weather turned."

I could almost smell the night air. Feel the chill on my skin. I'd been made for this. The call. "Wish I could've helped out."

"I wasnae about to interrupt your settling in. Besides, ye won't have to wait long. Calls happen at all hours, and soon enough the responsibility for handling them will be all yours. This month is quieter, but next, we'll see an average of two a day, mostly clustered around weekends. Have ye talked to Cait yet about providing childcare?"

I took a swallow of the hot drink to cover my sudden stumble.

Cait, my neighbour, wasn't talking to me.

Once her door was scrubbed down, she'd crouched to introduce herself to Isla. She'd waved to my daughter every time since but had given me the cold shoulder.

As Cait had predicted, my interference had caused her family to descend on her cottage. From my position of taking luggage into my and Isla's place, I couldn't avoid witnessing her frustration with the drama. Her da had stomped around, waving his arms and making a fuss. Cait had glared daggers in my direction every time we made eye contact, including this morning from her desk in her window, but I wasn't sorry.

Whatever fucker had targeted her would think twice if he'd been watching.

Then again, she'd hinted that this was a continuing situation.

The urge came over me to find out more. Later, I'd try.

"Naw yet. I'll talk to her today."

"Grand. I'll take ye to Castle McRae to introduce ye to your backup, should Cait naw be available, but ye can always bring your lass here to the hangar and she can wait for collection. We're a big family and we look after our own."

We drank our coffees, and Gordain gave me the lowdown on the job I was taking over. My responsibilities covered a vast area, extending outside of the National Park. I had sixty people under my command, mostly volunteers, in various locations, and a wide range of connections to other emergency services. We spent the morning covering the basics, getting me up to speed with their processes.

Midway through a walkthrough of recent incident summaries, an alarm blared.

Gordain's head swivelled, and he leapt to grab a phone. After listening intently, he barked a series of questions, ones I automatically wanted to know the answers to. The casualty's location, age, and their status.

My pulse picked up.

I'd suspected I'd have little time to acclimatise before my first call-out, and this focus was what I needed.

Gordain got off the phone and took up a radio, instructing someone to rally the on-call list. As he spoke, he gripped my shoulder and pointed at the equipment store. We entered, and he indicated to a kit already laid out. A jumpsuit, weather gear, and a backpack.

L. Ross, it read on the identity label.

The reminder of seeing my old name on the note that almost derailed our arrival here barely touched me. This was my element, and I was ready to do battle.

I stripped my jeans and jacket and quickly dressed again, following my boss out of the hangar and to a 4X4.

Gordain drove us away from the mountain rescue base, all action, though his posture was relaxed in the way of a man comfortable in his role. "A baptism of fire for ye, aye?"

"Give me the details."

He filled me in with short sentences. A woman in her fifties, fallen while walking. A common occurrence, even with experienced hill walkers. Her husband was present but couldn't get her down the mountain alone. Gordain had arranged for a medical pickup, with six of us heading out to collect her.

"For today, watch and learn," he said. "Ye need time on the hill to know the place, and this is the best way to get it."

We sped along. I eyed the weather—grey and with reduced visibility from earlier—and put myself into the mindset of my position of command. In no time, Gordain would hand over the reins, and I'd be doing this alone. I'd rely on the support I'd yet to meet.

"Who's in the crew today?"

"Cameron is your right-hand man. He's leading the advanced party directly there."

I cast my mind to the list of names I'd already memorised. "Isn't he young for that?"

Gordain raised a shoulder. "He's twenty-two but a team leader, trainer, and one of my most valued crew members. He's also the land manager for the entirety of the two McRae estates, and my nephew. Cameron's a highly capable lad. He nearly always answers the call."

I held back my doubts at such a youngster being second-in-command. At thirty, I knew my mind, but had I eight years ago? I wasn't so sure.

"Can I ask why ye left the military?" Gordain took a turn up a steep track, off the main road now. We'd been all business this morning and hadn't tackled any personal information.

"My daughter. I couldnae commit to a tour and leave her

for months on end. I had limited options, and my term had been served. It was time to leave."

"Where's her mother?"

I knew this question would come. I had readied an answer, but even so, it grated to give up any details on the subject. "My wife is naw joining us. I'm everything to Isla."

Gordain watched me for a moment before returning his attention to the road. "I looked into your background carefully. It was an unusual request ye made of me, and I needed to be sure of who I was bringing into my employ."

A pilot friend had told me about this job. I'd needed a place to take Isla, but changing our names meant difficulties with my references. I was an honest man, and the subterfuge rankled.

Gordain knew the truth.

Well, one truth.

He'd accepted us with the answer to a single question—was I doing anything illegal or immoral? I'd told him no and that I was protecting my daughter. He'd offered me the job.

"Ye made a good choice trusting me," I said.

"I'm sure I have. Kin comes first, and I live by that. The reason I'm giving up this job for the winter is because I need to support my family. Viola, my daughter, is newly pregnant. A secret within the estate, by the way. Her husband is a musician. A famous one."

I didn't have time to keep up with music, so I doubted that I'd heard of the son-in-law. "Congratulations. You'll be a grandfather. First time?"

"Aye, Viola is my one and only. They're going on tour for six months, and I'm taking over as head of Leo's security. He's had bad experiences with support in the past, and I willnae expose them or the bairn to risk."

"Ye cannae trust anyone like ye can family," I muttered.

A wave went over me, temporarily disrupting my keen eye for the rescue we were about to undertake. I lacked family, but at least I'd had that growing up. Isla missed out on it all.

I could give her everything but that.

"Exactly." Gordain sped the distance to the trail end, two other cars waiting and presumably containing today's crew. "Get ready to meet your new family, Lochinvar. They're all dying to see ye. First, sort out your childcare while we have signal. We willnae be off the hill in time for the end of the school day."

I winced but pulled out my phone, my signal reduced by the altitude.

The school would look after Isla for a couple of hours, then my neighbour would be the last resort.

Cait might still be unhappy with me, but I wasn't all that impressed with her either. But for now, I had no choice. Isla would always come first.

*C*_{ait}

Cait

 Outside my window, rain drizzled, ghosting over the open glen and obscuring the line between land and sky. Usually while working from home, as I did for three days a week, I'd feel snug and safe at my desk, but unease rattled me.

Annoyance, too.

The mystery of who'd graffitied my door remained unsolved.

I tapped a pen against my lip, staring into space. It wasn't as if I'd dated anyone I could've offended. And no one had approached me in forever...

Wait.

Yes, they had.

I snatched up my phone and scrolled through my messages. Three weeks ago, Jessica, an old school friend, had sent me a text on behalf of her brother, Jeremy.

He'd wanted to know if I was single.

I'd replied with a *thanks, but no thanks.*

My mouth dropped open. Could it have been him? Our

local police officer had suggested the act had all the hall-marks of dented pride.

With a zing of energy, I found Jessica's social media and then Jeremy's.

Ah, there it was.

Just a few weeks ago, he'd broken up with his girlfriend and lost his job. I breathed in through my nose and peeked at the subsequent posts. Online arguments abounded. Wow, this arsehole liked to air his dirty laundry in public.

Ha! His old job had been with a painter and decorator. Lots of access to paint.

It had to be him.

At the top of the page, I read the most recent post. It seemed Jeremy had taken a new job, far south over the English border.

I exhaled in relief and sat back. Was this problem solved? On paper, it could be. I hadn't been able to make the connection to the weird stuff happening at work, so it made sense for it to be a local lad with an axe to grind.

At least I knew it wasn't anything truly personal. Jeremy had been pissed off with everyone.

My email dinged, and I focused on my laptop screen. My boss had sent a meeting request.

From: Rupert Gaskill

To: Cait McRae.

Cait, there's something I need to talk to you about. It's a delicate matter but shouldn't take long. I wouldn't want to call you all the way into Inverness on your working-from-home days. Perhaps I could come to you?

R

I grimaced at the screen and considered my reply.

I'd worked at the University of the Highlands for two years as a researcher, supporting the development of courses for students—an entirely boring job that neither taxed me nor stretched my skills. I reported into a number of different professors and also to Rupert, the administration lead.

In all that time, Rupert and I generally met once a fortnight. He'd never been anything other than professional, thank God, except I'd been getting a weird vibe from him in the last few meetings.

His gaze set on me for a beat too long. The personal questions he'd ask from my university days to what I got up to on weekends.

Now he wanted to come to my home?

A shiver ran down my spine.

Surely he wasn't the one messing with me at work. I was probably imagining the strange vibe. Some people were just naturally chatty.

I made my response, booking a very public meeting room in my reply. *Of course, but I'll happily come in,* I wrote.

Slamming my laptop closed, I grabbed my phone and crossed the room to my kitchen, dialling my closest friend on the way.

Casey answered right away. "Hello!"

I opened the fridge and took out a salad I'd made. "Ever feel that you live in the twilight zone for strange things happening?"

"Uh-oh, sounds like a story."

"Oh yes. What are ye all doing for dinner tonight? I could use some company if you'd like to come here."

"Love to! Brodie's in his workshop, and I'm pottering around at home, so we'll be ready whenever you want us. Blayne might be late."

"No biggie. We can save him a plate."

My cousin, Blayne, had two partners. Brodie, who'd been his best friend for years until it had led to more, and Casey, who'd been an instructor at the snowboarding centre on my family's mountain. They'd had a three-person wedding and were expecting a baby in a few months. Their unconventional relationship worked, and they were the happiest people I knew. Their bairn was going to be so lucky.

I took inspiration from them that families didn't all look the same.

On the estate, we already had Archie, who had been born in the spring to Isobel and Lennox. Isobel's brother, Sebastian, often visited with his wife, Rose, and their baby, Persephone. And Viola, my other cousin, was newly pregnant.

Babies were my most favourite thing in the world, and I badly wanted to join the parent club. Though this was complicated by the fact I didn't have or want a partner.

Which was why I'd contacted a fertility agency.

Tonight, I'd tell my guests all about it. It was way more interesting than the random strange happenings.

"I might have to spill my news before he gets here. Is seven okay?" My phone binged in my ear. I glanced at the screen. "Oops. I have another call."

"Way to keep me on tenterhooks. See you at seven."

Casey and I hung up, and I leaned on the kitchen island and accepted the new call. "Cait McRae."

Wind buffered the other end of the line. "Cait? It's Lochinvar Ross. Your neighbour."

I rolled my eyes. We hadn't got off on the best foot, but I knew who he was. Nobody could mistake the big, scowling man. "Mr Ross. What's up?"

"Sorry to ask before we've had a chance to talk. I've been

called out to a rescue. The school will keep Isla until five, but if I'm later, can ye help?"

My parents and brothers often went out with the mountain rescue. Many of my relatives did. Call-outs could last for hours.

I was the anomaly within them—I hated hiking and had no sense of direction. I'd never even considered joining up.

"I can take her. I have friends coming for dinner, so she can help me cook. Is there anything particular I need to know? Is she fussy with what she eats?"

But Lochinvar's answer was lost to the bad weather. The call cut out, and I checked the time. I'd have to hustle to finish work early. Then again, this was the life of a parent, and I had to get used to it, even if I was only playing pretend right now.

At some point, I'd be balancing a child and a career for real. Like Lochinvar was.

I needed the practice.

*T*he school minibus rumbled to a stop on the road beyond the cottages' puddle-filled gravel track. I stepped outside, my big umbrella protecting me from the driving autumn rain. Una, the headteacher, exited the bus, Lochinvar's little girl behind her.

Una was a close friend to one of my aunts and had been my teacher, too. She waved, clutching the hood of her sou'wester. "Cait, are ye okay to take Isla?"

"Aye, her da called. Ready, Isla?"

Isla peered at me, but whatever resistance she might have had dissolved in the weather. She darted across the ground then dove inside my home. Una waved again and climbed back onto the empty bus.

I followed my charge.

In the lounge, Isla waited, dripping water onto the rug. "Did you say Da called?"

"He did earlier. He's working so isn't home yet. Ye can wait with me until he's back."

"Can I speak to him?"

"It could be tricky getting through. I'm sure he won't be long."

Isla's mouth turned down. Oh heck, I didn't want her to cry.

"Let's get you out of that wet coat then ye can help me in the kitchen until it's time to go home. Want to tell me about your first day at school?"

I eased her soggy raincoat off and hung it on a hook next to mine. Isla removed her shoes, her white knee-length socks dark with water. No words came from the little girl.

"Socks off, too. You can borrow some from me. I have some cute and fluffy ones with owls on."

Still nothing. I darted for my bedroom and grabbed the snug socks. On my return, Isla hadn't moved.

"Ye must've liked Una, aye? She was my teacher when I was a girl."

Isla reluctantly took the socks. She drew them on, far too big but better than being chilled, then she finally opened her mouth. "Did someone die on the mountain?"

My jaw dropped, and for a moment, I couldn't summon an answer.

"Did the man who ran the rescue die? Is that why Da has the job?" she added.

I blew out a breath and crouched to her level. "Oh,

sweetie, no. That's my uncle, and he's just fine. Your da will be, too. He'll be home soon and giving ye a big hug."

The poor girl. She had a new home, school, and life to contend with. No wonder she was worrying about her father.

Where was her mother? Maybe joining them later.

I dusted my hands together. "While we wait, we'll get dinner started. Ye can help bake cookies for after."

Cooking was my favourite hobby and one I practiced a lot. Where I failed as a mountain woman, I excelled with a mixing bowl. Cakes and biscuits were always welcome—I only had to shoot my brothers a text and one or the other would find a reason to drive by and help themselves.

First thing was to get Isla fed. My questions on her preferences fell short, so I took out the large tray of chicken I'd be cooking for tonight and fried her up a few pieces, mixing it in with pasta, peas, tomato sauce, and topped off with cheese.

The whole time, she only watched.

But she ate. As soon as the bowl touched the island where she sat, she launched into it. I continued with the preparation for the curry I was making for the adults, trying to hide my astonishment.

When she was done, colour returned to her cheeks. She drank her glass of water, and her eyes brightened.

She'd needed feeding, that was all. Relief warmed me.

"Does your da like curry?" I asked. "I imagine he'll be hungry when he's finished work. Shall we save him a bowl?"

She considered the question. "He likes home-cooked food. He says that lots. He didn't normally have time to cook when we lived on the base. Blair used to make dinner sometimes."

"Oh? What did she make that you liked?"

Isla raised a shoulder. "Lasagne, from frozen. I wish she could've come here with us."

Blair might have been Lochinvar's girlfriend, I guessed, as Isla didn't call her Ma. Best to leave that stone unturned, too. I went for the other question that sprang to mind.

"On the base? Was your da in the army?" Lochinvar looked the type. Some of my relatives had been military, and I knew the process-driven, serious ways it instilled.

Isla pressed her lips together then brought her hand to her mouth, her eyes wide.

"I'm not meant to talk about that," she said.

I blinked, entirely curious now. "Okay. Why don't ye help me with the cookies instead?"

Her eyes rimmed with tears, and she pressed her hand tighter.

Something was wrong here. Badly so.

I wiped my hands in my apron and approached her, sitting on the next stool. "Ye don't have to tell me anything. Ye haven't done anything wrong either. You're among friends here."

But she'd shut down once more. I made the cookies with her only watching, and for the next hour, she didn't make a single peep.

Nor did we hear from her da.

I knew the routine and had never worried for the safety of my family out on a rescue, even in the dark with the rain pouring. They were well-practiced. Then again, Lochinvar was new to the area. If he'd strayed from the crew...

I ceased my line of thinking and concentrated on keeping my guest happy and the dinner moving on.

It was only when my guests arrived that Isla finally perked up. She stared at Casey when I introduced her, taking in her obvious baby bump along with her pretty face and American accent.

Brodie gazed at his wife in devotion while she sat beside Isla at the kitchen island, then turned to me. "Blayne willnae be long. He texted to say he's in the car."

"You said you had news." Casey steepled her hands. "Don't make us wait."

I raised a shoulder, sliding a glance at Isla. I guessed it wouldn't matter if she heard. "I registered with a clinic. I'm going ahead with having my own bairn."

Casey's eyes lit. "Oh my God! That's the best news. How long do you have to wait?"

Excitement fizzed in me. "They have to do several tests before we agree to the mechanics of it, and they did warn me it could be a while until they have availability for my first appointment."

Isla wrinkled her nose. "Are you married?"

"Nope. I'll be a single mother, like you have a single father."

"My baby will have a mom and two dads," Casey added. "There are plenty of ways to make a happy family. Each is as good as the others."

The little girl blinked but didn't offer anything more. I served up dinner and put the TV on for her, but she chose to remain in the kitchen, snacking on cookies.

We'd finished our meal when an engine roared outside.

"Da!" Isla leapt down and ran for the door.

I followed, peering into the calmer evening.

Blayne climbed from his car, and Isla visibly wilted. It was past seven now, and I'd begun wondering about putting up a bed for her in the living room.

On instinct, I placed a hand on her head to reassure her. She drooped on me for a moment then returned inside. I waited for my cousin, and the huge man gave me a hug in the doorway.

But before I could invite him in, another vehicle arrived, spitting gravel under its tyres. The driver launched from the car, glowering at Blayne, his focus on my cousin's arm over my shoulder.

Lochinvar was home, and once again, the man was furious.

5

Lochinvar

Cold to the bone, I stalked to Cait's cottage, glaring at the man who I suspected to be her arse-hole boyfriend.

"Was it ye with the paint?" I barked.

The man, several inches taller than my six-three, tilted his head. "What?"

I prided myself on being a rational man, but the events of the afternoon and evening had set me on edge. The rescue had gone fine, at first. But the idiot husband of the casualty had taken it upon himself to walk to find help. He'd assumed we wouldn't be able to find them.

He'd left their one phone with his injured wife. Then the guy had slipped and broken his leg. Worse, he'd fallen into a rocky gulley and been unable to haul himself up to a visible position.

Our easy recovery had turned into a full-service five-hour search and rescue. Cameron, the young second-in-command I'd doubted, had a dog brought in, and his team eventually located the man. With night falling, it had been the dog's eager nose that picked up the scent. Otherwise we'd still be out there.

I was satisfied with how my first two call-outs had gone but deeply upset with myself for not being home for Isla on her first day from school. It wasn't like me to be unprepared, yet I hadn't been inside Cait's home with Isla, or had the chance to make my daughter comfortable with the possibility of spending hours there while I worked.

Unwarranted annoyance broke from my control.

"You're the boyfriend, aye? Did ye feel like the big man painting shite like that on the lass's door? Who the fuck do ye think ye are behaving like that?"

Cait palmed the back of her neck. "No. Lochinvar, stop."

"Why? Men dinna act like that. Boys do." I switched my gaze to Cait. "I hope ye aren't letting him inside with Isla in there."

Her jaw worked, but Cait seemed lost for words. Her eyes, however, glittered with irritation.

The tall man frowned at Cait. "Did someone paint on your door? What did they write?"

I pulled up short, my anger stalling.

"Da!" Isla pushed between the two people.

I caught her in a hug, lifting her to my arms like I did when she was tiny.

"You're cold. Are you okay?" she muttered into my neck.

"Were ye worried? Ye know I always come back." I held her close.

Cait loomed in my vision, Isla's coat and school bag in her extended hand. "You're welcome, Lochinvar. Perhaps next time I babysit for ye, for free, you'll have the good manners to thank me for it. And to not abuse my guests. Goodnight."

She dragged the man inside and slammed the door. A

moment later, as I was twisting the key in our lock, another lass poked her head out, a covered bowl in her hand. She handed it to me.

"Cait made extra for you," she said in an American accent. "Maybe return the bowl another day when she isn't spitting feathers about you?"

She closed the door, and I ushered Isla inside.

We set about our evening routine, and the scent from the bowl left on the kitchen table punched hunger through me. I'd snatched provisions on the hill, but a real dinner had been on my mind ever since the rescue had been concluded. I'd anticipated a frozen meal cooked in the microwave, but this had to be a thousand times better.

"Who was that other woman?" I asked Isla, poking my head into her room to find her rummaging around for pyjamas.

"That's Casey. She's having a baby, and the baby has two dads. One is Cait's cousin. We made cookies. Did Cait give you one of those?"

She hadn't, but no wonder. I dropped a heavy shoulder onto the doorframe, realisation dawning as my exhaustion set in.

I'd made an idiot of myself, jumping to conclusions.

Isla appeared by my side and peeked up at me. Our single-storey cottage was warm already, and my daughter smiled, relaxed and happy. Really, she should go straight to bed, but I sent her to the sofa while I took a two-minute shower.

When I'd dressed, hunger drove me to the kitchen. I found a spoon and took the cover off my bowl of food, exposing a still-warm chicken and vegetable curry with egg fried rice. I carried it to the sofa then tucked in.

It was all I could do to stop myself from groaning at the

sheer deliciousness. My neighbour knew how to cook, and I owed her one huge apology.

Isla cuddled into my side, her gaze on the cartoon she'd lined up on the TV.

Her eyelids drooped, but I needed this moment with her, to make sure she was okay and to remind myself of the reason I'd turned our lives upside down.

"I'm sorry about today," I told her.

My daughter yawned. "It was such fun. Brodie, one of the dads, taught me a card game. I'll show it to you tomorrow."

"One of the dads?" She'd said as much earlier, but it hadn't registered.

"Two dads and one mum. When Cait has her baby, she'll be just one mum, like I have only you."

"Cait's having a bairn?" Why didn't she mention that? Or my boss, for that matter. He'd told me about his daughter, so I would've expected his niece to come up in the conversation, too.

It made sense that Cait was the go-to babysitting service.

But Isla's eyes shuttered closed. I finished my last bites of the mouth-wateringly good meal and scooped up my bairn, her head lolling on my shoulder.

She needed her bed, but after all the events of the day, I didn't think I'd rest so easily.

───

*T*he following morning, I delivered Isla to school then jumped into my car. I had a later start today so would use the time to check our tracks.

I drove south for an hour, far from home if anyone could somehow trace me. In a supermarket, I picked up a cheap phone and SIM card, paying with cash. In the car park, I set it up and called a number I had long ago memorised.

After a couple of rings, a female voice answered. "Yes?"

"It's me," I said.

"Lochie! Finally."

I almost sagged against the seat, the relief of hearing a familiar voice, and a much-loved one, unsettling me yet again.

"Aye, well, I couldnae get away to do this. Give me an update."

"Little to report. A few people have asked where the two of ye have gone, but I've given each a different answer."

"Who?"

Blair gave me a list of names—all parents of school friends of Isla's. No one I'd specifically worry about.

I grunted appreciation. "Good. Thank ye."

"Do ye have troubles in your new life?" my sister asked. Like me, she had a blunt tone, one inherited from our long-dead ma.

I briefly recalled using that voice on my gentle neighbour. The few times I'd spoken to Cait, even in her irritation, she'd been soft-edged and warm.

I didn't know anyone like that.

Plus, she was pregnant, too, according to Isla. All the more reason to make good my apology.

Ahead, the supermarket entrance boasted bouquets of flowers in a display. Aye, that might help my case.

"Nothing worth mentioning. I'm hopeful we'll get to see out the six-month contract."

"And after that?"

"Somewhere else." I'd keep moving for as long as it took.

"Ye keep that little lass safe, Lochinvar," Blair ordered.

"I will. When do ye ship out?"

"Tomorrow. It's going to be a long time before I see ye both again."

"Email when ye can. I put a picture of ye in Isla's room. She willnae forget her only family."

"Not her only family, more's the pity."

"She'll never know those fuckers," I swore. "Not if it kills me to protect her from them."

"I know. When I come back from deployment, I'll be able to help again."

My sister had already done enough. Between the two of us, we'd raised Isla, both holding service positions. Blair was made for action, like me. She'd watched her buddies be deployed while she took a base job, sharing parenting time with me.

With the fresh threat to Isla, it had only made sense for us to leave, freeing Blair to advance her career.

Isla mourned her aunt, I knew that, though at the same time, Blair had never tried to be her ma. My sister didn't have a maternal bone in her body, as much as she loved her niece.

Maybe one day, we'd be safe and could settle. Perhaps I'd find someone who wanted the mother role. Who'd put up with my sorry arse.

My chest ached with a flutter of regret. Never once had I been in love, aside from the instant devotion I had to Isla when she'd been born. I couldn't regret a minute of the past six years, though. I'd do it all again in a heartbeat.

Everything my wife had asked.

"Stay safe," I said to Blair.

"Exactly what I was going to say to you, brother. Kiss Isla from me, and see ye on the other side."

*B*ack at the cottages, Cait's car was gone, so I left the bouquet by her door and headed off to work. Today, I was going over the training schedules before picking up Isla at four—a short day to make up for the long call-out last night.

I'd talk to my neighbour later.

One way or another, I'd make things right.

6

*C**ait*
    Along the dim interior corridor of Patterson House, a decaying college building in Inverness, I walked, my arms full of paperwork and my tablet. Rupert, my boss, had changed the location of our meeting to his private office and, despite it being mid-afternoon, disquiet hung over me.

Work was where multiple odd events had happened from the increasingly long list. My stolen coat bugged me the most. My mother had bought it for me, and it was perfectly tailored and a stunning deep purple. No one could wear that without me noticing.

Other, lesser happenings, like my lunch being taken, bothered me less. Maybe someone had made a mistake. My emails being opened before I'd had a chance to read them could've been a technology glitch.

Or it could be a pattern.

My nerves zipped with energy where I was giving myself the creeps. I blew out a breath and strode on.

Behind me, a *clunk* sounded. The windowless corridor plunged into darkness at my back. This part of the building was empty with the students away, but the motion sensors should keep the lights on.

A footstep thudded.

A glance over my shoulder revealed nothing, yet my pulse jumped.

I hustled faster, my heels clicking on the tiles.

Overhead, the lights failed, too. Now in almost complete darkness, I spun around. Another footstep fell, loud yet the owner invisible.

Someone was coming.

The hair on the back of my neck rose. Sweat broke out on my brow.

"Hello?" I called.

No reply.

I took a quick breath and kept moving, passing gaping, empty rooms. With every step, my wariness grew. My shoulders bunched automatically, and I could almost sense the touch of a stranger from the dark. Grasping me with a bruising grip. Hauling me through one of the doors along the route.

God, this was freaking me out.

With my papers clutched to my chest, I peered back again, not stopping. Still nothing but the tapping echo.

A door slammed.

I let out a shriek and took off, sprinting to the faint light at the end of the corridor. With a burst of energy, I flung myself into the stairwell and stared back.

An empty hall yawned.

No one pursued me.

My heart banged into my ribs, my breathing coming hard. *Fuck*. What the hell was that? My imagination or worse?

I set my jaw and swung to hit a fist to the manual light

switches this end of the corridor. The overheads sprang to life.

"There," I called into the empty space, feeling ridiculous. "Do ye think you're funny? Come on out, if ye dare."

Nothing moved, and my bravery slipped.

I turned and jogged the two flights of stairs to the office suite.

Jill, Rupert's PA, waited at her desk. This woman had never once smiled or been friendly to me, but boy was I happy to see her. She peered up and gave me a slow once-over. Her blonde bob had the slick shininess of a fresh hairdressing appointment. I half considered complimenting her, but she'd probably sneer.

The fear in me receded, and I forced my mind back to the business of the day.

"Hi, Jill. Is Rupert in?" I said in a rush.

"You booked this meeting, didn't you? Mr Gaskill is waiting."

Okay then. I thanked her and pressed the office door aside, leaving it slightly ajar behind me.

Rupert lifted his head from his screen. "Caitriona. Thank you for coming."

"Just Cait, please." I'd told him this a hundred times. Few people used my full first name, and I didn't want him to be one of them.

He gestured to the door. "Could you close us in? What we have to discuss might be...private. Better not to have anyone overhear."

Ugh. I obliged then took a seat.

Rupert rounded the desk and settled into the chair right next to me.

His knee touched mine, the smooth material of his brown suit trousers brushing on my tights.

As subtly as I could, I shrank back.

"Your email from last week," he started, his Birmingham accent making his words friendlier than I suspected they'd be. "I know at the time I acknowledged the request, and of course you have the right to pursue this avenue, should you choose, however, I wouldn't feel I was doing my duty to you as your employer if I didn't offer the best of my advice."

Oh God. I'd informed Rupert, the other managers, and HR, that I'd need time out for appointments with the fertility clinic. It was part of the maternity terms and conditions, and I was entitled to the leave.

No part of my message invited discussion.

"That email was a notification only," I said firmly.

"I understand, and parenthood is a blessing. One that shouldn't be entered into lightly. Cait, we've known each other for a number of years now. You joined us as a fresh-faced graduate, and you're still very young..."

He left the sentence trailing, like I should take something from his words.

"I'm sorry, was that a question?"

Rupert put his hand on the arm of my chair and inched forward.

Shite.

My discomfort deepened, and heat prickled me, returning in a rush from my earlier scare. I leaned back farther.

"I have two children," he said, his eyes wide. "Beautiful. I pride myself on how well-made they are."

Well-made? Was this guidance? Or...an offer?

"Both are bright. My son is strong-willed but dutiful. My daughter always receives compliments on her pretty face and lovely hair."

"Why are ye telling me this?"

"Caitriona, it's important for you to understand that you have options. Children don't always turn out how you expect, no matter the planning. My brother, for example—"

I stopped listening, caught on the word 'options'.

Abruptly, I stood, then slipped past Rupert to the door.

The urge to apologise came over me, and I forced it away. He'd made me uncomfortable, and I wasn't at fault.

"Like I said, the email was a notification only. Thanks..." *Don't thank him.* "I need to leave."

Riding a wave of panic, I collected my possessions and exited. Jill stared from her desk, no doubt taking in my hot face, but I didn't stop. Not for her, or for the other voice that hailed me as I left the building.

Whether my boss was or wasn't my stalker, he'd just revealed an unhealthy degree of interest.

I marched straight back to my car and drove home, trying not to cry.

*O*n my doorstep, a bunch of flowers lay propped against the door. I stopped in front of them, too alarmed to search for a note.

Had Rupert done this? Was it even him behind the weird acts? I clamped my hand to my mouth, nauseous.

Footsteps had me spinning around.

Lochinvar approached, a hand out. "Christ, lass, what's wrong?"

Thank God.

Instant relief replaced the myriad other emotions. Which was strange, because after the drama he caused with yet another of my relatives last night, I ought to be annoyed.

An acute sense of safety warmed me instead.

I folded my arms against the intrusion. "Lochinvar. I wanted to talk to ye."

He ran his gaze over me, lingering on my belly, then dug his fingers into his black hair. "Aye, I did with ye, too. Step aside, will ye?"

"What?"

He gestured for me to move, then when I did, he stooped and collected the bouquet. "Those are from me. And Isla, too. A thank ye and an apology."

He held out the bunch of pretty, autumn-coloured blooms, and I stared.

"Those were from ye? Did ye think it might be a bad idea to leave them considering what I found at my home last week?"

He blinked, realisation dawning over his big features.

In a rush, my indignation returned. The events of the day had done a number on me, and I was ready to unleash it all. "While we're here talking about bad manners, what the hell was that about last night? Ye launched at my cousin, were rude to him, and yet again inserted yourself into my business."

The enormous mountain man drew a heavy breath. "I know."

"Do ye really? Seems to me ye bulldoze your way through situations however ye please."

"It had been a tough evening, the rescue a difficult one. Forget that. I have no excuse."

I didn't want him to be reasonable. I was fed up, but more, my blood zinged with increasingly frantic energy. Some new sensation I couldn't understand but which urged me to continue this fight.

The last thought brought me up short. I had no reason to quarrel with this man. None at all. His crazy acts simply put him into a category of people I wouldn't be friends with. I pulled back my shoulders.

"I get that we have to be neighbours, and I'm more than happy to look after your daughter, but I'd appreciate it if ye left me alone from now on."

My chest heaved, and Lochinvar's gaze darkened.

A moment passed between us where tension rose, tangible and warm. I flitted my gaze from Lochinvar's piercing eyes to his clenched jaw. The way he looked at me...

He proffered the bouquet once more, and I gritted my teeth.

I was so sick of men offering me things I didn't ask for or need. My rational mind completely left me. "Do ye know what ye can do with those flowers?"

Lochinvar's eyebrows rose, and he burst out with an amused chuckle.

He laughed? Oh hell no.

I spun on my heel and entered my home, slamming the door behind me.

For the next several days, my wish was granted. Whenever I saw Lochinvar outside the cottages, he'd dip his head in acknowledgement but not speak.

The intensity of his gaze didn't let up, though.

Blayne dropped me a text to say Lochinvar had tracked him down and given him a well-worded apology. My cousin was easy-going but also a good judge of character. His description of my neighbour as a 'solid guy' didn't go unnoticed.

One evening, the school brought Isla to me. It was only

an hour before her father appeared from the mountains, bringing the scent of the wild outdoors with him.

He ushered Isla into their home but paused on his doorstep.

Why was I still waiting? I stopped all the same.

"I ken ye don't want me to make conversation, but if there's ever anything ye need, go ahead and ask. You've helped me a lot, and I can do the same for ye."

The calm of the past few days had mellowed me some. I had no clue what had prompted Lochinvar's gesture, but it was kind. Neighbourly.

"I appreciate that. Thanks for the offer." I gave him a quick smile. "Goodnight."

No answer came, and I didn't wait around for more.

7

Lochinvar

Dawn spread over the landscape, faint light peeking under a heavy sky. I exited my Mountain Rescue Jeep and inflated my lungs with cool, crisp air. Snow would come soon, though we were barely halfway into October. With it, the complexity of my work would rise.

Wintery days brought freezing temperatures and drenching fog that rose from nowhere. With Gordain now having stepped back, I had a wealth of tasks to get on with. Planning. Training. Rotas. Volunteers and professionals I still needed to meet.

So why the fuck was my brain locked on to the enigmatic Cait McRae?

It had been a few weeks since our last conversation outside our homes, and beyond that, we'd barely spoken.

Everything about the lass intrigued me.

Her style—flowery dresses with a denim jacket and brown boots. Her fair hair usually tied up. Her friendliness to everyone who came by.

The scent of baking that wafted from her place. The way

she'd warmed to my daughter and made our introduction to our new home ten times easier.

The way, over a month, no boyfriend had appeared, despite the fact Cait was pregnant.

Those little details had started to fascinate me. I shouldn't have let them. I couldn't allow the distraction.

I grumbled to myself and stomped down the mountain track. From the only other car in this isolated spot, a dog barked.

Her owner popped the door and climbed out, releasing his animal from a harness.

The brown-and-white Collie, a member of our crew, bounded up to me then shot away to sit by the door of the building we'd come to see. She gave another bark, and Cameron McRae ducked his head in greeting.

"Mr Ross," he said. Then he indicated to his dog. "Ellie's keen to get inside."

"Lead on. Show me the place," I asked.

Cameron directed me into the small cottage I'd wanted to see. Hill House was vacant of residents and used as an area command centre. In its position high above a glen, it had excellent views but was cut off by a rocky ridge above and thick forests meeting heather-strewn slopes below. It made a good base for rescues in this part of our reach.

I stooped under the low doorway and poked my head into the basic downstairs rooms. Cameron pointed out the generator for power, space for multiple agencies to meet, and supplies for restocking. It all appeared in order.

He led me into what must've originally been the front room.

As well as wanting to see the house, I also wanted to get to know this lad. Despite my reservations, he'd impressed me over the past month and, as Gordain had noted,

Cameron showed up for almost every call. He'd been a key asset. His animal, too.

From under the table, the dog watched us, all aquiver, and with her attention locked on her owner.

I lifted my chin to Cameron. "How long have ye had her?"

"Three years."

"She has a good track record."

"Aye. Same as her owner." He gave me a thoughtful look but didn't elaborate on his statement.

This was a big part of my needing one-on-one time with him. I'd seen him follow instruction and manage others with quiet words, typically with a serious expression to his blue eyes that belied his age. Gordain had told me how Cameron had been six foot at thirteen and joined the volunteer team at sixteen, despite being too young to go out on the hill. He knew the locale like the back of his hand, and nothing fazed him. He didn't yammer on like other people his age, and his capabilities were plain.

With anyone else, I'd expect to have this explained to me in detail in an attempt to impress. Not Cameron.

He reminded me of myself.

I liked this stoic young man. Right now, he was about the age I'd been when my life had turned upside down.

"I've been covering off the terrain over the past couple of weeks," I said. "Hiking the areas that come up most in incident reports."

Cameron dipped his head in approval.

"The peak beyond this cabin features a lot in winter. Can ye tell me why?"

He rubbed his square jaw, his gaze flitting to the window. "When there's snow on the ground, the wide glen with the access road makes a picturesque walk. Ye can go deep into the mountains from here, and there's a hidden waterfall within an hour's trek. Signal's shite, though, and the weather can change in a heartbeat. The windchill knocks people on their arses. The cold drains their energy, and they find they can't get back to their cars. Then if the granite's naw sticky, the tracks have poor footing. Under snow, it can be a death trap."

Cameron talked me through the rescues he'd attended here, and I ran over the details of the reports I'd read. They were typically the more straightforward kind—extracting a hypothermic or injured person to medical care via a rolling stretcher—though there had been a winch operation by helicopter once or twice, too.

We were well into the detail when his dog sat up, her ears pricking. She barked once.

Cameron stood and moved to the window. He peered out then went to the door, checking the road. When he returned, his eyebrows drove together. "Strange. Ellie's telling me someone's here. She did the same a few weeks ago when we were on a supply run, and she's rarely wrong."

"Could be a passerby?"

"Aye. Maybe they're out of sight." He didn't look convinced.

I had no idea why, but Cait's graffitied door sprang to mind. "What day were ye here before?"

"I'll check." Cameron pulled his phone from his jacket pocket, the screen lighting up with a picture of a smiling lass.

"Your girlfriend?" I asked.

Pink spots appeared on his cheeks, and he huffed a laugh, quickly moving on to his calendar app. "I wish."

The urge came over me to warn him to keep himself to himself for a few years more. Not that his life was any of my concern, but entanglements brought an end to youth. Freedom replaced with constant vigilance and worry. I'd never regret my life, because Isla was my world, but I wouldn't wish it on anyone else either.

"Here." Cameron gave me the date: the day we'd arrived in the Highlands. The same time Cait's door had been painted.

My sense of misgiving increased. This time, I wasn't about to expose Cait's business to yet another of her relatives. Her cousin, Blayne, had accepted my apology, and he'd shown deep concern over what had happened. As anyone would. I wished I knew what action Cait had taken. Whether she'd discovered anything.

If it hadn't been a local, could the perpetrator have hidden out here?

The dog gave another bark. Cameron stood taller.

"Does anyone use this building bar us?" I scanned the rooms again.

"No. They shouldnae." He gestured to his dog. "Ellie, seek."

As if rocket-powered, she launched away and scampered up the stairs, her claws clacking on the bare wooden treads.

We jogged after her.

The dog made a beeline for a doorway. In the corner of a bedroom, a sleeping bag laid rolled up on the floorboards. She sat next to it and barked once.

Cameron ruffled the fur on Ellie's head in praise. "No wonder she was quivering. I instructed her to rest, but she was on edge."

I picked up the sleeping bag, revealing empty packets of energy bars and a flattened can. A quick examination provided no further clues. No name label that would be there for the property of a scout. No red paint smears, though the likelihood would've been small.

"Was this here before?" I asked.

"Naw last month, I ken that for sure."

"Do ye know of any reason someone would stay here overnight?"

"Not on-crew. It's not kitted out for that. We'd change teams and send people home," Cameron added.

"I'll take it away and bin it. Dinna want to encourage anyone to come back." I bundled up the mess and took it to my car.

For the next hour, Cameron escorted me on a circular walk around the hill before we went our separate ways.

I drove back the few miles to my cottage, my mind churning over and making connections.

I didn't believe in coincidences, but I couldn't be sure if this was relevant to Cait's problem. Or how I'd find out.

Cait's car waited in its usual spot, next to where I parked. She was home. I had an hour until I needed to collect Isla so mulled over going to speak to my neighbour. Yet feverish energy infected me, and I couldn't shake it off. I needed to burn it up before I could stand in front of the woman who'd claimed my peace of mind.

I knew my protective instincts were stronger than most.

Too often, women and children needed defending from men. It was a fact of the world that laws couldn't always provide. Some lowlifes could only be prevented from acting out their evils by the strength and aggression of better men. I'd been taught that as a boy, afraid of my father even as I'd escaped with my mother and Blair, and believed it to this day.

Not that I thought women weak. Ma was the strongest woman I knew, and she'd raised Blair and me as equals, working endless hours to provide for us. But the simple truth was, in general, men were physically stronger.

Brutal, sometimes.

Cait lived alone in her cottage. Even on this remote and wild estate with her kin nearby, she was vulnerable. She'd already been attacked with the word scrawled on her door.

And she was going to have a bairn.

That set every alpha male instinct in me to high alert.

Fuck, I almost shook with the will to command her to listen to me. To let me include her in my daily concerns.

If I went to her like this, tense and stubborn, we'd end up fighting again.

Outside the back of the cottages, a short, walled-in patio kept the forest at bay. Beyond, a cleared area of hillside made a good spot to chop wood for the fire. Isla and I had a well-stocked store already, but there was nothing wrong with adding to it.

I stowed my jacket on the wall and unlocked the shed to grab an axe, hefting it over my shoulder as I strode to a waiting tree stump in the clearing. In short order, I split a thick pine bough into chunks, then set about making kindling.

The *thud* of the axe resounded and ricocheted in the damp, muffling air.

Heat built, and I shed my jumper and t-shirt, leaving myself bare-chested.

Sweat coated my skin. I swung the weapon and took out my emotions on the wood. Fuck people threatening others. Isla, Cait—they'd both been victims.

I put more power into my muscles.

The pine halved, pieces flying.

How fucking dare someone daub paint on the lass's door. What a brainless, cowardly arsehole. If I ever found out who did it...

Movement at the cottages halted my efforts. I focused and found Cait at the window. She stared at me. I stared right back.

Ah God, she was pretty.

On her shoulder, a wee bairn snuggled. A soft shape in her arms.

My stomach tightened.

Whose bairn that was, I had no idea, but it looked content. I heaved in a breath, utterly caught on the vision before me. Likewise, Cait seemed stuck. Her gaze coasted over my form, and I straightened, letting her take her fill.

With the axe across my shoulders, my arms hooked over it, I knew the effect it had on my muscles.

She touched on my broad shoulders, abs, and over the smattering of black hair on my chest. She followed the trail down to where it disappeared under my combat trousers. I felt every inch of her attention as if her fingers slid over my skin.

I had no business engaging in this moment. No reason at all to let myself succumb to a deep, rolling wave of attraction.

Nor could I stop it.

Abruptly, Cait turned away, and I was released, my rising instincts only worse than before.

8

Cait

I carried Archie to the sofa and moved him to my lap so I could see his face. He scrunched up his nose and flailed his arms and legs.

On autopilot, I tickled his hands and feet in a game, but my mind was entirely elsewhere.

Fixed on Lochinvar, half naked and savage.

He'd swung that axe like the logs had attacked him and he was fending for his life. Powerful swings. Deadly accuracy. In olden days, he would've been a mighty warrior.

Each hack sent a shockwave through my body. But it was *his* body that I'd got stuck on.

He was beautiful. Lean, tall, and muscled, his biceps the size of my head. Bulging, so strong. I couldn't take my gaze off him, nor the dark hair that continued on his chest and downwards.

Despite my lack of sexual feelings, I'd appreciated male beauty before.

This was nothing like that.

I'd wanted him to continue stripping.

Brand-new feelings sparked low in my stomach.

What the hell was that?

Too hot, and entirely confused, I glanced at the clock on my wall and heaved a sigh of relief. Lennox would be home soon. I had an excuse to leave.

"About time I got ye back to your father," I told Archie.

In a minute, I'd collected his belongings, strapped him into his car seat, and got on the road, not sparing a look at the neighbouring cottage.

Even as I drove, I couldn't shake the feelings in me. I'd been electrocuted. Scalded.

Something was very different.

At Isobel and Lennox's place, I carried their son inside, reuniting him with his father. Between them, my cousin and his wife juggled Archie's care, and I was always happy to help out with babysitting the six-month-old, like I'd done today, taking the afternoon off work.

Lennox waved a hand in front of my face. "I asked if he drank all his milk. Are ye okay?"

"Fine." I jerked my head up and frowned. "Why?"

"You're red-cheeked and distracted."

"Am not."

My cousin grinned, locking on to my distress in the way that close family could. "What's going on? What have ye been up to?"

I backed to the door. "Nothing concerning ye. I have to go. Bye."

Through the blustery afternoon, I drove erratically and parked with a wary peek at the cottages. It was too early for Lochinvar to collect Isla, so he was probably still in the house.

Could he sense my weird level of interest through the walls? I didn't want him to.

A thought struck me.

When I'd been ogling him, he hadn't moved. He'd witnessed my act and let it continue.

I wished I'd caught his reaction. Maybe he'd been horrified.

Then I recalled the slight movements he'd made, how he'd stood taller, his axe held behind his shoulders so his biceps popped.

Perhaps he'd felt what I had. This curious...thing I couldn't explain.

Without any intention of vanity, I knew how I looked and how that affected some people.

I'd always been pretty.

I'd never encouraged the attention.

For the first time ever, I was almost desperate to know if Lochinvar Ross found me attractive.

On the cusp of rising energy, I skittered into my house, keeping my gaze on my brown leather boots. Then, in my bedroom, I changed into my form-fitting pink-and-black yoga kit and stepped outside to the patio at the back of my cottage.

There, I rolled out my yoga mat and stretched, warming up. As I did almost every day, I moved through the poses of my regular routine.

The big difference here being the fact I was in the fresh and chilly autumn air and not my living room.

It was only when I moved from Downward Dog into Cobra—from my backside being high in the air to pushing up on my arms—that I dared risk a glimpse at Lochinvar's window.

There he was.

His dark glower glued to my body.

Ha! We'd switched places. He'd shown his cards. Satisfaction warmed my tensed muscles.

I held the pose and shivered.

I wished I had the cocky swagger to send him a wink, but instead I rolled into Plank and hid my flushed face.

By the time I stole another glance, Lochinvar had gone.

---

*A*cross the car, Casey gave me a curious look. "You're on edge. Did something happen?"

"Ye could say that." I heaved a breath, concentrating on the road and our trip into Inverness.

For days and days, I'd nurtured the fizz of feelings I'd experienced, though I hadn't crossed paths with Lochinvar once. He took Isla to breakfast club at the school and hadn't been on an evening call-out. I'd had to travel for work so missed their comings and goings.

Yet the fresh sensations hadn't gone away.

Tonight, Casey and I were meeting up with Viola, as Vi was about to leave for Leo's world tour. I'd planned to share my odd reaction with them.

Leo had a rehearsal in the city, so Casey and I were crashing that, but first, we had another chore.

My godmother wanted to see me.

I'd been putting off the visit.

Georgia Banks was my birth mother's cousin. Growing up, she'd been my only connection to that side of my family. Yet I typically shied away from meeting with her. Learning about the person who'd supplied half my DNA only went so far, and Georgia had a knack for unsettling me. She had put herself in the role of amateur psychologist, linking everything I did, thought, and felt to the fact my birth mother had gotten pregnant with me in secret and then died not long after my birth.

Seeing her left me flat, but at least I had a fun evening to anticipate after.

"Let's get Georgia over and done with first, then we'll chat," I told Casey.

She agreed, boosted the music, and we sped on.

We arrived at Georgia's home in the outskirts of Inverness at six. My aunt ushered us inside with hugs and a warm welcome.

As a kind of personal shield, I'd gotten into the habit of always bringing Casey with me, and my friend settled into a chair, accepting a mug of tea while making chitchat about her pregnancy.

"Cait, there's a reason I asked you here today." Georgia reached for a bag from beside the couch. "Ever since you told me that you wanted a baby, I'd planned to give this to you."

She passed over her gift.

I received the white knitted blanket and smoothed over the wool. "This is lovely. Did you make it?"

"I did, but nearly thirty years ago and for my own two. They both used it, and you would've, too, as a newborn, had your mother told me about your existence. It was too late by the time we found out about you."

I summoned a smile. "My future baby thanks you for the kind thought. It's beautiful." Then I rushed on to prevent Georgia from lingering on the last part of her statement. "I've booked in with a fertility clinic. They have a long waiting list, but I'm on it. My parents are super excited to be grandparents. Ye know Da doesn't like to be outdone by his older brothers, and they're all grandads already, or about to be."

Georgia heaved a wistful sigh. "Your mother would love to know how happy a family you have. If only her heart hadn't given out, she'd still be with us now."

Casey widened her eyes at me, her expression knowing. "I think—" she started.

"Of course," Georgia interrupted, "you wouldn't be going down this path of single parenting if she hadn't died."

Oh boy.

Her gaze distanced, as if she was reliving a long-ago scene. "I can't help but look back with frustration at what Kaylee did. Her fascination with your father, getting pregnant on purpose, hiding you from him. From all of us. No wonder you don't want a man. She really screwed you over."

I'd never followed her logic on this. My internal workings had nothing to do with my start in life. Da had claimed me when I was only months old, and he and Scarlet, my stepmother, though I'd never called her anything other than Ma, were all I knew.

Yet every time I saw her, Georgia picked at the wound.

"Cait will make an amazing mother," Casey stated.

"She will. It's just such a shame. Did I tell you how I found out about it all? Lord, it was a shock! Kaylee being told she wouldn't get pregnant and all."

My armour dropped, and I stared. "She was told she couldn't get pregnant?"

"Yes. Surely I've told you this?"

"Never."

"I can't remember the specifics, but she knew it from her teenage years. Something to do with her heart, I'm sure."

Kaylee's heart problems were responsible for ending her life, and I'd had scans growing up to make sure I hadn't inherited the condition, but what if there was something else? Da wouldn't know. He and Kaylee had been friends but nothing more.

"Georgia, this is really important to me. Can ye please try to remember exactly what Kaylee told ye?"

"Hmm? Oh my, it's such a long time ago. I can't be sure. It won't matter considering the path you're taking, the doctors doing all the hard work. Now, back to the time I first heard about you."

The conversation continued in this vein for another hour until we could politely extricate ourselves.

I kissed Georgia goodbye, thanked her again for the blanket, revved the engine, then peeled away from her street.

"Argh," I bit out, then banged the steering wheel.

"Holy shit," Casey drawled. "Read the room, Mrs. How does she think that kind of conversation is helpful?"

"I have no clue. What was that new sly addition? Kaylee was told she couldn't conceive?"

"She could have misremembered."

"Maybe. There's always something she's alarmist over, and it's always the same: I'm broken for life. She drives Da nuts. After her visits to the estate, he'd sit me down and talk through each of her statements. Undoing the 'facts' she'd tried to instil in me."

"What kind of facts?"

"She internet-researched stress in pregnancy and lectured me in how it affects babies. She also believes that Kaylee being there then vanishing hurt me. But you know my mother. She's the most amazing woman. I couldn't have asked for better."

Casey rubbed my arm, but there was nothing more to be said. Georgia had dropped her new bomb for me to worry over, and there was nothing I could do about it.

We zipped into town and to the rehearsal space where we were meeting Viola. A burly man answered the door of the closed gig venue, admitting us when I gave our names and IDs.

Inside, a small audience waited in front of the empty stage.

Viola waved from a table, and we made our way over, swapping hugs.

"I'm so glad you're both here!" the former snowboarder sang, balancing on the crutch she relied on after a bad accident a few years ago ended her career.

I gestured to the crowd. "Who are all these people?"

"Leo's record company and their families. Relatives of his band. He's performing a couple of official warm-up gigs, but this is just for industry folks. Oh, Da's here, too, somewhere. He'll come over when he sees ye. I've told him to stop hovering like I'm about to expire."

Casey settled into her seat and smiled. "It's lovely that he cares so much about you. I wish my dad gave a shit. Actually no, maybe I don't. It's far nicer being away from my family than having to deal with their drama day in, day out."

We all chuckled.

Viola pointed at the bar across the hall where a barman waited. "Mocktails? I'll go order them."

Casey stood. "Let me. I need to pee anyway. You both have the joy of advanced pregnancy and peeing every thirty minutes to look forward to."

We gave our orders, and she disappeared.

Alone with Viola, I finally let myself relax.

"How was Georgia?" my cousin asked.

"We went over her favourite topic of me staying single because I'm scarred, then she intimated my birth mother had some problem with conceiving. Right out of the blue, and with no further information. What am I supposed to do with that?"

"Jeez. The woman's a riot. Considering ye exist, maybe that wasn't true."

I blew her a kiss. "I'll try to believe that. Tell me about the tour plans. Edinburgh first, right?"

Viola rolled her dark curls into a hair clip and got into their European itinerary. Between Leo's rock show performances, they'd get to go on several cool tourist trips. Her father would provide their security, and we all smiled at how fierce he'd be to any avid fan who came too near.

Casey returned, and we were midway through a conversation on travelling when Leo appeared on stage. The audience applauded, and Casey and I catcalled and whistled.

Viola only gazed at him, her expression settling into one of utmost devotion. I liked her husband so much, and he suited her perfectly.

It was hard not to envy their happiness.

For their surprise wedding, he'd planned a whole mini-festival of family and friends then performed a song in which he asked her to marry him there and then. It was the most romantic and sweet gesture, their love so easy and full.

I'd been content with living a loveless existence, but at times, it hurt that I was different. Maybe Georgia had it right, and I was just broken.

Except, I loved my family and my friends. Was my malfunction tied in with sex and desire?

My mind drifted back to the *something* I'd experienced when spying on Lochinvar.

I tested myself. Aye, it had been real. I could still sense the edges.

He'd jolted feelings from me that no one else ever had. It

was unlikely to be close to the sorts of emotions Casey and Viola felt for their men, but it had happened.

"Cait?" My cousin waved. "Where did ye go?"

Leo's song had ended, and the waiter arrived with our drinks. I blinked and accepted mine, my cheeks heating.

"Sorry, I got distracted. Actually, can I ask a question?"

They swapped a glance and leaned in.

"How old were ye when ye started noticing boys?"

"Eight or nine," Casey replied. "Early bloomer."

"Older for me. Maybe eleven? I wasn't really into them until a few years later, though," Viola added.

"And what did that feel like?"

Casey's attention turned speculative. "Warm and vital. A need. It wasn't an erotic feeling until I was a teenager, but I was totally drawn in. Why? Is this to do with what you said in the car?"

Viola's head swung. "What did she say in the car?"

Casey grinned. "Not much. She was being mysterious."

I peeked around and sank lower in my seat. "A few days ago, I found myself stuck staring at a man chopping wood, half naked. He was beautiful, and I think it woke something in me."

Both of their jaws dropped.

"Like a sexy feeling?" Casey asked.

I swallowed. "I don't know. Possibly?"

Viola cocked her head to one side, her examination of me piercing. "Was it the guy, or did it just happen at random?"

"I'm not sure."

Subtly, she gestured to the bar. "The bartender is fine. Anything going on when ye look at him?"

I cast my gaze over the lean man pouring drinks. His wide mouth slid into a grin at whatever his customer was telling him, and his eyes twinkled under a thatch of light-brown hair.

He was cute, but nothing sparked in me.

"Nope. But I don't know if it was the guy so much as the action."

"The wood chopping? Ooh, you like the mountain man type. Rugged. A little bit wild. Just my type, too." Casey sipped her drink, her hand to her rounded belly.

I pondered this. "I grew up with mountain men, so I don't know about that."

Casey snorted. "But those are your relatives. Presumably Mr Mystery is a new man in town."

Viola lifted a finger, drawing both of our attentions. "Who are we talking about?"

The heat in me grew, more from embarrassment than anything. I felt like a teenager with her first crush. Maybe I was. Except I was in my twenties.

It was easier when I didn't feel anything.

"Lochinvar. My neighbour."

Leo strummed his guitar and commenced another song, acoustic this time so we could still hear each other.

My cousin's gaze gentled. "At least he's a safe target."

"What do ye mean?"

"He's a married man."

I gaped then coughed to hide it. "He's married?"

"His wife isn't with him, but she exists. He talked to my father about her. I don't know the specifics, but he didn't say 'ex'. That's a pretty big indication he's still wed." She glanced around. "Let me call Da over. He can tell us more."

"No!" I squeaked, picturing my uncle's face. I was the only single woman amongst us, and it would be obvious why she was asking.

Then horror struck me. "Oh God, then I did something

both bad and stupid."

I explained about the yoga display and how I'd tested Lochinvar's reaction in return.

"Gotta say, whether he's still with his wife or not, most men would probably stare at ye." Casey grinned.

"He shouldn't have. I hate that he did." I slumped onto my arms, the euphoria from my revelation now tainted and cheap.

If this was just the start, I had a lot to learn.

"Aw, honey. Don't let this faze you. What's happened to you is wonderful, and there are plenty of great guys out there. Go on a date, try yourself out," Casey encouraged. "See where this takes you."

A screech came from the back of the hall. "Leo, I love you!" A woman burst from the shadows and tore through the space.

Before she even reached the stage, Uncle Gordain stepped in front of Leo, just as a huge bodyguard intercepted the fan. With an easy swoop, the bodyguard lifted her from her feet. Arms bulging, he carried her from the hall, the woman yelling her protestations of love.

"Oh God." Viola dropped her head back to stare at the ceiling. "Why does this happen every time? Da's going to be unbearable now."

She and Casey laughed, but my mind had stalled on one thing.

Oh God.

The idea of Lochinvar grabbing me in such a dominant move sent a thrill straight through my nervous system. He'd have no problem throwing me over his shoulder. Stealing me away to his cave.

My breath caught, and I was lost.

Maybe the mountain man thing was true after all.

9

*L*ochinvar

Around me, the mountain rescue team strode up the damp track, their red jumpsuits bold against the dull green-and-brown landscape, beating a path up the steep glen to our target. I'd invited the younger members of the group on a training session, and they were a tight unit, easy with each other.

With Cameron taking the lead, I slowed to bring up the rear, intending to watch today.

For the past two weeks, I'd been away from the estate most days, visiting farther-flung teams, driving out early and returning just in time to get Isla from school. I'd spent hours on the road, climbed numerous peaks, and met dozens of volunteers.

Despite the hard work rate I set myself, it hadn't dented my interest in my favourite distraction.

Cait was on my mind too much.

I was also horny as fuck—a need I couldn't shake no matter what I did.

Yet that glimmer of attraction I'd seen in Cait had died.

Ever since I'd caught her watching me, she'd greeted me with cool indifference, and it bugged the fuck out of me.

I needed to know what had happened. What had changed.

I couldn't ask.

It was for the best that she'd lost interest. I only needed to do the same.

Ahead, a shout came. We'd reached our target.

In a grouch, I strode to Cameron. "The casualty's been located. What will ye do now?"

Today's exercise was a complicated one. The victim—a roped-up mannequin—perched on an outcrop midway down a waterfall. From our position on the slope, the water fell mostly out of sight, the river flowing under the hill and thick brown undergrowth concealing the rocks where it emerged. The churning of the falls hitting the ground far below was the only warning many would get.

Under snow, it would be almost invisible.

I'd planned the exercise based on real events. Last winter, a man had broken a leg plunging down the crevice. It would only be a matter of time before it happened again. People ignored personal safety, particularly if there was a photograph to be had.

Cameron paused for a moment then nodded. He strode away, calling on a team to set up the ropes, ready to carry a rescue load. Two of the older members of the team had advanced rigging training, and they approached the gorge with care, talking through the process as they went.

I stood back and let Cameron manage the action, his face damp with the light rain, and his manner confident as he ordered the crew around the slopes.

Some were his relatives, including twin red-headed brothers of nineteen, Max and Maddock McRae. I'd yet to be as impressed with them as I was their cousin, but had spent little time with them. I presumed they worked or were at university, but more importantly, I often saw them heading into Cait's cottage.

"Max and Maddock, on me," I barked.

Both raised their heads from watching the rigging set up over the falls, and joined me.

"What are our principle methods of locating the casualty following a report?" I questioned.

"Fuck," one drawled. "Good thing ye prepped for a test."

His brother didn't flinch. "Source of the initial report is best, followed by Phonefind or What3words, if the person needing help has a working phone. A local team member would be another good source."

I acknowledged his good answer, peering between them. They were utterly identical. The same dark-auburn hair, green eyes, and pale, freckled skin. I guessed their ma could tell them apart, but I had no chance. I wondered at how closely they were related to Cait—they bore little resemblance to her.

"Which twin are ye?" I asked the helpful brother.

He grinned. "Maddock."

The other lad chuffed a sarcastic laugh, his attention switching to the wide glen below, as if he wanted to be anywhere but here.

Irritation rose.

I couldn't have passengers on my crew. Either he was here to work or he was gone.

"Then ye must be Max," I snapped, my patience already thin. "Why don't ye tell me what you'd do as a runner, attending the scene today ahead of a main party?"

He heaved a sigh like I was annoying him. I glowered deeper.

"Lochinvar, can ye come here?" Cameron called.

I turned on my bootheel and stomped away.

"Saved by the bell," Max quipped behind me.

Stowing my annoyance away for later, I homed in on the rigging crew. "How's it going?"

Cameron pointed at the neat rope work on the ground. "Grand. We've tested the rigging, and all is well. But I dinna think we should carry out the rest of the exercise today."

For fuck's sake. "Why not? We're here and ready. It's a waste of time if we pack up now."

He lifted his chin, indicating behind me. "The fog."

I spun around and took in the view.

Or lack of one.

In my distraction, I'd completely missed how the light rain had turned into a thick cloud. The summit of the hill was completely obscured, and the slopes of the glen drifted away even as I stared.

Fuck.

The crew waited on my word.

I twisted back, my mood increasing, but at myself now. This was no way to lead. I'd dropped the ball. "Good call. Pack up. We'll make a fresh attempt another day."

Cameron gave the orders, and I dropped my head back and gazed at the white-out sky, summoning my strength. I had to get a handle on myself or I was going to go insane.

An angry shout came from my left, and I whipped around to seek the source of the ruckus. The twin lads squared off against each other, antagonism decorating their expressions. Then Maddock, the more helpful of the two, murmured something low and taunting. Max's lip curled, and he snapped out a punch at his brother. Maddock ducked then shoved Max hard in the chest.

"Ah fuck, naw again," Cameron muttered.

He jogged over and dove into the fray, knocking a furious Max aside before separating the two men. Another man joined him and frogmarched Max away.

In turn, the remaining crew collected up the gear, packed it away, and descended the hill to our cars. I sought Cameron.

"What the hell's up with those twins?" I asked.

He raised a shoulder. "Personal issue. They've always brawled, though not usually like this."

"We cannae have fighting in the service," I warned. "Even with trainees. It's risky and unprofessional."

"Agreed," Cameron said. "It's up to ye if ye let them continue. But so ye know, Maddock is away at university most of the time, so they aren't usually on call together."

At the cars, I paused. I'd travelled to the site in the rescue service's Jeep, my own car at home, but now, I needed nothing more than a good run.

My muscles screamed for further punishment. My body ached for it. The truth surfaced.

Ah fuck, but I wanted sex.

To chase Cait down and get that look back in her eye. To have the pert blonde woman under me, moaning my name. *Christ.*

"I'll make my own way back."

Cameron squinted at me. "Are ye sure? It's a fair walk home. Easy to get lost."

And the visibility was shite. I was a fucking mess to even consider it.

"Fine, drop me at the road. I still need to use up some energy." I slammed myself inside, not speaking again until we were off the hill.

Cameron halted to let me out, then I was alone in the

misty valley. Just me, the empty, winding road, and my spiralling thoughts.

---

*F*orty minutes later, I regretted my choices. The fog had thickened to below ten metres visibility, and fine droplets had leaked inside my waterproofs. I couldn't lose my way as the road led straight to the estate, but I craved my warm home.

Almost as much as I craved other things.

A low rumbling pulled me out of my thoughts. Already on the verge, I stepped back, wary of idiot drivers speeding despite the conditions.

Orange hazard lights blinked, illuminating the water-filled air. The vehicle grew closer, its rate slow, fog lights glowing. I watched it approach.

Then recognition slapped me in the face.

It was Cait's car.

She sat forward in the driver's seat, peering out, though not spotting me on the bank. The car slid past.

Fuck this. I had to talk to her.

I lurched to a jog and caught up, then banged on the boot. The car shuddered to a halt, but the *click* of the locks resounded.

Smart woman.

I strode to the front window and ducked to look inside. "Cait, it's me."

She clutched her hand to her chest in relief, then hit the button to lower the window. "Ye scared me. This weather is insane. Why are ye out in it?"

"A poorly judged walk."

She burst out in a laugh. "This is why I never go hiking. It's dangerous. Need a ride?"

Wrestling my rucksack off, I climbed in the passenger side, too big for her little car and too wound up to speak.

Cait gazed at me. "Are ye okay?"

"Naw really."

She blew out a breath, her cheeks pink. "Let's get home. You'll feel better once you're in."

She was still being cool with me. I couldn't bear it.

The closer we got to home, the greater my emotions spiked.

At the area we parked, under a stand of trees, Cait took the keys from the ignition and tilted her head at me. "Getting out?"

"No."

She frowned but waited, a witness to my suffering.

I scrubbed my hand over my face, all too aware of how weird I was being. Yet it couldn't be helped. Bathed as I was in Cait's company, her scent, and her half-amused look, my surge of need eclipsed all reason.

"Ye want me," I uttered.

Fuck, that wasn't how I meant to phrase it.

"I mean, I want ye."

"Want?"

"Aye. Want. Lust after. Stare at."

Cait dropped her focus to her lap. "Oh. We're doing this?"

She could've denied it. Told me I was mad. Kicked me out of the car. But Cait only sighed.

Then words fell like lead weights from her lips. "You're married."

Utter relief danced through my veins, warming me from

my damp clothes. I wanted to laugh. "Divorced. A long time ago."

Cait's mouth opened, and her gaze flew to mine.

Stark, heated chemistry swarmed, filling the car. Only half of it coming from me.

My phone buzzed.

I swore but collected it from my pocket.

"The school," I mumbled then answered, my heart pounding for too many reasons.

"Mr Ross, it's Una. We won't be running our after-school club today due to the weather conditions. I can't ask my staff to stay late in this fog. It willnae be safe. Are ye able to collect Isla or shall I take her to Cait's?"

"I'll be there," I replied, my throat tight.

We hung up, and I returned my attention to Cait. Likewise, she jerked her vision up, as if she'd been examining me.

"I have to fetch my daughter."

"Okay."

"This conversation isn't over."

Cait blinked but didn't reply. She climbed from the car and went into her house, and it took every ounce of my self-control not to pursue her.

Instead, I slammed myself into my 4X4 and got back on the road.

Isla needed me, and she would always be my first priority.

10

*C**ait* Lochinvar's car disappeared into the mist, and I slouched indoors and fell onto my couch, draping my arm over my eyes.

For a good fifteen minutes, I just laid there, mulling over the same points.

He was *not* married.

He wanted me.

Casey had called earlier to ask if I'd thought any more about going on a date. She believed getting myself out there was the best test, but my mind and body rebelled against the idea.

I'd dreamed of Lochinvar.

In it, he'd tracked me down and caught me in his strong arms. He'd torn my clothes from me, and I'd...let him.

Liked it.

Woke up in a sweat.

If this was my sexual awakening, it had waited a hell of a long time to come about. I rolled up and padded to my bedroom, stripping my work suit, shirt, and underwear. Then I dove into a hot shower.

The water cascaded over my body, hitting areas that previously never registered as so sensitive. Now, I was keyed up and...what was the description my friends used? Needy?

Yeah, that.

I slid my hands down my naked flesh, lingering over my nipples before delving south. Touching myself had never been high on my agenda. I could orgasm, but it wasn't the big deal everyone else made it out to be.

Right now, it wasn't my hands I wanted there.

Lochinvar's face appeared in my mind. His thick body. His piercing stare.

His mouth.

I glanced over my clit and hissed at the sensation.

Shite. That felt good.

Yet...I didn't want to do this alone.

I killed the shower and stepped out, dragging my dressing gown over my wet body. On my bed, I towel dried my hair, considering those fresh thoughts of my burly neighbour.

A thudding shook my front door.

I jumped, and goosebumps rose on my skin. Keeping low, I snuck to the bedroom window and peered out.

Lochinvar's broad back loomed next to my door. I sighed in relief and skipped to answer. The moment I did, Isla flew inside.

"Da's had a call," she announced.

I lifted my gaze to her father. He stared at me, and his focus sank to my neckline, and lower before jerking up.

I shivered.

"Isla's right. I have to go. An entire hiking group is lost in the fog, high above Glen Durie. Will ye be okay?"

I swallowed, that pesky neediness spiking. "We'll be fine."

He took a step back. Then another.

"Wait," I said. "What should I do if you're not back by Isla's bedtime?"

His gaze darkened. Without a word, he reached for his keys and removed the one for his cottage. I accepted it, his fingers brushing my palm.

Electricity licked me.

Lochinvar gave me one last searing, lust-laden look, then left.

---

*O*ver the course of the nearly two months since Lochinvar and Isla had moved next door, the little girl had warmed to me. She still clammed up if accidentally touching on her past, but on the whole, I'd uncovered a sweet if somewhat stubborn child.

Very much her father's daughter, though they had no outward similarities.

I dressed in a hurry and joined her in the living room. "Hungry? It's early, so we can make something that takes longer. Maybe lasagne from scratch?"

Isla beamed and nodded, her fair curls bobbing, and she leapt from the couch and followed me into the kitchen. She seemed to enjoy the process of cooking, watching more than contributing, and she took one of the two stools at the island, placing her chin on her hands.

Normally, I'd chat away, but my brain was mush, my thoughts gone with her da. Instead, I turned on the radio and danced as I fried the mince with onions, garlic, herbs, and three kinds of tomatoes. I had Isla stir the white sauce so it didn't curdle then help me grate the cheese.

Without even thinking, I constructed an enormous lasagne, mentally allocating the largest portion to her father.

Isla declined from helping with the salad, her protective walls rising once more, but dutifully tried all the vegetables when our meal was ready.

We ate, working through Isla's spelling homework, then took to the couch. My home wasn't yet kitted out for a child, and I didn't have games or books. I didn't want to sit her in front of the TV all evening, so there was only one thing for it.

The lion's den.

Anticipation swirled in my belly.

I was beyond curious about this little family. Worse since Lochinvar's confession. They were so close. He often took Isla with him on weekend hikes, then returned with his tired girl on his shoulder. She didn't lack for anything, and it was as if they'd always been a unit, not one that missed the mother of the family.

I wondered if Lochinvar had a picture of his ex-wife anywhere.

I should mind my own business. Yet the wondering wouldn't cease.

"Your da gave me the key to your cottage," I said. "Would ye like to go there?"

"Aye!" Isla leapt up.

I slid my boots on as she buckled up her school shoes.

"You're sounding more Scottish." I ducked into the kitchen to collect the covered plate I'd readied for Lochinvar, then turned to witness Isla scowling.

"I am Scottish." She stomped outside and waited while I

locked up then moved to open her door. "Just because I never lived here until now."

Her statement begged a question, but my lips were sealed.

We entered the house, and Isla discarded her bag and outerwear then darted down the hall.

Switching on a lamp, I peered around the living room. This cottage was the bigger of the two. Like mine, it had a wide front room that took up the width of the single-storey house, with the kitchen to the left. I'd seen the place be decorated, and not much had changed. A bookshelf held children's stories and a few thrillers, but no framed photos perched on top. The coat hooks hosted light jackets and pairs of huge male or tiny female shoes waited underneath.

I followed Isla and hovered at the end of the bedroom hall. "Are ye okay?"

"Da says I have to get changed out of my school things when I get home. Can ye help me?"

I stepped to her door and peered in. Isla was halfway into a fluffy unicorn onesie. The wide hood sported a twisted horn and pink satin ears. The sleeves and legs ended in darker material, mimicking hooves. One of her sleeves was inside out, so I reached to reinstate it.

"You're adorable. Did ye know the unicorn is the national animal of Scotland?"

Isla's eyes widened. "Do they live here?"

"Only in myths and legends," I said. "But we have a unicorn pool at the base of a waterfall. I'll take ye there one day."

"For my birthday?"

"When's that?"

She hesitated, linking her hands behind her back. "In December. Next month."

"I'll talk to your da about it."

She gave a little yip of excitement and skipped past me to the lounge.

But before I left her room, I caught sight of a picture frame by Isla's bed. A woman smiled out, a much younger Isla in her arms. Without going over to take a closer look, I could only see her grin and compare it to Isla's. But they were very alike.

That must be her mother. Presumably the woman was still alive, too, as Lochinvar hadn't called himself a widower. Only a divorcee.

God, Isla must miss her.

In the lounge, Isla had set up a game for us to play on the rug.

My heart swelled with affection. As much as I felt a pull towards Lochinvar, the same applied to his daughter. I knew they weren't staying past the length of his contract. Uncle Gordain would return by the end of February and take his job back. I couldn't imagine alpha male Lochinvar accepting a lower position.

They'd leave for certain.

That set the terms for how I saw the Ross family.

I could be a friend to Isla in that time. Maybe something different with her father. But only short-lived.

Fine. Boundary set.

The evening drew on, darkness falling. The fog lifted to drizzle, yet Lochinvar still didn't appear. I braided Isla's bountiful blonde curls then dozed on the couch with her. Ideally, she should've gone to bed, but she begged to wait up to see her father.

The snick of the door woke me with a start. The TV had frozen on an 'Are you still watching?' screen, and Isla snored, fast asleep, snuggled close.

Lochinvar stood over us, his features barely visible in the shadowed room.

Electricity danced over my skin.

He made a low sound, then slid his arms under Isla, his cold knuckles running across my arm. In a fluid motion, he lifted her to his chest, murmuring something soft as she stirred, then he carried her from the room.

I sat up, my pulse skittering. Did I leave? Staying felt...dangerous.

But I was no coward.

After a minute, the huge man reappeared. Without lighting the lamp, he took a seat at the other end of the sofa from me. The scent of him, of cool, fresh mountain air, spread my way.

"How did it go?" My voice came out timid. Not like me at all.

Lochinvar studied me. "Good. Four souls saved. Are ye pregnant?"

I blinked at the change in topic. "Why did ye think that?"

"Isla said."

I pieced together conversations we'd had. God, that must've been from when I'd told Casey and Brodie about my baby plans. "No. I'm not."

His eyes gleamed.

Though he didn't move, confusion and apprehension grabbed me, tightening my throat. I'd been in the position before when a man had been so obviously about to make a move on me. I hated the nervous awareness. The expectation the moment set.

The undoubted failure on my behalf to make it work.

"I'm going to have a baby with fertility treatment," I added fast. "Donor sperm."

Lochinvar tilted his head. "Ye dinna want a man?"

"Never been interested before."

The statement fell between us, loaded with meaning.

"Before me."

"Maybe."

"Are ye a virgin?" he asked, his tone not one of teasing or accusation, but of gentle interest.

"No. I tried sex at university."

"But ye didn't enjoy it," he stated. "Or more likely those ye experimented with were clueless."

Sweat broke out on my brow, but I didn't need to confirm his words.

Lochinvar pressed on. "What's different about me?"

"You're rougher. Wilder."

His analysis continued. "Did this start with me chopping the wood or before?"

"The wood. The axe."

"Ye like that harder side. The violence."

Again, not a question. I slowly nodded anyway, then gave up my truth. "I have a fantasy of ye. It's dark."

"I can let my tastes run dark, if ye want."

I shivered at the promise. "It's of ye pursuing me."

The admittance smarted. I was giving him power over me. Power he could use to humiliate me or reject me.

Lochinvar paused, considering this, then placed a hand on the sofa back and leaned in. He was so big, so broad.

My skin zinged in awareness.

Fear sprang, loading my muscles.

Fuck, he was going to kiss me. I wasn't ready. Didn't want this.

He brought his mouth close to my ear. "Get up."

"What?"

"Go to the door."

I obeyed, my frightened soul needing direction. I stepped into my shoes, no clue what was happening.

Lochinvar stalked over and grasped my waist. He manhandled my stiff body out of the way, then unlocked the door, opening it. With a finger, he pointed outside into the frigid night.

He...kicked me out?

"What...?" I stammered.

"Run, Cait."

What the hell was he doing? And why was this working? I skipped backwards. Lochinvar took a long tread after me, his jaw clenched tight.

Those black eyes glittered.

I was looking at a predator. A threat. A dangerous animal.

Excited, I turned and bolted. My pulse skyrocketed, and I flew over the ground. Every sense trained on the danger at my back. My spine tingled, fear merging with a different state. This was nothing like the emotion I'd felt in that hall at work. No, this was...exhilarating.

I reached the cars when a heavy arm caught me.

A helpless sound burst from my throat, and Lochinvar spun me around. He gripped my biceps so I couldn't escape and pushed me against his vehicle. Only his hand stopped me from banging my head on the metal.

With his huge frame, he caged me in, eclipsing the night.

I panted, every place we touched blazing to life with sensation. All fresh. All real and vital.

I struggled in vain.

Then Lochinvar crashed his lips onto my neck.

I opened my mouth in pure shock. The energy behind his almost-kiss-almost-bite bruised me, his beard abrading my skin. But the pain was nothing to the splintering joy.

I tried to move his lips to mine, but he didn't budge. All I could do was receive. His mouth slid to under my ear then to my collarbone, his teeth testing my flesh.

Lochinvar's leg forced its way between mine so I rode his thigh, my feet barely on the ground. A burst of sexual feeling spread from my core. I writhed to chase it, though barely able to move from the position he'd caught me in.

Then he dropped me.

Lochinvar stepped back, breathing hard. I staggered, nearly falling, and my chest rose and fell where I couldn't pull in enough air.

Neither of us spoke, but the dark light in his eyes only intensified.

Lochinvar gave a snort that sounded like satisfaction, then he turned and strode to his cottage. His door slammed, and I was left alone.

The night air cooled my ardour, and I stared, seeing nothing.

It hadn't been a real kiss, nor gentle and sweet.

What the hell was it? And why did I only want more?

11

*L*ochinvar

At the window, I watched Cait until she got herself together and returned to her home, closing herself safely inside.

In all my thirty years, I'd never experienced anything like I had in that moment.

Never been so rough.

So in need of dominating a woman.

Fuck, but I liked it.

Loved knowing I'd turned her on when no one else could.

My hard-as-nails cock agreed.

Yet I knew beyond a shadow of a doubt that I had to protect myself, too—why I hadn't kissed her sweet mouth. It would be too easy for me to barrel ahead with this and get burned.

I locked myself in the bathroom and started up the shower. Under the hot water, I took my cock in hand and braced an arm to the tiles. Lust surged with every stroke. In my head, I fucked into Cait's tight body, the woman wet and willing beneath me.

She'd want me to be hard on her, giving her the wild mountain man experience she'd imagined. The version of me that turned her on.

The way no other man had.

Ah God, that fucked with my head.

It had been too long.

"Fuck," I gritted out, as muted as I could make it.

A minute more of fucking my hand, then my balls tightened and I came.

Spent, I let the water spray down on me, washing my moment of madness away.

Not that it had made a dent in my need for Cait. No, that burned ever stronger.

"Aye, lass," I murmured. "Ball's in your court."

Like for any other hunter, it was a waiting game from now on.

12

*C*ait

It took days for my self-assurance to return. I read articles on attraction and kinks. I might be submissive, I considered. Needing my partner to call the shots.

That didn't seem quite right. Lochinvar made no further moves on me, though interest came off him in waves. So it was on me to push for more, and I intended to. Not so submissive of me.

I concocted a plan. An extension of my fantasy.

I just needed to get the nerve to ask him for it.

On Friday morning, he delivered Isla to school then returned home, taking a phone call in his car outside the cottages. Unlike the previous week, a sunny day had dawned, though with an underlying icy chill.

I wanted to go for a run.

Or a chase.

In my mind, Lochinvar would catch me and force me to the ground. We'd have sex, then, once he'd blown my mind, he'd let me go. Not that I'd be truly trapped.

I breathed through my nose, turned on, yet unable to

frame a way to ask him to pursue me. Instead, I dressed in my running kit and stepped outside.

A moment of waiting then Lochinvar climbed out of his 4X4. He cast his gaze down my body, lingering on my curves encased in the tight-fitting material.

"Going somewhere?"

"For a run."

"Where?" he demanded.

"Into the forest. Do ye have anywhere ye need to be?" My heart pounded.

Lochinvar's stare intensified. I didn't budge.

Then he stormed inside his home, the door left ajar.

I waited for a beat then took off, my trainers crunching the died-back undergrowth as I rounded the low wall to the forest behind my home. An animal track made my path, and I dragged in a lungful of clean air.

This had been my running route for years. Few others came out this way, the view obscured by the thick trees.

The perfect place for an ambush.

And I was certain Lochinvar would follow.

A crack of branches snapping quickened my already racing pulse.

I put power into my legs, flying up the hill and onto a flatter track. The scent of pine rose from where I crushed dense piles of fallen needles under my feet. Woodland animals scurried from my path.

A glance over my shoulder revealed a shadowed figure in pursuit. A big, dark man.

Fuck. He'd come.

My breathing stuttered, but I pressed on, jogging faster. My hunter sped up. The distance between us slimmed.

That same thrill of the chase blazed through me.

Ahead, a stand of evergreens waited, exactly where I

knew it would be. I left the path and plunged inside the thick lower branches to a small, hidden clearing.

At almost the same second, a hand gripped my trailing wrist.

"Ah!" I squeaked and stumbled.

I hit the soft ground.

Lochinvar fell on top of me, dropping on his hands and knees over my body. For a second, he did nothing but check my expression.

Then he took my throat in a light hold. His other hand coasted to my waist, and without ceremony, he yanked down my running shorts.

I slammed my eyes closed, entirely overwhelmed. In lust, fear, and a myriad of other emotions.

Lochinvar stripped my shorts to my ankles and forced apart my knees.

Without a word or further pause, his mouth landed on the juncture of my legs.

Heat blitzed through me. I yelped, and he moved his fingers from my throat to cover my mouth. Silenced, I squirmed under his heavy form.

Lochinvar gave me no half-measure. He licked then sucked on my sensitive clit. An animal sound ripped out of him, and he hoisted my hips then drove his tongue inside me.

Blooms of warmth spread in my veins, despite the icy day. The forest, the sounds of nature, it all paled to the background, and all I could feel was him. Nothing I'd ever done to myself felt this good. No one had ever touched me with the same reaction.

My breasts grew heavier in my sports bra. My muscles heated, tensed to the point of hurting.

Then he pushed a finger inside me, adding a second.

Some magic place exploded with feeling. I bit on the hand over my mouth.

Lochinvar pumped in and out of me.

Oh God. Oh Christ.

If I cursed out loud, I had no clue. Only the rushing of my own blood filled my ears.

He continued sucking, using his whole mouth to assault my private area. Each hit inside touched a blissful patch of flesh. My body supplied a rush of delicious chemicals far greater than ever before on my solo adventures.

I struggled. He held me harder.

Then inside, I tightened.

Lochinvar made a deep sound of need.

Somehow, this was the trigger. I whimpered then surged, arched my back, pushing against Lochinvar's intrusions.

And came.

I splintered into pieces, a mess of nothing but powerful, orgasmic waves. They broke over my mind, and I swam in sheer heaven.

Distantly, I was aware of Lochinvar working me through it. He swore, his tone utterly awed and delicious. The pressure of him pinning me down released. I was spent. Boneless. Unable to crack an eye.

In minutes, he'd done what took me an hour alone, though I'd never once reached the same heights.

But then I returned to myself. Suddenly cold, I scuttled up, drawing my shorts over my nakedness.

Lochinvar sat back on his haunches, his chest heaving with deep breaths. He scrubbed over his mouth then raised his gaze to mine.

What did I say? Thanks? That was great?

But then he gestured, pointing to the route home. I took a step, and he moved out of my way.

I jogged home, my brand-new sexual partner keeping a safe distance and making not a single demand of me.

We returned to our cottages as if nothing happened.

Finally, in the shower, removing pine needles from where they stuck to my skin, I had a realisation. That had been immense. Exciting. A revelation.

And I absolutely wanted to try it again.

13

*C*_{*ait*}

*C*ait

From her cosy seat in her lounge, Casey stared at me, her mouth open in a perfect O. She'd moved into her new home—built by the family on the site of an old barn—just a week ago, and the place was still in the process of being furnished. The kitchen, lounge, and one bedroom had been completed, the nursery was next. They were living the dream.

"He chased you? Then pounced on you?"

"Yep. Right there under the trees."

From the iPad screen, some fancy hotel suite in the background, Viola gawked. "Holy fuck. And he didn't kiss you?"

"Nope. Well, not on the mouth. He dove right on in and got to work."

"Did he come himself?"

I hesitated, considering that fact for the first time. "No. He didn't even touch himself that I saw. Only me."

"And it was good?"

"Insanely so."

Both women gave up twin sighs.

Casey mock-wiped her brow. "That is extremely hot, and I will never be able to look him in the eye again."

I grinned. "Have ye met him properly?"

"I have. He was here talking to Brodie about joining the mountain rescue. With Blayne's new job, he's away too much to commit, but Brodie's going for it. I might, too, when our baby is older." She considered me. "I liked him. He's frank and honest, and the no-bullshit approach suits you."

I liked that about him, too. As well as a lot of other things. A week had passed since our...dalliance, but not a moment of it had escaped my memory. I pulled a face, trying to frame my next sentence. I needed my friends' input. They were so much more experienced than me.

"I was thinking about asking him for something else. Another round, but maybe with a difference. I don't want to only be able to get off after being chased."

Viola snorted. "That would be a fun relationship."

"Well, it can't be a relationship. He might be single, but he's only here for another three months."

"Okay then. Why not try straight-up sex? In a bedroom, not the cold ground," Casey asked. "Lay him out, take the reins, so to speak, and be the one in charge."

I squinted, assessing my reaction. "I never liked that in the past. What if it's the same and I get spooked?"

"Then you ask him to tie up your hands and blindfold you, and you'll be back in your comfort zone."

Viola groaned. "Oh man. Talk about zones. I'm right in the horny one, and Leo isn't back until late tonight. I decided against going to every gig because the noise levels might not be good for the baby, but now I'm regretting my choices."

Casey laughed. "I'm the other side. I can barely move, so sex isn't an every-minute need anymore."

It was true. At eight months, she was huge.

"On that," Casey added. "Any news on baby planning, Cait? Did you reconsider your fertility clinic idea?"

I frowned. "No. Why would I?"

"Because now you've jump-started your sex life, sex can lead to love, which might mean you eventually find someone who you want to make a family with."

I followed her logic. It made sense. And yet... "That could happen, or not. I've never had feelings for a man. I haven't suddenly fallen head over heels for Lochinvar because he made me orgasm. Even if I did find someone, that could take years. Then years more to trust them and know they'd be a good parent."

"Fair point," Viola concluded on-screen. "I can remember ye telling me at seventeen that ye wanted to be a mother. Maybe even younger."

"Exactly."

Casey gave me a soft smile. "Is that so? I knew I'd want a family in future but not this soon. I can't regret my baby—I love him or her so much and they aren't even here yet—but I would've liked time with my men to grow our relationship."

An option I wouldn't have.

She continued. "If you do find a partner in future, he'll accept you as a single mother. If he doesn't, he isn't the right guy."

I exhaled a slight sense of misgiving. I had a plan and it was a good one. Sure, there were downsides, but overwhelmingly it would be good. Nothing had changed in who I was or what I had to offer a child. There was still the question of whether I'd have problems, too. No, my mind was made up.

"I'm going to contact the clinic again to ask if there's been any cancellations."

I found my phone and tapped out the email, hitting 'send' to commit myself once more.

Viola asked Casey pregnancy questions, and I let the knowledge fill me. Soon, I'd need that, too. It was going to happen.

14

Lochinvar

"Da, was Ma's hair blonde or brown?" Isla chirped out.

I stumbled in my footsteps. We were yards from the school, other families milling at the gate. Taking Isla's small hand, I led her a few yards away.

"Blonde, like ye. Why are ye asking?"

"We did a class on gen...genets."

"Genetics?"

"Yes! Ma must have had blue eyes, too, but really, I should have brown like yours." She gazed up at my black hair and dark eyes.

"She did, I mean does." My heart thudded. My mouth dried.

Isla didn't remember her ma, hardly surprising, and although I'd expected questions, I was in no way prepared to answer them. She was only six. No, near seven.

Even so, I thought I'd have more time.

"We'll have a proper chat about it at home. Look." I

gestured at the school. "Everyone's going in. Ye better hurry."

"Bye, Da!" She flung her arms around me then ran to join the end of the line of children from her class.

I moved to the gate and waited for a moment, watching her.

Isla looked just like her mother. Even had one or two of her mannerisms, which could only come from her genes. The family history that could one day hurt her.

That could make her despise me.

Guilt choked me. The crocodile of kids filed inside, and I just stood there.

"Mr Ross?"

I glanced to find Una, the school head, yards away.

"Did ye need to speak with me?" she asked.

"Naw. I'm going. Just keep her safe, aye?" I had no idea where the request came from.

The teacher's face crinkled in concern. "Safe? Of course. Is there something I need to know?"

Isla's school had locked doors, strict rules, and passwords for collecting kids, CCTV covering the entrances. I'd assessed it any number of times.

But this threat today came from within. There was nothing I could do to protect my daughter from that.

"I...need to go." I muttered an apology, ducked my head, and left.

---

*a*t home, I had the rest of the morning free. There were jobs to be done at the cottage, a loose shelf in Isla's room, a radiator that wouldn't heat, so I buckled my toolbelt around my waist and set about my tasks.

An hour later, a light knock at my door interrupted my work.

Without even rising from my crouch, I knew the identity of my caller.

Cait McRae haunted my thoughts more now than ever. I'd waited on her, but the need in me had risen to insane proportions. I was barely keeping a lid on it and relied on my cast-iron will to stop from marching to her house and demanding more.

I'd half expected her to come home with another guy, killing dead my infatuation.

I stood and dragged my shirt off my hot body but left the toolbelt over my jeans. Then I strode to open the door.

Cait peeked at me, her hands in the pockets of her floral dress. She went to speak, swallowed, then tried again, her gaze stuck on my chest. A faint blush stole up her throat.

Frustration felled my defences, and I reached out and pulled her inside, slamming the door behind us. Then I released her and waited, folding my arms.

"You're busy," she said.

"I'm not."

"I should be working, but..."

"Ye want something from me?"

Her throat bobbed. "I do."

The room spun around me. All I could see was Cait. So pretty. The more I knew her, the lovelier she became. Whatever she needed, I was ready.

"Spit it out, woman. Make your demand and I'll answer."

She toed the floor. "Can we go to your bedroom?"

Fuck. I tilted my head, surprised. "Ye want me? In a bed?"

Every wish I'd made regarding the woman had just come true.

I continued, not intending to make this harder for her,

especially considering I was already hard and more than ready to go. "We'll go to yours."

"Why not here?"

"I'll be able to smell ye after, and it'll drive me mad."

Her cheeks flamed, but she nodded and turned. We were inside her place in seconds. Cait disappeared into the hall. I strode after her and closed us into the bright room.

She sat on the edge of her bed. Her hands shook.

Ah Christ, she was nervous.

I drew the gauzy curtains and dropped my toolbelt to the rug with a thud. Cait watched me, no attempt at seduction in her, but fear plain.

I didn't want her to be frightened of me.

There were any number of ways I could go about this. Knock her onto her back and take control like in the forest. Or a gentler, slow easing into sex.

Maybe neither of those were what she sought.

After a beat, I sat beside her then shuffled back, lying out on her mattress with my eyes closed.

Cait's breath hitched, and she shifted her weight. I imagined her looking me over, my bare upper half ready for her examination, my jeans tented from where I was hard for her.

She didn't speak, so I explained. No need for misunderstandings.

"I imagine ye never had a man in your bed. I'll keep my eyes closed," I promised. "Put a blindfold on me. Do whatever ye want to me. Ask whatever ye like."

Rustling sounded, and she moved on the bed. The room was warm, but I suppressed a shiver.

"Talk to me, Cait."

"Can I really blindfold ye?"

"Aye."

Soft material landed on my face, a scarf, I guessed, and I raised my head to let her fasten it.

"Can I touch ye?" she asked.

I wanted to tell her if she didn't, I'd go insane, but in this new scenario, she didn't want the hunter. She wanted permission to play with the wild animal she saw in me.

She needed a safe body.

I simply inclined my head in the positive, my breath held.

Careful fingertips landed on my forearm and traced through the black hair. They ran up my biceps and gripped the hard muscle, testing my strength.

I drew my arms over my head, resting them on Cait's soft pillows.

Every nerve ending stood to attention, awaiting this woman's moves. My cock throbbed, and the anticipation hurt.

Cait followed my arms back to my linked hands, then into my hair. She drew her nails over my scalp. I hissed, enjoying the sensation far too much.

She ghosted over my features, stroking my beard, then both of her hands landed on my chest. With the lightest touch, she pressed on my nipple.

Pure shock zapped me.

I stifled a groan, but my muscles tensed.

Cait stalled. "Is that...? Did I...?"

"Naw. It's nice." What a fucking weak word.

She made a pleased sound.

"Use your mouth," I suggested.

Her breath played over my skin, then Cait's hot mouth replaced her fingers. She licked me then hummed. "Salty."

From where I'd built up a sweat. Damn. "I can shower," I muttered.

"Don't."

She licked me again, the end of her tongue glancing over my nipple. And again. That tiny sensation became my world. I groaned, unconcealed this time, and Cait increased the pressure. She swapped sides, using her thumb to work the nipple she'd left.

I'd never cared much for foreplay, not the receiving of it, but Cait's careful exploration was the sexiest experience of my life.

My breath hitched, but I held my position. She kissed my chest, while I slowly went crazy from holding back.

It was too important that she own this.

For one, I had no clue what I was doing besides being here for her. I hadn't been involved with a woman for the longest time. Cait had come to me for a second go, which changed us from a one-off to...something else.

I should be over the fucking moon that she'd selected me, but a low warning still sounded in my mind.

I didn't care about being used.

I just had to keep emotions from the fray.

Surely no challenge for a man used to exerting control over every part of his life.

Her ministrations continued, and my hunger grew. Cait pressed her lips to my cheek then turned my head to do the same to below my ear. Then she sucked my earlobe.

"Fuck," I bit out, almost goddamn dizzy.

"Did I hurt ye?"

"No. I just had no idea that was a pleasure zone."

"Neither did I." She pulled away and paused. "What do I do now?"

"I told ye, anything. Take off your dress."

"I already did."

Ah Christ. She'd been in her underwear the whole time? My cock leaked, painfully enclosed in my jeans.

"Undress me."

Her hands traced over my abs and down my happy trail to my waist, then undid my buttons and zip. My cock strained to greet her, and Cait hummed again.

"Can I get ye completely naked?"

"You're killing me. Aye, woman."

Her musical laugh had me pressing my lips together to stop from grinning. Sex had never been so much fun, and we'd not got to that part yet.

God, I hoped we'd get to that part.

Cait moved off the bed then stripped my jeans and boxers.

I lay there, bare and proud, jutting out for her.

"Do ye have condoms?" I asked.

"I do." She left the bed again, and a drawer opened then closed. Plastic wrap crinkled, and then foil tore. "I've never put one of these on before."

"Roll it down me, but make sure ye leave a gap at the end."

Cait seized my cock. I'd been expecting the contact, but after all the attention she'd given the rest of my body, I was primed beyond belief. I jerked, my legs bowed out and my heels pressing into her quilt. My action dislodged Cait's hold.

"Christ." I barked a laugh.

She giggled. "Trying again."

This time, I locked my jaw.

I expected the condom to be rolled on, but instead, Cait's tongue slid over my engorged cock. "Fuck," I yelled, then fisted the blanket beneath me and turned my head. Heat drove through me.

I needed to see her do this. Wanted to witness her mouth on me in this way. But still, under the blindfold, I kept my eyes closed, the darkness adding to the sheer erotic scene.

All I could do was feel. Her fingers indenting my hip and thigh. Her hair tickling my skin. The warmth of her tentative blow job. Maybe her first. Urges to fuck her mouth came at me again and again.

My breathing came ragged.

Cait took me deep into her mouth.

My balls tightened.

"Stop." I pressed the heel of my hand into my eyes. "Any more and I'll come. I dinna want to do that yet."

"But ye liked what I was doing?"

What a question. My restraints broke. I reached for her, blindly seeking her hand. Then I linked our fingers and wrapped them around my cock, crushing hard.

"Fuck me, Cait," I begged.

The longest moment in the history of time passed. I'd made a mistake. Blown it. Scared her.

Then Cait threw her leg over mine and climbed on top.

15

C ait

Naked aside from my bra, I straddled Lochin-var's thick thighs and got into position. Despite my university hookups, I'd barely tried anything other than lying under a guy.

This experience had already blown my mind.

I wanted Lochinvar badly. Needed him inside me.

I reached between us and held his dick in place then sank down onto him.

He made a guttural sound of pleasure.

I stiffened and held still, braced on his chest.

His groans earlier had lit me up, and I'd enjoyed his body tensing when I touched him, but now...

The alien stretch of his huge cock alarmed me. It didn't hurt, but it was...odd. No explosion of lust eased the feeling. No sexy transformation changed what I already knew.

I didn't like it.

Before, when I'd tried this, I hadn't felt able to stop my lovers just because I didn't exactly enjoy what we were doing. I'd let them continue until they were finished. Then I'd slunk away, hating myself.

Lochinvar would expect me to be moaning porn star-style. Yet here I was, being weird.

A clammy chill rippled over me.

All the good feelings I'd gained fled.

"Cait?" he asked. He repeated himself when I didn't answer.

Tears welled in my eyes.

Then Lochinvar did something curious. During all my actions, he'd only touched me once, to guide my hand to his dick. He'd linked his fingers behind his head straight after.

Now, he released them and reached for me, bringing me down to lie on him. I obliged, huddling into him, my knees around his hips and my cheek to his chest.

He hugged me, his muscular arms banding around me.

We were still joined, but he made no complaint.

"Everything's okay," he half whispered.

"I'm sorry," I replied, my voice cracking.

"For what? We're only lying here."

His fingers drifted over my spine in soothing repetition. After a minute, my pulse slowed and I exhaled. I trusted this man. Everything he did was in service to someone else. His daughter. My family. Lost or injured people in the mountains.

Me.

"I'm freaking out," I said.

He didn't reply. Just waited.

Moments passed. We remained in the pose.

Slowly, by degrees, my panic ebbed away.

Lochinvar adjusted me on his chest. The action shifted me on his hard-as-steel dick.

Both of us stilled.

This time, it felt different. His tiny move hit something inside me. A pleasure point. I lifted on my palms and wriggled, trying to find it. Renewed, I rose on my haunches and slid him out then in a few inches.

Yes! There it was again.

Lochinvar pressed his lips together, his nostrils flared.

Hmm. Guess he liked that, too.

I rode him a few more times, chasing the sensation. The solid weight of him changed from feeling weird to essential. None of my previous lovers had been as big as him. None had touched the places he was.

A deep ache formed, but the edge of frustration still affected me. Bringing myself to orgasm like this seemed a million miles from here.

"Need some help?" Lochinvar asked, his low voice rumbling.

"How? I mean yes."

Slowly, he sat up until we were face to face, me bright-eyed and too aware, him unseeing beneath the silk scarf blindfold. Then he touched me, my shoulders first, then down my sides. He explored my body with his caress until he came to my bra fastener.

"Can I take this off ye?"

"Do it."

My bra fell away, and he eased back on one arm, palming my breast with his free hand. He ducked to kiss the swell of the other before sucking my nipple into his mouth.

"Oh," I uttered at the whoosh of lust.

Lochinvar curved his arm around me, taking my weight. He kept on with his attention to my hard nipple but under me, jacked his hips. That same place inside me bloomed with pleasure, doubled now.

I yelped and he did it again. Lochinvar commenced a

steady motion, teasing my nipple while fucking me. Hitting the spot over and over. After a moment, the warmth returned to my veins. I gave up a sound of need, surprising myself.

"Grab on to me," Lochinvar asked.

I wrapped my arms around him, and he left my breasts, his head against mine. Then he pressed his lips to my cheek.

Holding me up, he thrust into me. "Ye dinna have to come. I willnae either. Just feel. Dinna fret."

He wouldn't? I didn't have to? But I wanted it, been cut up because I couldn't. Then again, I'd had little to no sexual interest before.

My thoughts dissolved as Lochinvar picked up the pace. He clamped me to him, fucking me with increasing power. I hid my face in his neck and held on, allowing the moment to dominate my mind.

Every other thought fled.

Each crash of our bodies put pressure on my clit. Without thinking, I wedged my hand between us and strummed myself. Lochinvar choked on a sound of need.

Like before, his suppressed noise ignited a flurry of fireworks.

He loved this. It was working for him. I'd gotten that masculine groan from him.

Something surrendered in my mind.

Oh God.

Breathless, I chased the feeling, rubbing my clit while he fucked me. Our rhythms joined in perfect unison.

Then, from nowhere, I smashed through a wall of pleasure.

Some kind of strangled cry burst from me, and I pulsed around his dick, coming. There was no space for thought.

None. Only a trembling rush of deep satisfaction. Brilliant sparks danced in my vision.

I clutched Lochinvar, shock battling with the need to laugh in delight.

He moved faster. Slack-jawed, I came back to earth.

I'd done it! I'd come.

I'd had sex and liked it.

So much heat had been generated I was surprised the windows hadn't steamed up.

Then Lochinvar growled and changed his stroke. Still so hard, he pushed his forehead to my shoulder. His breathing accelerated. His firm muscles trembled.

Oh God, I needed him to get there, too.

I held on, silently urging him. My heart rate skittered along, too fast yet perfect.

Lochinvar gripped my backside. "I said I wouldnae come…"

"Forget that. I need ye to."

He withdrew and slammed into me hard.

We both groaned.

A knock rattled the front door.

"Caitriona?" a voice called.

Lochinvar halted, sweat pouring off him. "Someone just called ye."

"Oh my God. That's Ma."

He loosened his hold, his mouth open, his body poised to ram into mine.

"I'm so sorry," I babbled. "I invited her for lunch. She's early."

He clenched his jaw, eyes still closed. Then he released me to the quilt. "Fuck." He scrubbed a hand over his face. His dick bobbed, still so hard. "Give me a second."

I leapt off the bed and snatched my dressing gown from the wardrobe, wrapping it around myself in a hurry.

"Ma has a key," I explained. "If I don't answer, she'll assume I've gone for a walk and let herself in."

Peeking back, I witnessed Lochinvar tear off the condom and finally remove the blindfold from his eyes. Light blazed in them. He lumbered up on legs as unsteady as mine, then pulled on his boxers, jeans, and socks. Finally, he buckled on his toolbelt, presenting a vision I'd see in my dreams tonight.

"I can't find your t-shirt," I squeaked.

"Didnae have one."

Oh shite, he didn't.

A grin tweaked his lips. Despite the fact we'd been interrupted at a crucial moment, somehow, he was finding this funny.

"I can't believe this is happening," I griped.

His amusement increased the more I flapped. "Regretting me already? That's a blow to my pride."

"No!" I clamped my hand over my mouth, laughter bubbling up. "Go out the patio doors."

"Aye, if ye like."

Argh. I didn't like. I wanted to continue.

Ma knocked again, and I closed my eyes for a second. "Coming," I called out the bedroom door.

"Okay," she yelled back.

"Yeah, ye were," Lochinvar quipped.

I ran my fingers through my hair. Then I took a deep breath. "I feel like a teenager."

"Don't. You've done nothing wrong."

True, except in sexuality terms I was so far behind I couldn't help but be awkward. I took another calming breath and let my smile out again.

"I'm sorry ye didn't get to...finish." I waved a hand.

"So am I. But that wasnae the point, no?" He leaned to peek out of the window at Ma and his forehead wrinkled. "That's your ma? Scarlet McRae, aye? I met her on a training day. She's a volunteer."

"Yep."

"The red hair... Are Max and Maddock your brothers?"

"They are." I unlocked the patio door.

Lochinvar stayed still. "How did that colouring skip ye?"

Ma had freckles and flame-red hair, my brothers' a darker auburn. However, she and I had no features in common. I was blonde, two inches taller, my face rounder and more symmetrical, my eyes wider, and green to her blue. No one would ever pick us out as kin.

From anyone else, Lochinvar's question would bother me, but right now, it didn't. "Technically, they're my half-brothers. Ma isn't my biological mother. That was someone else. But Scarlet raised me. Genetics don't automatically make a family, right?"

A flash crossed his gaze.

Of recognition, fear, and deep discomfort.

Before I could ask or say a word, Lochinvar spun away and exited my room, stalking over the patio to his place.

Leaving me wondering what the heck I just said.

I skipped to answer the door to Ma, then made out I was just hopping into the shower, leaving her to make our lunch in the kitchen.

I stripped and washed up in record time, all manner of interesting aches in my body. I'd barely had a chance to process what happened, but fresh pride stole over me while

I dressed. I'd had full sex, with a minor blip where my brain checked out, but Lochinvar had helped me through it.

Without getting his.

Again.

I should buy him flowers or something.

Chuckling to myself, I thought back to what Aunt Georgia had said. How my birth mother had screwed me up. In your face, Georgia.

I just hadn't started yet.

*L*ochinvar

  At the store in the hangar's operations room, I stomped about, checking inventory. Outside in the main building, crew shouted to each other and metal clanked, accompanying me as I worked. I'd ordered new kit and binned some old. Then there were boxes that had been stuck on a high shelf, presumably for a reason.

The boxes bothered me—I didn't like an untidy store. Or loose ends left untied, like the lass I needed to talk to but hadn't found the chance.

A figure stopped in the doorway. "Mr Ross. Ye wanted to see me."

My glance revealed Max, who I now knew to be Cait's brother as well as the not-so helpful one of the twins.

In the past weeks, he'd been present on a couple of missions but had given me less of the backchat as when he'd been with his twin. His surliness hadn't shifted, though.

There was more going on than I understood, and I intended to work it out. For his sake, and nothing to do with how I liked his sister.

I gave the lad the once-over. "Thanks for coming in. Here, help me with this."

He followed my indication to the first of the boxes then planted his boot on the bench to grab it from the shelf. "Where do ye want it?"

"On the table. I need to work out what to keep and what to bin."

Max carried the box to the wide table where we often sorted kit then ripped open the tape. We peered at old, holed jumpsuits and cracked helmets.

"Ye ken how sentimental your Uncle Gordain is?" I asked.

"Aye."

I grunted, an internal debate playing out. At over halfway through my term here, I had taken ownership of the role of head of service and fucking loved it. The volunteers listened to me, I'd updated the ways of working with success, and our last few call-outs had been textbook.

My secondary role of overseeing the hangar's operations was easy as pie, the place practically running itself.

I'd even gone up in the Sea King with one of the pilots, the buzz unbeatable.

Almost.

Staying wasn't on my agenda—there was no role for me here beyond Gordain's return, and that end date would come quickly enough.

"What are ye going to do with it?" Max asked.

"Chuck it all, perhaps."

He raised a shoulder. "Your call."

It was, but this wasn't my change to make. I was only a small part of the history of this place.

"Stick it back on the shelf," I ordered. "I'll mark it up for Gordain to decide on when he returns."

Max obliged then followed me out to the ops room. "Is that why ye called me here? To not clear out boxes?"

I huffed at his cheek. I had two ways to play this youngster. Either call him out on his attitude problem or try to help him change it.

I folded my arms and eyed him. "I want to designate ye as a runner. Ye live locally, and you're usually the first here."

Runners answered the call instantly and attended the scene ahead of the main crew. They'd stabilise an injured or cold person until they could be brought off the hill.

Max was a biker, I'd discovered. Speed appealed to him.

The brawny young man blinked then pushed back his auburn hair. Doubt filled his expression. "I'm Max. Did ye mean to ask for Maddock?"

"Naw."

He considered this. Apparently, I'd stumped him.

"I'll pair ye up with Cameron for the next few times we need this kind of role. You're both fast, sharp-eyed, first-aid trained, and ye know the ground."

"Will ye ask my brother, too?"

"I didnae plan to." Needing a coffee, I passed Max and slapped the lad on the shoulder. "Ye can answer now, or later, if ye want to think on it."

His frown deepened. "Aye, no need to think. I'll do it."

Inside, I warmed, but I kept my expression stern. "Good. I'll talk to Cameron."

"I'll see him after work in a couple of days. Family dinner at the castle," he explained.

A family dinner. There were so many McRaes around, I could only imagine the scene of them all sharing a meal. The good feeling. The loud conversation.

A powerful pang hit me of how I missed out. Of how my daughter did.

Yesterday, I'd driven south to check my messages.

Nothing had come in from my sister. She wasn't the greatest at communications, but this wasn't like her. I could only assume she'd been deployed somewhere with limited opportunities to send an email.

I stared at my black coffee. Christmas would be upon us soon enough. Snow had claimed its place on the higher grounds. Isla's birthday was in a week, and I had no idea how to make it special for her. With no note from her aunt, she'd feel it hard.

Dimly, I was aware of Max saying something, but I'd lost myself in my thoughts.

Cait's voice joining his pulled me back in a rush.

Cait was here.

"Maximus. Shouldn't ye be at work?" she asked her brother.

"Lunchbreak, Caitriona." He pulled a face at her. "Why are ye here?"

Kah-tree-nah. Such a pretty fucking name.

Under the bright operation centre lights, Cait's eyes sparkled. "None of your business. Are ye going to Uncle Callum's dinner?"

"Aye. He'll only moan if someone doesn't show." He switched his gaze to me. "Did ye need me for anything else, boss?"

"Naw the now. Thanks for stopping by."

Max left. I stared at Cait in no small amount of wonder. In my months here, she'd never graced the hangar, yet here she was.

Her gaze took in my jumpsuit. The oil on my hands from where I'd poked around one of the helis. She lingered on my lips.

We'd never kissed, despite everything else we'd done.

I wanted her to launch at me. Wind those long legs around my waist and take my mouth with hers. Do everything I'd been dreaming about since our tryst last week.

Except that wasn't Cait's style.

It had taken everything in her to instigate sex with me. Bravery that I admired and imagined didn't come easily considering the background she'd explained.

Every inch of me screamed *fuck it, take her in your arms.* But I couldn't.

Anything more with this lass and I'd be in trouble.

A kiss, and I'd be over the edge.

She was so warm. If I fell for her, I'd be fucked. Already, a small kernel of something had taken root. A deep and tender...what? Longing. If I focused too hard on it, it caught my breath. I couldn't afford to give up that air. For a long time, I'd run on pure energy, the inner part of me cold and untouched. Cait's heat would melt that, leave me weak.

The conclusion hurt, but it only intensified my resolve. I liked her. Too much. So I had to end this now.

"Hi," she whispered.

"Hello, Cait."

She tilted her head. "If ye want, ye can call me Caitriona."

"Is that what your family call ye?"

"Aye. Only them."

Ah God, she twisted a knife without even knowing.

"What do your family call ye?" Curiosity decorated her sweet tone. She pulled her fleece-lined denim jacket tighter around her.

"Lochie. Well, Blair does. My sister. She's the only one left."

"I'm sorry. Where is she?"

"Deployed."

In a heartbeat, I'd told her more about me than anyone else knew. Information that was dangerous in the wrong hands. Not in hers, though. Without asking, I knew she wouldn't share a word.

Since last week, I'd been more and more tempted to confide in Cait. I needed advice on my daughter, and with Cait's situation, her specific family circumstances, she'd know far more than me.

Maybe I could do that on a friend basis.

If only I could get over the longing first.

A laugh came from outside in the hangar, and we straightened, though none of the passion had turned into action.

Cait blew out a breath. "I came here to do two things. First, to check on ye and ask a question."

"Check on me? Why?"

"Last week, I left ye..." Her cheeks reddened. "Unfulfilled. I regretted that."

"It's okay, sweetheart. I didnae mind."

She gazed at the floor. "It won't happen next time."

Heat flooded me. I spoke through a tight throat. "Next time?"

"I want to offer ye a deal."

"Cait, stop."

Cait gave a laugh. "Ye don't even know the terms."

Her amusement flickered as if she sensed my mood change. Still, she pushed on.

"I want to try what we did again. Test out a couple of different scenarios I've been thinking about. If ye agree."

Hiding my instant lust, I forced a calm face. "I'm sorry, I cannae."

"Why?"

"I'm leaving soon. It isnae a good idea."

For a long moment, we just gazed at each other. I resisted the urge to drag her to the operation room's floor and have her here, and she simply took me in.

Her shoulder sagged. "Then no deal. Right. Um, the second thing is to extend an invitation. Callum, Da's oldest brother and the chief of our clan, is hosting a meal at Castle McRae tomorrow. Ye and Isla are included in the invitation. It's last-minute, so ye might have plans..."

"No plans. We can be there."

Cait linked her gaze to mine once more, and neither of us moved or spoke. Cruel tension ached where I held myself firm.

"Good," she finally said. "It's at five-thirty because of the bairns. Callum and Mathilda's daughter, Skye, is visiting with her family. She has two children not far off Isla's age, so there will be someone for her to play with."

Another pause. Another long stare.

"Caitriona," I asked, using her longer form name without conscious thought.

"Yes?"

"I'm sorry about your deal."

"So am I." She pressed up on her toes, kissed my cheek, and left.

17

Lochinvar

A morning on, and I was made of regret. Not that I'd change my mind about Cait's offer, but I'd woken in the night so aware of the woman beyond the cottage walls, I nearly lost my mind.

"Ready?" Isla pogoed on the spot, her hiking shoes dropping wee clumps of mud on the stone step.

"Ready, Captain," I confirmed. "Lead the way."

Isla stepped out into the winter sunshine and promptly knocked on our neighbour's door.

Cait answered, a smile at the ready for my daughter. For me, I got a sly look and a faint blush as welcome.

"We're going for a walk," I explained. "You're coming with us."

Cait blinked. "That's very kind of ye, but—"

"Ye hate hiking. We know. So we're going to make ye love it."

I wanted Cait as a friend, and her guidance on a subject I couldn't bring myself to consider, so we had to start over.

Her wry expression told me everything I wanted to know.

Bossy, she implied with a raised eyebrow.

Undeniably, I replied via a chin lift.

"Please?" Isla begged. "Please, please, please."

Cait's bemused expression shifted to acceptance. "Well, okay. But don't let me choose the direction or we'll be horribly lost."

She ducked back inside and reappeared in sturdy boots and a warm jacket. For once, the weather was in our favour and, though the air was chilly, the sun blazed.

With Isla leading the way, we set out from the cottages.

The splendour of the Highlands had never appeared as pretty as today. Soon, we crested the hill our cottages perched on and descended the other side, a glistening loch in the distance.

Cait kept pace with me, unspeaking though eyeing me when she thought I wasn't looking.

"Are ye from the north?" she asked eventually. "I'm guessing from your accent that's so."

"Aye. When I was born, my parents lived in Aberdeen, then Ma took Blair and me back to her hometown of Torridon, north of here."

"Your father didn't go?"

I rubbed over my beard. "He was a violent drunk. We basically fled. He didnae follow, or not that Ma ever told me. Both of them died before I was twenty."

Cait didn't reply, and I glanced over to find her wide-eyed.

"God, that's awful."

I raised a shoulder. "Ma did what she had to do in taking us away."

Cait shivered. "Ye get your protective instincts from her then."

I'd stopped to offer her a hand over loose rock but stared.

"The mountain rescue? Plus you're obviously military."

She placed her hand in mine, and awareness zinged over me, spreading from where our skin touched.

"Am I now?"

"Oh, come on. Sure, you're a private man, but some things can't be hidden."

We continued walking, and I had to force myself to let go of her fingers. The swell of enjoyment that built in me, though, I didn't shy from.

"What military man signs am I giving off?" I raised an eyebrow.

Ah fuck, I was flirting.

"You're highly organised, punctual, made of energy, and when you say you'll do something, it's done. I have relatives who were the army or RAF, so I know the type. Oh, and your sister is in service. Not exactly a stretch to get there."

"Fine. Ye got me. I was RAF."

Cait beamed. "That was my guess. What kind of job did ye do?"

"The last military search and rescue operation. Mostly now it's provided by civilian contractors, like the one I run for Gordain."

"It makes sense for ye to be here then."

"What do ye do for a living?" I changed the subject, earning a chuckle from Cait.

"I work an incredibly boring job at the university in Inverness, designing courses for students."

"Ye dinna enjoy it?"

"Nope. I don't hate it either."

"Why do ye do it?"

"The steady income, I get to work from my cottage, and it doesn't take up too many brain cells. I need those for other things."

I chewed on this for a minute. A desk job was a mystery to me. I couldn't imagine being still for that long.

Cait picked up on my hesitation. "What? Ye don't approve?"

"Life is too short not to do what ye love."

She stared at me then we both burst out in laughter. Doing what she loved could've been part of her sex deal, considering how much she liked the act. The tension in me ramped up, and I breathed in through my nose, far too enamoured with the pretty woman at my side.

"Truth is, I've never wanted anything more than to be a mother. Scarlet has this amazing career as a business-woman, and plenty of my aunts and cousins run their own companies. I always wanted to be closer to home. To raise bairns. That probably sounds unambitious to ye."

I rubbed my chest against a lingering ache. "There's nothing easy about being the centre of a family. It's a noble calling."

"Ye think?"

We shared another look, and Cait graced me with her beautiful smile.

Isla buzzed back over. "What are you two laughing about?"

In a sweet move, Cait captured Isla's hand, and they strolled along, swinging their arms.

"Your da was teasing me because I'm already lost and we're not even half an hour from home."

Isla cackled. "I've only lived here for a few months and I can find my way easily. You're a grown up."

"Isla," I warned for her cheek.

My daughter and Cait exchanged a glance, amusement on both their faces as they conspired.

My heart skipped a wee beat. It was too nice, and too easy. Cait's company had turned the hike into far greater fun than usual. Isla and I were too used to each other. She needed someone to complain about me to. Or laugh at me with.

A short while on, Isla darted ahead, leaving us alone.

"I wanted to ask a favour," I said.

Really, I wanted to kiss her, but that wasn't an option.

"No deal," Cait deadpanned.

I heaved a regretful sigh. "It's about your family dinner at the castle. I know half the names, but the relationships aren't all clear."

"Do ye want me to run through everyone?"

"Please."

"There are a lot of us McRaes. Let me see." She held up a hand. "My da is one of four brothers. The eldest is Callum. He's married to Mathilda, and they own Castle McRae. Callum's head of the clan, too. They have three children, Lennox, who's married to Isobel. He runs the snowboarding centre, she operates a classic car garage. They have a baby, Archie, who is just the cutest. Then Skye lives with Artair on a remote island in the Inner Hebrides, that Artair owns, by the way. They have a son, Mathe, and a daughter, Adaira. Lennox and Skye's youngest sibling is Blayne. He's married to Brodie and Casey, and they're expecting a bairn in a couple of weeks."

She tilted her head to make sure I was keeping up.

"Go on," I prompted, updating my mental map.

"Next brother is Gordain. He's married to Ella, and their daughter is Viola. Vi got hitched to Leo last summer, and they, too, have a bairn on the way. Aunt Ella's brother, James, is married to Mathilda's best friend, Beth. Isobel is their daughter. They also have Sebastian, who's married to Rose and has baby Persephone."

"I dinna think I've met them yet."

"Aside from Isobel, the Fitzroys all live in England in this enormous mansion. Now, back to the Scots. Da has a twin brother, William. Both men are on your crew."

"Aye, I know many of these names, but this is really helping."

"Good. William is known as Wasp. He's married to Taylor."

"Cameron's parents."

"Exactly. Last but not least, Da married Scarlet, and they have me, then my younger twin brothers Max and Maddock. Maddock's at uni, and Max works in Isobel's garage." She dusted off her hands.

"Ye have so many relatives."

"I do. We make up our town, pretty much. I can't really compare it to growing up elsewhere, as I was only ever here, but I know I had a charmed childhood."

I stared at Isla, not for the first time wishing I could give her something similar. Brothers and sisters. Cousins to play with. Big family meals to attend.

"I've noticed friction between your brothers," I probed.

"They've always fought. Both are competitive little arse-holes." She grinned. "Neither will tell us what the latest problem is about. It's like they have their own twin-world and are content fighting over it. We only intervene if there's blood drawn."

"Blayne's relationship is a strange one," I moved on.

"It is, but it works for them."

"I've never even managed a two-person relationship. Three is incomprehensible."

Cait went silent. Her forehead creased in a frown.

"Apart from your wife?"

There was no good answer to that. I shut my mouth and kept on walking.

In the distance, a chopping sound rent the sky, then moments later, a helicopter swung into view. I tracked it, identifying the Eurocopter as one from Gordain's hangar.

"Do ye fly?" Cait twisted to watch it pass.

Relief flickered, and I was glad to focus on something else. "Naw. Winch man."

"You'd hang out of one of those? Jeez."

Isla raced off to investigate something to our left, and I stopped, Cait doing the same.

"It isnae that bad. It's easier than flying, that's for certain. The only time I worried, we were hovering over a fishing boat in a storm. The coastguard was busy, it being a hell of a night, so the RAF was called in."

"Tell me about it."

Cait's attention fully on me was like a beam of sunlight. Her gaze holding mine, her focus set—I wanted to keep it. The whole morning of conversation felt like we were deepening our understanding of each other. I'd intended not to let anyone close, yet I talked to Cait with ease.

The sense of safety in another soul knowing my life was addictive.

"The boat had capsized a few miles off the coast, the crew clinging to the hull. I went out and collected them one by one. The howling tempest battered us the whole time, and I could hardly see for half of it, rain pelting down, sea spray flying up in a wall of water."

She shivered. "I bet ye didn't even hesitate."

"Never have. Ye cannae think like that when lives are at risk."

Cait's gaze flitted from my eyes to my lips. "Ye know, Lochinvar. We're very lucky to have ye here."

The chemistry between us swelled all the more.

Ah fuck. I wanted her so badly it hurt. An acute and physical ache deep inside.

"Lochie," I corrected.

Before, I'd told her my nickname but hadn't given her permission to use it. Something had shifted now, and I needed her to use that name.

"Like I said, Caitriona," she replied softly.

"Da!" Isla's shout broke the moment.

We hurried across the slope, and I took Cait's arm so she didn't fall.

Isla stared down the glen, hopping from one foot to the other. "There are two people over there. One just fell down a slope. They haven't got up, and the other person is calling them, and their dog's going bananas. Look, can you see them?"

I followed her gaze. Sure enough, a woman hovered at the top of the slope, her dog dancing around her. Below, another person lay crumpled on a rock-strewn slope.

The second figure raised their head, red on their face and on the rocks.

Adrenaline flooded my system, and I took two steps, then spun around to Cait and Isla. "They need help. I have my radio so will call it in if I need a spare pair of hands. Cait, can ye take Isla home?"

Isla snorted. "Do ye mean can I take Cait home, Da?"

Cait's warm gaze touched on me. "We've gone in a straight line in broad daylight. Even I can find my way back.

Go do your thing. We'll bake something for when ye get back."

With a wrench, I tore myself away and left to help the injured party. If I hadn't, I probably would've done something stupid like begged Cait to offer her deal again.

I could hide my feelings and not burden her with what she didn't want. I'd enough self-control not to show anything on the outside. God knows I'd had practice at managing my emotions.

Aye, I could take the hit and survive it.

I let the energy of my task in hand take me over, pushing thoughts of Cait's deal out of my head. And what I'd do if she asked again.

18

*C*aitriona

I paced my living room, my day's work mostly already done though it wasn't yet lunchtime. Yesterday, after Lochie had been called to action, Isla and I had returned to bake brownies. Her da showed up two hours later, a happy outcome to his mission with the injured man taken to hospital by his girlfriend.

The little family stayed for tea and cake.

Aside from me dropping and cracking my favourite mixing bowl when Lochie had stood too close to me, it had been so lovely.

God, I wished he hadn't friendzoned me.

My phone dinged, and I leapt to grab it. Earlier, I'd sent Viola and Casey a group message with a specific request. My message was top of the screen.

Cait: Give me your top three sex positions. Stat.

Viola: Stat? Like you're about to have sex? Put your phone down, woman.

Cait: No, no. I mean for future reference.

Casey: Ooh, I like this game. Um, let me see. We're talking one-on-one, so in no particular order: the guy standing up with me in his arms, legs around his waist; me flat on my back, not allowed to use my hands (try it and you'll see); sixty-nine until one of us can't stand it and takes full control.

Viola: Upright, on my knees, Leo behind me.

Casey: That is super hot. Making notes.

Viola: Mine's hot? You wrote an essay.

Casey: It's one of my favourite subjects. I have a lot of opinions.

I sighed, overwhelm creeping in. There was so much I didn't know. Where the heck did I start? I might not have a sex partner in mind, but knowing this felt important.

Cait: I offered Lochinvar a sex deal. He turned me down. I still want to have a few ideas, though. In case I ever find another man to try them out on.

Viola: Lochinvar turned you down? Is he mad?

Cait: I think I scared him off. I didn't get the chance to explain I'm not asking for anything more. He said we'd just be friends, I think to put me in my place.

Viola: Talk to him again. You obviously like each other, and you're compatible.

Cait: Do you know what's scarier? If he actually says yes.

Viola: If he does, then tell him that this is difficult for you and I bet he will have ways to make it easier. He's probably thought about it a lot.

Casey: Agreed. You're focused on the mechanics, but what you're exploring is attraction. It's intangible and should be fun. Think of Lochinvar as a friend, like he wants, and not an object.

A door slammed, and I peered out of my window. Lochie strode from his car toward his cottage, a heavy-looking bag in his hand. His gaze locked on to me behind the glass. A smart salute came my way.

Heat washed through me.

Then Lochie carried on into his home.

Fuck! Why couldn't this be easy?

With a groan, I withered to sit on the couch. Should I offer again? He'd been willing before I'd said anything about my stupid deal.

If I'd somehow come across wrong, I should correct that. Then he'd have the full picture. And might change his mind.

Reassured, though still trembling at what I was about to do, I stood.

A rap sounded at the entrance to my home, and I hopped, my heart pounding.

I stashed my phone, brushed down my dress, then opened the door.

On the other side, the huge mountain rescue leader waited.

His expression jumped between determination and plain, unconcealed need.

"Caitriona," he said.

"Lochie."

I ushered him forward and shut us in, my fingers trembling.

He held up the bag. "I brought ye something."

Taking it with care, I peered inside. It was a mixing bowl. A pretty one, with white interior and blue flowers on the outside.

Lochie didn't budge, his muscles rigid. "Ye broke yours yesterday. I thought it would be missed so I drove out and bought a replacement."

What an utterly friend-like thing to do.

"Thank you, that's really kind." Wilting all the more, I stepped into the kitchen and placed the bowl on the counter before I dropped this one, too.

Then I rotated slowly, eyeing my neighbour as he advanced, hands in his pockets.

"You're kind to my daughter. And to me."

I couldn't summon a reply, so caught as I was in the intensity of his stare.

"I made a mistake." His voice turned to gravel.

"What was that?"

"Saying no to your offer. I havenae been able to think of anything else since."

A shiver ran up my spine.

Both of us took a deep inhale. My body warmed, wetness pooling between my legs.

"Maybe instead of a deal, we can do this just once." Lochie took a step forward. "Will that work for ye?"

I closed my eyes, gripping the table at the small of my back. "It will. Do ye mean now?"

He moved closer, and the hairs on the back of my neck rose in my alarm.

"Aye. Are ye nervous?" he asked.

"I can't help it. There's no reason I should be. We've done this before."

"We have, but that doesnae make this any less extraordinary. Can I ask ye something?"

I peeked up, heat rising and prickling my skin.

"Ye mentioned scenarios. Are there specifics ye want to try?"

Not one single item from the list Casey and Viola gave me came to mind. My brain fuzzed up, my mouth cotton wool.

I couldn't answer, but this didn't stop Lochie.

He advanced another step. "Because I had some ideas. They're basic, but I think you'll like them."

A short pause followed, then, without warning, he

seized my waist and boosted me to sit on the kitchen island. Then he leaned in and pressed his lips to my cheek, his thick body between my open thighs.

"Want me to lead this?" he asked, rough.

God, I did. It wasn't embarrassment affecting me this time but simple overload. There were too many ways this man could ease the ache deep inside me, and I had no clue where to start.

"Yes," I managed.

Lochie kissed under my ear then breathed in. "In my bed last night, I thought about ye, and not for the first time. Do ye know how crazy it's making me, the fact that I can do to ye what no other man can?"

He ran the tip of his nose across my cheek, his lips skating mine but not landing until they reached my other cheek.

"I want to see how well that connection works. What ye prefer—a fast and hard fuck to get ye to come, or a slow, easy screw, building up over time."

I gave up an undignified little moan.

Lochie smiled, the Devil in his eyes. "Which do ye want to try first?"

"Either. Both."

"Good. Hold on."

He scooped me up and straightened, turning to carry me from the kitchen. I clutched onto him, my legs around his waist. In my dim bedroom, he settled me onto the bed, his knees on the mattress. Then he reached back and dragged his long-sleeved black t-shirt over his head.

My mouth watered at the reveal of hard muscles, those enormous biceps, and his dark chest hair.

"Ye like my body," he informed me.

I gazed, mesmerised. "I do."

"Wouldnae hurt if ye told me."

I blinked.

Oh!

It hadn't even occurred to me that he'd care how attractive I found him. A man like him, so big and confident. So in control.

I took a fresh look, seeing past lust to all the parts of Lochinvar that had caught my attention.

"You're beautiful," I said, entirely honestly. "Not just your body, but your mind, too. You're strong and capable, and your body is honed to perfection. I'm so attracted to ye."

His fingers skimmed my legs, taking my dress with them until my underwear was on display. He had been blindfolded last time we were in this room.

Lochie stared, his nostrils flaring. "Anything else?"

His hands continued up, over my waist to caress my breasts through the layer of fabric. I exhaled and pushed into his touch, but he moved on, taking my dress straps in his fingers.

"You're patient with me. And generous. I never cared what men thought about me. No one ever made me feel…"

"Anything." He drew my dress straps down my arms.

I'd left off wearing a bra, as I was working from home and my blazer hid my chest, and Lochie's eyes widened.

His lips curled in obvious satisfaction. "No one ever made ye feel anything, but I have. And I intend to push that as far as it'll go. Now get this dress off before I tear it from ye."

My heart leapt, and I jerked to perform his command, sliding down the short zip at my side. Then I wriggled, pulling the dress over my head with Lochie's help.

In just my lacy, damp knickers, I propped up on my elbows, my chest rising and falling with my fast breaths.

Lochie's dark gaze soaked me in. Previously, I'd worried about him seeing me, but now I loved it. Undisguised admiration filled his expression.

Still kneeling between my legs, he lowered his head to mine, and he laid a soft kiss on my lips.

God. Oh God.

I hadn't expected it, assuming he'd steer clear of kissing me like he had done before.

It was our third sexual experience, but our first kiss.

My whole focus narrowed in on that touch. Lochie moved with care, though clearly driven on by lust and need. His warm mouth coaxed mine to life.

On instinct, I opened for him, my hesitant tongue meeting his.

Heat eclipsed all sense. His taste drove me insane.

He held my frame against his much bigger body. Greeted me with the slide of his lips on mine.

Finally, he slowed, giving us both space to breathe. With our faces close, he kissed my cheek, his smile spreading.

"Wow," I managed.

He went to speak but evidently changed his mind as he returned for another kiss, and another. I closed my eyes again and focused on the sheer pleasure I received from just his lips alone. How was this even possible?

I raised my hand to trace over his bulky shoulder. That had surprised me, how firm his body was. So different to my pliant one. His muscles tensed under my touch.

"That's it, woman, work me out," he muttered.

"Are we really only going to do this once?" I asked.

"Ask me in a minute. I willnae be able to refuse ye anything."

He left my mouth to kiss a path to my breasts, licked my nipple then sucked it, using his fingers on my other breast. I revelled in the sensation, loving how instantly my body responded to him, my nipples hard and my skin so sensitive to everything he did.

Heat swirled, and the ache in me built. I hooked my leg over his backside in an attempt to bring him closer. "Take off your jeans."

"All in good time." He continued his pleasuring of my nipples, switching sides with his mouth and using his thumbs to elongate them. "Ye have fucking perfect tits."

"I do?"

"Tits, body, everything." He blew on my nipple, and we both watched it pebble even harder. Lochie switched his gaze to capture mine, holding eye contact as he lowered for another lick.

With my jaw slack, I basked, the pressure I'd felt previously, the expectation to moan with exaggeration, simply not there. We both wanted to find out what I liked, and this was so much closer to the fun my friends had suggested we could have.

Lochie nudged my breast then, at the same moment, landed a hand between my legs and bit lightly on my nipple.

"Lochie!" I arched up, senses alive and sparking.

He grazed me with his teeth, his hand not moving but firmly held over my skimpy underwear, the heel of his palm clamped against my sensitive nerves. He made a sound of approval. "Rougher," he said to himself, as if confirming the answer to a question.

Then he bit me again, harder, testing his teeth. But at the same time, he shoved aside my knickers and thrust a finger into my wet core.

I moaned.

Lochie pumped his hand inside me, simultaneously kissing where he'd bitten. "So wet and ready for me."

My mind scrambled. This was how I pictured other people having sex, not me. 'Wet and ready' had never been the case in the past, but my body lit up for this man.

Abruptly, he jerked up and stood. He undid his jeans and dragged them off his long legs before reaching into his pocket to extract a condom. Keeping his gaze on mine, he held it up.

I lifted my chin, beyond excited to continue.

His hard dick bobbed under its own weight, and I gazed on in fascination. Lochie sheathed himself, then he sat on the bed and grasped my waist. Without pause, he drew me up to his lap so we were face to face, then positioned himself at my entrance.

He pushed home while I scrambled to wrap my arms and legs around him. His sheer strength kept me from falling. His hard dick disappeared into me.

With a moan, I buried my face in his shoulder, holding on for dear life. This time, the intrusion of him stretching me didn't feel so alien. I anticipated the pleasure to come.

No, it was already there.

I clutched him harder, every tiny movement sending thrills through me.

Lochie held me tight, his breathing fast.

But then he pulled away, ducking to meet my gaze. He put space between our torsos then indicated down. "Watch."

Holding my thigh, he slid his dick in and out of me.

We both stared.

"Think back to last time. What did ye like? Shallow or deep?"

"I don't know. Everything."

He rolled his hips in a short plunge, several more following, all hitting the same place and sending delicious sparks out in spirals.

I gave up an indecent sound. Then I copied the motion, grinding down on him. Lochie huffed a breath but let me try it out. But my concentration on getting it right lost half the energy.

"Better when ye do it," I conceded.

"Course it is, for ye."

He gently guided me to lie back and hauled my leg over his shoulder. "Now deep."

Long, lengthy strokes followed. I closed my eyes, the sensation instantly too much and not enough. Lochie strummed my clit as he worked.

Tight heat built deep inside me.

"God," I exclaimed.

Lochie's reply was an amused rumble. He kept up his steady assault, fucking me, so slow but with potent effect. Unlike before, I was ready for an orgasm. No doubt nor worry constrained me. This was going to be so easy.

I gasped at a firmer hit. "Can we try hard and fast now?"

"Naw."

I blinked open my eyes. "What?"

Lochie grinned, the effect devastating. Sweat gleamed on his broad chest. "Next time."

I grumbled to myself, delighted, and closed my eyes, letting him continue his rhythm. Despite his words, the power behind his moves built. Each time he drew out, I whimpered. Every single one of his thrusts blazed heat through me.

He drew my legs over his shoulders and ground into me at the deeper angle.

I was lost to the waves of sensation.

Yet every time I neared that addictive release, he eased up again, his clever fingers retreating from my clit to massage lower, or to ghost over my breasts.

I loved the attention, the ramping up of warmth and tension. Nothing had ever felt this good.

Soon, I was a mess, writhing and willing to beg.

"Please," I said, breathless.

"Please what?"

"Make me come."

"Persuade me."

I gazed at him, wondering how the heck I could do anything he wasn't already doing. Then I dropped my legs and pushed up on an elbow, reaching to bring his face to mine. Lochie followed my touch, and I dug my fingers into his hair and kissed him.

Whoa, kissing while having sex took on new heights.

Now, our bodies were aligned, and the angle changed once more. The weight of him, though he mostly supported himself, added a new element to the mix. My skin lit up everywhere we touched.

He worked my body, but I was going to own this kiss.

In the same way I'd never been interested in sex, kissing hadn't been high on my agenda. Instinct more than practice had me tilt my head to better our connection. He opened his mouth as I did, and I stroked my tongue over his.

Lochie's movement stuttered, and elation thrilled me.

I'd done that. Distracted him. Me, a woman with zero skill.

Again, I caressed his tongue with mine, and he slowed his thrusts even more, his hips flush to mine. I kissed him, and he ground into me, deep inside and with pressure on my clit from his solid body.

Against my chest, his heart pounded.

God, this was good.

So busy trying to seduce him with my mouth, I lost focus on my own pleasure, and my orgasm smacked into me unawares. A flood of good feeling burst out in an explosion, and I cried out, arching into Lochie.

"Fuck, Caitriona!" he growled then jacked his hips once and buried himself hard inside me.

Even in my zoned-out, trembling state, I felt his dick pulse.

His climax boosted mine, and I throbbed around him, my head dizzy and my mind lost to reason.

Utter relief mixed with my other more potent emotions, and I half laughed, half moaned at the joy of it. Lochie captured the sound with a new kiss, this one claiming, and rougher. He rolled off me but kept me to him.

We cooled, tangled and satisfied.

A smile broached my lips, and I peeked at the man with his head tucked by mine.

He regarded me in return, a contented, smug set to his features.

"Slow and easy worked well," I said.

"I meant to turn ye onto all fours, but that didnae happen."

"Something for next time. Or the time after."

Lochie's gaze moved over my face, taking in each element as if he hadn't allowed himself such a close study before. I relaxed and did the same.

He must've trimmed his beard as it was neat and well-managed, cut to the shape of his jaw and accentuating his masculinity. His dark eyes held intelligence, I'd already witnessed that, but they also beamed with kindness and determination. I bet he could be stubborn, if he chose to. A strong nose and cheekbones, broad forehead divided with a worry line...

I reached out and placed my fingertip in the divot.

His lips curved. "Ye can't get to thirty and lead a life like mine without some damage."

"You're seven years older than me."

"Does that bother ye?"

"Not at all."

I should be getting up. I'd been slack at work this morning but had an afternoon of video calls and a packed morning of meetings in Inverness tomorrow to prepare for.

Yet I stayed, cosy in my bed with a man who could play my body like a musical instrument.

"The first time we did this, I thought I'd scared ye off," he said. "I was rough. More than I liked."

I raised a shoulder. "I asked for that."

"Which did ye prefer, like this," he gestured down to us, "or with the chase?"

"This. The chase definitely did something. Maybe it woke me up. I don't know. But today was just..."

"Incredible," Lochie murmured, his attention laser-focused on me.

God, he'd liked it. I mean, it could be obvious from the fact he'd climaxed, but I had a gulf of missing knowledge on this subject and assumed nothing.

"Ye liked it, too," I said carefully.

"Are ye joking?" He reached for my hand and placed it over his already-hard-again dick. "You're the most beautiful woman I ever saw, Caitriona."

I froze, going rigid at his words.

Lochie pulled back, that narrow focus becoming even more keen. "What's wrong? Ye dislike the compliment?"

"I... No."

"Why?"

I pulled back my instincts and looked inward. I was a logical woman, so what was causing this? I picked over my words. "Without intending to sound vain, I know I'm pretty. Da was a model in his youth, and when I was younger, it's all people used to say. That I was so beautiful I'd be picked up by a modelling agency. Not that my parents would ever allow it. But my father's looks are what caused my birth mother to become obsessed with him. There's a long story to what she did, but to shortcut it, she befriended him, got pregnant on purpose, then hid the pregnancy."

Lochie's eyebrows dove together. "Where is she now?"

"She died not long after I was born."

He blew out a long breath. "You're worried about me being obsessed with ye?"

It sounded so stupid when he said it. "No. It's habit, I guess. I had a shite time as a teenager with boys being arse-holes to me because I wouldn't date them. Some of their behaviour could've been called obsessive. My older cousin had to give a warning more than once. Then when I went to university and tried sex, the first guy, Dean, broke his hand smashing my bathroom mirror after I told him I didn't enjoy our night. The second, Ashley, spread rumours that I was a lesbian because his pride had been hurt. The last, Jude, a drama student who lived in the same dorm, was the only one who didn't go weird. I was honest with him about why I wanted to try, so he had no expectations. More recently, with work and my door... I think I trigger something in people. It's always happened, and now I work hard to avoid it. I never let a man think I might be interested, until I tried again with you."

Lochie listened, taking in my explanation. He paused, that intelligence working over my points. "Those boys were wee bawbags for how they treated ye. No lass should take abuse for not wanting a man."

I shivered, and he reached to grab the quilt and pull it over me.

"But I'm naw a lad," he continued. "I can guarantee I'll be the man ye want me to be."

"You're leaving, too," I said softly. "I think that's part of what makes me feel safe with this. In February, you'll go."

"I will."

Silence filled the room, and my thoughts drifted.

"Will ye tell me what happened at work?" Lochie asked. "I know about the door, but ye implied there was more."

I flapped a hand. "I worked out the door thing. It was just some rejected local guy letting off steam. He's long gone."

A trilling sound came from the living room.

"That's my laptop. Shite, what's the time?" I leapt up.

"Quarter to one."

I wrapped my dressing gown around my body and padded out to peek at the screen on my desk. Rupert was calling. I swore and returned to the bedroom.

"It's my boss. We have a video meeting in half an hour. He's early."

"Is he one of your problems?"

Pacing the room, I let the call ring out, though it raised my hackles. "Actually, yes. He is."

Lochie grabbed me on a pass and brought me to his lap. He fitted his mouth to mine. His kiss chased away my momentary angst.

"Today was incredible. I willnae call ye beautiful again until ye ask. I cannae fucking wait to do this again."

It was a moot point, my deal. Whatever had changed his mind didn't matter. We'd set boundaries and both knew the score.

Hunger rose, instant even after everything we'd just done.

I kissed him back, losing myself on his lips for several minutes. Reluctantly, I dragged myself away.

"I need a shower then I have to get on with work."

"Go to it."

Lochie reclined on my bed, donning a self-aware grin at the utterly splendid sight he made.

I washed up then returned, slipping into my smart-but-comfortable dress and blazer. Lochie spread out, watching my every move, that smile not shifting.

Ready, I still had ten minutes until I needed to meet with Rupert. Lochie looked in no danger of going anywhere.

"Ye can nap here while I work, if ye like?" I said.

He breathed in, inflating his mighty chest and giving me shivers at the same time. "I have work of my own, but thanks for the offer."

He stood and pulled on his clothes.

My laptop rang again, disrupting my happy viewing.

"I better answer it this time."

"I have an idea," Lochie said. "This guy's interrupting your lunchbreak, aye? Take the call."

I narrowed my gaze. "What are ye going to do?"

"Show my face. Scare him off. It's the only language some men understand."

I'd been independent so long that this should rankle me. Yet I knew on some level he was right. There was a certain type of man who didn't take no for an answer, and I didn't want to find out if Rupert was one of them.

"Fine," I muttered and moved into the living room and to my desk.

Rupert's beaming face appeared as I clicked to accept

the call. "Cait! I hope you don't mind me interrupting your lunch."

"I was busy, but I've just finished."

Lochie loomed behind me, visible on the screen. He didn't grab me or kiss me, but he made an obvious move to tuck his t-shirt into his jeans. His black hair was still ruffled from where I'd entwined it in my fingers.

"Caitriona," he rumbled. "I'll be going."

"See ye tonight."

Out of sight of the camera, his look turned smouldering, then he winked and let himself out my door.

On my laptop. Rupert blustered something, but I was barely listening. I only tuned back into the call when he got to the point of what we needed to discuss.

My attention was quite happily set on the new me that was emerging, thanks in no small part to the handsome rescue captain who could work my body like he owned it.

19

Cait's Watcher

The university office's lights blinked off around me, plunging me into darkness. Anger rippled, the rage budding under my surface, hot and hungry. It was getting harder to control.

Needing a reminder of good things, of Cait's measured, pleasant words, I opened her email with shaking fingertips. It had been a while since I'd taken a rightful look through her affairs. She tried to make a game out of it, but she had such a terrible choice in passwords. It barely took the evening to work out this one. I let a smile broach my lips at how she played me.

Then I scanned the list, and one email caught my eye.

I read it.

Again.

Again.

Oh, my sweet girl. She'd booked in for fertility treatment.

She meant for us to have a baby.

I tapped my nails on the desk. My fury eased a degree now I could recall my plans.

Once I'd shown her the truth, she'd be so happy. I'd make the best coparent for her children, and of course, she'd agree.

But first, we had to dance.

20

Caitriona

Lochie's name appeared on my phone early afternoon the next day. "Caitriona," he greeted me. "I've had a call. Can ye take Isla after school? I know you're in the city so no problem if naw."

I glanced at my list of appointments and calculated how long each would take. "I can do it. It's the dinner at Castle McRae tonight. Did ye remember?"

"Aye. I'll probably be late, but half my crew are going, so they'll work harder to finish quicker."

I chuckled. "I'll take Isla there, and we'll see ye when you're done."

"Grand."

We said goodbye, and I hung up, smiling to myself. This evening's gathering would be a nice end to a crappy day. Again, my emails had been opened before I'd got to them. Including one from the fertility clinic, confirming my registration. I'd spent two hours with an IT guy who insisted no one else had access rights, even though it had happened twice. He implied it was my mistake, the jerk.

It looked less like a glitch now and more a pattern.

"Cait?" a voice interrupted my thoughts.

I glanced up to find Jill, Rupert's PA, across the open-plan office where I'd taken a desk for the day.

"Hiya." I rubbed my eyes.

Jill's mouth formed a grim, firm line, and she brushed over her skirt, her polished nails pointed. "I need to speak to you about working arrangements. Mr Gaskill is reconsidering the policy on office attendance. Your current pattern of spending a day per week with colleagues is insufficient."

I tilted my head. "I work every day with colleagues, not just one. Working from home is part of the terms of my employment by the university. Rupert has no say over that."

Technically, I was employed by the faculty, and not Rupert whose job it was to coordinate non-teaching staff.

Jill shook her head once, her sharp-cut bob slicing the air. "Rupert oversees your day-to-day activity and has made his decision."

Then I caught on to what was happening. This was because he'd seen Lochie in my home. I jerked to my feet, embarrassment and annoyance heating my blood.

"Why?"

"Excuse me?"

"On what basis did he make that decision?"

She blinked several times. "I'm sure he isn't required to explain himself to us—"

"Actually, he is. If Rupert wishes to change my ways of working, he can put it in writing and apply to Abigail Grant for a change. Then it can go via HR for consultation."

Along with Rupert, Abigail had interviewed me for my job, and it was her budget that funded me. I rarely saw her, but we'd met recently to talk about my family plans. She'd have my back.

Jill hesitated, and I forced myself to breathe normally.

"If that's all, I have work to get on with."

In the same way as it had done before, Jill's gaze slunk over me. She took in my pretty but smart floral dress, and the half-filled coffee mug on the table, then turned and left me alone.

My hand shook when I tried to get back into the email I'd been typing. I'd always been proud of my strength of mind, and how I didn't let anyone push me around, but that hadn't been pleasant.

Luckily for me, the rest of the day sped by without further incident.

At four, I left, needing to be early to collect Isla.

I clipped through the big hall at the entrance to the university, smiling at people I recognised. A familiar blond caught my eye ahead of me. In a few steps, I'd caught up.

"Jude?" I said.

The man turned. "Oh my God! Cait?" He grinned big and flung his arms out to wrap me in a hug. "It's been so long. How are you?"

Jude had been a friend at university and one of the guys I'd slept with. I'd seen updates from him on social media where he'd been travelling the world for the past year.

"I'm good. What are ye doing in Scotland?"

"Visiting my uncle and…" He held up a hand, waggling it. "Then I'm going to meet my fiancée. Huh, that doesn't work so well when you're a guy. No flashy ring to show off."

I smiled happily. "You're engaged? That's amazing. Do I know her?"

"Chelle Brooks? I don't think you shared lectures, but you probably met."

I cast my mind back, recalling an unassuming, fair-haired, nerdy woman. She'd hidden behind her glasses and hadn't spoken much, but I pictured her serving coffee in the student union café, a band t-shirt under her apron. She couldn't be more different to Jude's athletic, sporty type, but then again opposites attract.

"I remember her. Congratulations. When's the wedding?"

A shadow cast over us. I peered to see Rupert standing next to Jude.

Oh, how could I have forgotten? They were related. Rupert was the uncle Jude waited on. In fact, Jude had been the one to tell me about the job at the uni.

"Wedding?" Rupert intoned.

My good humour fled. I lifted my chin and turned back to Jude. He glanced between me and his uncle, his eyes widening.

"I've somewhere to be right now," I said, "but I'd love it if you and Chelle could come to dinner one evening. We can catch up."

"That would be great. In the next few days while we're in the city?"

"Perfect. Friday at seven?"

"Deal."

He reached to high five me, then I purposefully walked away, not giving Rupert another glance.

In my car, I sped into the National Park and towards home. A little early, I went straight to school and presented myself to the receptionist, handing over the collection password despite being no stranger.

"Ah, Cait, I'll grab Isla for ye," said the sweet lady who'd worked there for longer than I could imagine.

She returned in a minute with Isla bouncing along beside her.

"Cait!" She darted forward and hugged me. "Do you like what I made? It's a collage."

I examined the gluey picture with its jewel-coloured shapes. "Ye clever girl, it's beautiful."

She glanced down, suddenly shy. "I made it for ye. Da said I could."

My heart warmed, the stress of the day evaporating. "I love it. When we get home, we'll put it on the fridge."

She jumped right back into Tigger mode, hopping along as we left the school. "Can we make cookies?"

"Not today. We'll get changed then we're going to the castle for dinner. There will be other kids, and your da will get there soon."

She slipped her hand into mine. "Can I sit with ye?"

"Aye, I'd love that."

No small wonder filled me at the turnaround in Isla. Her personality had emerged over the months she'd been here. She was a joy to be near. Sunny and caring.

At the cottages, I took the key Lochie had previously left with me and let Isla in to get changed while I went into my own home. We met again outside, and I grinned at her pink-and-purple unicorn onesie.

"Will ye be warm enough in that? It can be draughty in Castle McRae."

"Don't worry, I've been there before so I remember. I put on leggings and a jumper underneath."

Such a clever girl. I gave her a hug, and we got on the road again.

At the castle, Aunt Mathilda ushered us inside. Christmas decorations glinted here and there, though the big tree had yet to go up outside. Half of my relatives were already present, but as Lochie had noted, several were absent and out on the rescue, including both my parents. I introduced Isla to my cousin Skye's children, then let her run free with the pack of kids loose in the castle.

I joined Casey who, at nearly nine months pregnant, needed all the entertaining. Food was served as a buffet, so I was well fed by the time the doors opened to admit the mountain rescue.

Never before had I been one of the people waiting on their other half. Lochie wasn't mine, not really, but I stared in hunger at the huge man heading up the crew spilling through the door. Still in their jumpsuits, they'd clearly had a good result from the operation, considering the broad smiles and camaraderie. Brodie joined Casey and Blayne, kissing both. My parents made the rounds then headed for the food.

Lochie greeted his daughter with a hug.

Then he came for me.

I wanted to kiss him so badly it hurt.

I chewed my lip instead. He followed the action.

"Did all go okay?"

"Aye."

"We've eaten. Isla's been happily running around with the other kids."

He didn't reply, but his gaze darkened.

My insides tightened, and the room narrowed to just us. The very air stalled in my lungs. I needed him. Now, or tonight as a minimum.

His dilated pupils said he agreed.

A clap broke our intense focus.

Uncle Callum took to the middle of the floor. "I need your attention for a minute before I lose ye all to dinner and chat. I called this meal, interrupted as it was, to allow my son to make an announcement. Lennox?"

My cousin took the floor.

Ah, I knew what this was. Isobel had told me they were trying for baby number two right away, even though Archie hadn't even turned one yet. I'd appreciated the warning, as previously baby announcements had stung.

This one wouldn't. Not now I had my plans.

I let my ready smile appear.

"Thanks, Da. Where's Isobel? Ah, come here, woman. We're happy to announce we're expecting again. Archie will have a wee sister in late spring." He beamed, and Isobel slipped under his arm, tiny against him but clearly so happy, and with Archie burbling on her shoulder.

Applause, whistles, and congratulations flowed.

"Couldn't ye let the woman rest?" someone called, and everyone laughed.

"Other way around," Isobel quipped, causing a riot of catcalls.

The party continued with food brought out for the rescue team members. My father joined me and Lochie, gesturing at his side with some concern. Lochie brushed off whatever my father was asking and changed the subject.

In my head, I kept coming back to Lennox and Isobel.

Though that expected sting hadn't appeared, a new one rose its ugly head. Their happy-couple state drove envy through me. When my turn came to make my announcement, my family would be over the moon, as they were now for Lennox and Isobel, but I'd be doing it alone.

Nothing had changed about that fact. No matter my new sexual discovery, I still couldn't have the love that they shared. It shone from them, beautiful and all encompassing. That part of me wasn't going to budge, I knew it to my bones.

Another option presented itself.

Could I fake it? Enjoy sex with a partner and raise a child with someone I respected, even if I couldn't love them?

No. I hated lies.

But maybe an arrangement could work.

Mathe, Skye's son, jerked to a halt in front of me and grabbed my skirt. "Isla's crying."

"What happened?" Lochie stepped up.

The whole time, he'd been at my shoulder, quietly chatting with Da and finishing his meal.

"She got wet earlier and now she says her head hurts," the little boy added.

We followed him from the room, and my wayward thoughts disappeared, replaced by something more worrisome still.

*L*ochie
　　　My raging lust for Caitriona turned to cold concern as I took in my wee lass.

"It rained on us outside, and I got wet," Isla explained, on a go-slow from descending the bunk bed ladder in the kids' room on the first floor of the castle.

Tear tracks streaked her cheeks, and my chest constricted. She rarely cried.

"When did ye play outside?" Caitriona asked.

"After dinner. Before dessert."

I raised an eyebrow at Caitriona, and her forehead creased.

"Around six, so a couple of hours ago," she said. "Isla, I said ye could play in the castle with Mathe and the others, not go out."

"It was only to run to the wall and back. It rained hard. We liked it." Isla stopped on the ladder, her face pale.

I looked into her eyes. "Want me to carry ye?"

She nodded and drooped on me, her furry onesie dry to my touch.

But then damp crept through to my shoulder. "What are ye wearing underneath?" I asked.

Isla buried her face and didn't answer. I lifted her to the floor and unzipped her unicorn outfit to find a woollen jumper and leggings.

Sodden.

"Ah shite," I muttered. "Have ye been in these wet clothes for all that time?"

Caitriona crouched beside me and touched Isla's top, rubbing it between her fingers. "I'm so sorry, I didn't know."

"I hugged her earlier and didn't notice. The fleece hid it."

I raised my gaze to Skye, Caitriona's cousin, who I'd met only five minutes ago. She'd followed us upstairs after her boy. "Do you have anything I can borrow for Isla? I need to get her dry."

"I'll grab something of Mathe's."

With Caitriona's help, I stripped Isla and dressed her again in the borrowed clothes. She stood, miserable as we did it, her mouth turned down.

Abruptly, Isla lurched and vomited on the floor.

"Christ." I clutched hold of her so she didn't faceplant into the mess.

Skye yipped and danced over to a chest of drawers to grab a box of tissues. "I've got this. Get the poor wee thing home to bed."

"Thank ye." I turned to Isla. "I'm going to carry ye to the car. Is your belly sore?"

Her bottom lip trembled, but she shook her head.

Skye watched on in concern. "Do ye have anything in case she gets a fever?"

I brought Isla to my shoulder and stood. "Naw. I can

count on one hand the number of times she's been ill. Since she turned five, nothing's touched her."

Caitriona pressed her cousin's arm. "Do ye have medicine Lochinvar can borrow?"

The second woman produced a bottle of paracetamol syrup, and handed it to her. I thanked her again, then clutched my lass in my arms and strode downstairs.

The family and my crew members expressed surprise that we had to go, and Cameron frowned, his gaze locking on to the site of my earlier injury.

Caitriona rushed out an explanation, but I was already out of the door, frustrated at myself.

Isla was my one concern. My everything. In my arms, she now dozed, but her breathing was too fast, and with every inhale, my fear increased.

She could catch a fever. Or pneumonia. The castle wasn't the warmest place. All those hours, she'd been in clammy clothes.

Caitriona chased me to my car. "Here's the medicine. Should I come with you? Can I help? I feel so bad."

"Don't," I half-snapped then forced myself to swallow my fear. "We'll be fine. I'll see ye tomorrow."

I peeled out of the car park, focused only on my daughter.

---

*I*sla slept, but I couldn't. I sat on the floor by her bed, elbows on my knees, taking her temperature with the back of my hand every now and again.

Dwelling on the past, present, and future with increasing apprehension.

Tonight, though the rescue had been a success, I'd taken

a fall. Nothing severe, but I'd slipped on rocks and landed hard, bruising my side.

An unluckier version of that fall could have knocked me out. A worse accident could leave Isla an orphan. It happened to rescuers. Rarely, but this risk was there. I'd heard nothing from my sister, so who would care for my daughter if I couldn't?

Caitriona would, I knew that. At least for a while. But she didn't have the full story on who we were and why we were effectively in hiding.

Plus I'd been rude to her, and it fucking bothered me that she might be worried about us.

On the bed, Isla flung out an arm and twisted over. I'd saved the medicine in case she became feverish, but a quick check confirmed no temperature spike. Nor had she been sick again. This time, it appeared she'd gotten off lightly.

I sighed over my sleeping lass. If Isla became ill, had a medical emergency, my deepest-held secrets would be out. It wouldn't be by choice, and I couldn't handle that loss of control.

The two strengthening arguments added to my resolve.

I couldn't be an island with her. Or for myself. It was driving me insane.

I eased up and quietly left the room.

At three in the morning, I found myself outside Caitriona's door.

I'd barely tapped when it flew open. Dressed in leggings and a long t-shirt, Caitriona shot her gaze to mine.

"Is she okay?"

"Aye. Dinna fret."

She paused then dipped her head, some of the worry leaving her expression.

Unhinged, I grabbed her hand and pulled her with me, barely giving her time to close and lock her own door.

Back in my cottage, at Isla's room, Caitriona swept past me and touched my daughter's forehead.

Such a simple act, yet it drove nails into my heart.

Her shoulders sank, and she gazed at me, seeking confirmation of her own findings. Aye, Isla was fine.

But I was far from that.

I beckoned her out and into my bedroom, gesturing for her to sit on my bed. Under the lamplight, Caitriona pushed her loose hair behind her ear then perched on her hands, warily watching me.

"I was rude to ye," I said.

"Ye were. But I understand."

"I apologise all the same. Isla is my whole world. I made a mistake tonight…"

"In trusting me to care for her?"

"No. That isn't what I meant." I wanted to sit next to her and hold her, but I had information to share, and it needed a rational mind. Caitriona scrambled my brain at the best of times. I pressed my shoulders against the wall and summoned my will.

"In my not looking out for her properly. That has been my single most important goal for years."

As if she could sense the weight of words waiting to be aired, Caitriona let me speak.

"When I first knew of Isla's existence, it was four weeks before her birth."

"Ye didn't know your wife was pregnant?"

"Liv wasn't my wife then. We married three weeks later, then our bairn came four days on from that."

"Where is she now? Liv, I mean."

"Prison."

I let that settle for a moment, my muscles held tight. Caitriona swallowed but waited for me to continue.

"Liv was my childhood schoolfriend. She grew up in a village near to mine. Poor, like us, but to a far worse family. Her father was a notorious drug dealer and a shite example of a human being. Her older brothers followed in his footsteps. Violence, gang war, ye name it, he brought it to their home. To a lesser extent, Liv did, too. Stealing, getting into trouble. Then she vanished when she was seventeen. She was twenty-one when we met again."

My heart pounded, and my stomach crushed in a ball. After the next piece of information, I couldn't go back. Caitriona would know it all.

She lifted her head, confusion in her eyes. "But ye said she was pregnant when ye saw her again."

"Aye." I could barely force out the word.

Caitriona froze up. "Oh, Lochie. Fuck. Are ye saying what I think you're saying?"

"Isla isn't genetically mine."

Shock widened her eyes before a fiercer expression took over. "She is yours. In every other way, that bairn is your daughter."

I loved the vehemence of her tone. It matched the rising wave of emotion in me. "She is. Legally, with my name on her birth certificate. I was the only person her ma trusted to care for her child, my child, as Isla became. Her genetic father was a lowlife, a lad from a rival gang. He turned his back on Liv."

"That poor woman. Why is she in jail?"

"When she found out she was pregnant, and her boyfriend dropped her, she made the mistake of contacting her family. Her father demanded she return to the fold and raise the bairn as one of them, and she went, but once there, they began using her to make deliveries. Long hours behind the wheel, heading south into big cities. You can guess why."

"Drug deliveries?"

"Aye. They imported from Europe, docking small boats at remote Highland coastal towns. Then Liv became their mule—a slight, scared woman who no one would suspect. She wasnae innocent, not by a long chalk, but it was something else that made her run from them again. When they found out who'd fathered the bairn, they talked about using that connection. It scared the shite out of Liv to think of her newborn as a pawn between gangs. She was desperate to break the cycle."

Clamping her hands together, Caitriona just let me talk.

"On her last trip, Liv came to me. She ditched the car with the drugs and fled to the base where I worked, begging for help. At the same time, the police swooped in and raided her family's property. They arrested her da and brothers and put out a warrant for Liv. She was terrified, and I couldnae refuse her. The only way for me to take full ownership of the bairn was as her husband. She hid out, and we barely got away with the wedding. The birth happened under police custody."

I'd stored my explanation away carefully, knowing one day I'd need to present it to my daughter.

"Isla is seven in a few days. Why has her mother been in prison so long? She wasn't the instigator."

"At that point, I had no clue how deep Liv was in on it. She told me she'd be let go—I think she even assumed it—but it wasnae to be. Liv's sentence was for eight years. They had evidence of her actions but also her contact with the other gang. They painted her as a go-between and proved the driving part after discovering the abandoned car with a damning fingerprint. Then she turned to drugs inside and got a consecutive sentence. She stopped permitting my visits some years ago now."

"So ye were left holding the baby."

"Aye. I thought it would be for a month or two, but it pretty quickly became apparent that was a fantasy."

"By which point you'd fallen in love."

I stared at her. How easily she understood me.

Cait cleared her throat. "What happened with Liv's family? Did they get sentenced, too?"

A prickle ran down my spine. "Her father is still inside, but her brothers were released earlier this year."

Caitriona's fingers dug into my bedspread, and I could see her putting pieces together. Why we moved. Why we were here.

"Is Isla in danger?"

"Liv believed so. Despite naw wanting to see us, she was clear over her warning. They want Isla. Threatened Liv for keeping her from them. I suspect that they might still try to use her as she's part of two warring families."

"Then you're in danger, too."

That hardly mattered, but I nodded acknowledgement.

"The best I can hope for is they give up trying to find her. They have no idea that I am involved, and I've been very careful to keep us off public records in any searchable form."

With her gaze dropping to the floor, Caitriona asked her next question so quietly I had to strain to hear it over my own rushing blood.

"Is Lochinvar Ross even your name?"

"Yes and no. Ross is an assumed surname. Lochinvar is my name, but not my first. I was called Bram after my father, though my family always called me Lochie."

"Will you tell me your real name?"

"Bram Lochinvar MacNeill."

She raised her gaze and repeated the name. "Why are ye telling me this?"

"I've lost contact with my sister. She's a serving officer so it happens, but I need someone else to know Isla's story. In case anything happens to me. Or to her."

For a long moment, Caitriona searched my gaze. I couldn't read her mind on this. Of anyone I'd ever met, Caitriona was the most level-headed and honest. She called things as they were, and I trusted her.

Relief trickled in and replaced my anxiety from reliving the past.

"I'm glad ye told me. I can't imagine how difficult a decision it must have been to take on Isla in those circumstances."

It had and hadn't. "I fell for the bairn instantly. The rest became a necessity."

"Does Isla know?" she asked.

Ah fuck.

My skin turned clammy.

"Naw yet."

"Any of it?"

"Only that we changed her surname and had to move for safety's sake."

Realisation dawned in Caitriona's eyes. "Ye think I can help her, because of Scarlet? Because my mother isn't my biological ma?" She swung her gaze off me. "Is that why we're friends?"

"Ye think I'm using ye? No. I had no idea of your background until after we started... Whatever this thing is we have."

She slumped. "Right. Sorry."

I dug my hands into my hair and wrenched it, then gave

up my cool-headed act and dropped to the floor in front of Caitriona. On my knees, I took hold of her shoulders. "Dinna apologise. I've just burdened ye with years of my problems. I've done it for selfish reasons, too. I have to keep Isla safe, which means someone else needs to know the facts."

"I'm glad ye did. I care about her." She linked her gaze to mine.

I leaned in and pressed my mouth to hers.

Caitriona cupped my jaw, her fingers sliding over my beard. She made a small sound of need, and sparks blazed between us.

Always a man of action, I came alive with fierce and instant heat.

I stood, bringing her with me, and backed her to the wall. Caitriona clung on to me and, as we kissed, I picked her up by her thighs. She wrapped her legs around my waist, squeezing me, and I surged against her.

Passion exploded. My breathing came hard. Caitriona wrenched my t-shirt from me, then moved to undo my jeans.

I paused to let her do it and pressed a kiss to her throat. "Hard and fast this time."

Her quick nod gave me the green light.

Dropping her to her feet, I dragged down her leggings. She was bare underneath, and I cupped her between her legs, sinking my fingers into her arousal, acutely aware of how I'd done this. Turned her on. I'd never get over the fact that she wanted me. Was wet for me alone.

Caitriona moaned softly. I badly wanted to taste her, but there was only one way this was going down.

Kicking away the rest of my clothes, I removed Caitriona's shirt, taking a second to admire her perfect tits, then grabbed her back into my hold. My nails-hard dick sought entrance to her soft body.

"Condom," she whispered.

Fuck. I muttered an apology then dipped to take what I needed from my jeans. Suited up, I got back into position with her legs around my waist, then oh-so slowly, slid into Caitriona's tight heat.

We both suppressed a groan.

My dick pulsed, thickening even more. I withdrew then slammed home. Caitriona gasped then grabbed my hair to yank my face to hers. She kissed me, swallowing my next groan. This was too good. Too natural and right.

I picked up speed, jacking my hips to fuck the way I'd promised. Before, I'd made love to her, but this was pure animalistic need taking over. I'd trawled through painful memories and stirred the beast inside me.

Heat eclipsed sense. Getting Caitriona off became my goal.

In and out I surged, charging myself up. My woman received me, taking everything I had to give. Our kiss turned sloppy until we abandoned it, and I tucked my head into the crook of her neck.

I slammed into her. Over and over, crashing down with increasing power. Even in my worked-up state, I could feel her clamping down on me inside. She clawed at my back, silently urging me on.

In my position of pinning Caitriona against the wall, I could only fuck, following an undeniable need to give this lass my all. Whatever we were to each other, I'd crossed a line tonight and there was no going back.

Nor did I want to.

The change in my lonely life had undone some closely held part of me.

A fresh wave of lust rinsed through me, and the base of my spine tingled. Fuck. I could go for hours if Caitriona wanted, but I also needed to come. Soon.

I slowed to change the angle, checking Caitriona's expression in the dim light of my bedroom.

"Don't stop," she begged, hoarse. "I'm close."

Ah God.

Her words released the control I'd so carefully guarded. Now, I pounded her, hitting home with all my force. A tremor took my muscles, not enough air in the room to fill my lungs.

"Lochie!" Caitriona arched in my arms, then squeezed me, coming hard.

With barely held relief, I gave up my control and followed her over the edge, surging once more then stilling. Inside her, I came, spilling the contents of my balls. My orgasm obliterated my thoughts, and I soaked up the sensation. The utterly addictive feeling of pleasure. Aye, this was so needed, so perfect.

Together, we breathed, coming down from the high. As soon as my head cleared, I carried Caitriona to my bed and set her down. Then I disposed of the condom and climbed under the covers, drawing my woman back into my arms.

She reached for me and held me close, her head on my chest.

We let the world, the good and bad and everything in between, drift away.

 *aitriona*

"Daddy!"

At Isla's voice, I jerked upright, disorientated for a moment.

I was in Lochie's bed, in his cottage.

Naked.

The door handle twisted, and I sucked in a breath then dove back down, whipping the covers over my head.

"Can I watch TV?" the little girl chirped.

"Aye. I'll be out to make your breakfast," Lochie replied in a low rumble.

After a beat, he pulled the blanket from my face. An amused smile curved his lips. "Morning."

"Shite. I didn't mean to sleep over."

"It's okay. She didnae notice."

He ran his arm around me and hauled me onto his chest. Then kissed me firmly.

Dazed, I blinked at him. "Whoa. Good morning."

Lochie's smile spread, and I caught it, grinning back like

a dope. After everything he'd said last night, I knew him so much better. And liked him all the more for it.

Bram Lochinvar MacNeill. Harbourer of a fugitive, and devoted father.

"You're still talking to me after last night," he said.

"Why wouldn't I?"

Lochie raised a shoulder, his confidence hanging on an edge.

"I do have a question," I said.

"Shoot."

"Why did ye agree to Liv's request when she showed up? It was a lot to do for someone ye hadn't seen in years."

He sighed. "I know. It was. But I'd always felt such guilt over the way she'd left."

"Was she your girlfriend?"

"No. She wanted me, and I was always leaving for the military, so I refused her." Lochie threw back the sheets and slapped my backside. "Come on. We'll have a job sneaking ye out, so why don't ye stay for breakfast?"

I nodded slowly. Lochie's bedroom didn't have a door to the outside like mine did. Theirs was in the kitchen and presumably locked. We climbed from the bed and collected our clothes, dressing while shooting glances at each other. Once ready, Lochie opened the door then peered out. He waved me to follow, and we walked the short hall.

In the living room, Isla perched on the couch, her back to us.

Her da silently walked past, and I tiptoed until closer to the door.

"Isla, Cait's joining us for breakfast," he suddenly announced.

The little girl's head swivelled. I froze on the spot.

"Hi, Cait. Can you braid my hair before school? Da isn't

very good at it." She held her gaze on me, ignoring the cartoon playing in the background.

"I'd love to," I replied.

Lochie subtly reached for my hand and pressed my fingers. "Are ye cold? Grab my hoodie from the chair. I'll make coffee."

He disappeared into the kitchen, and I released a breath. My thin t-shirt wasn't warm enough for the chilly morning, so I grabbed the hoodie then took a minute in the bathroom before joining Isla.

With a happy smile, she offered up a brush and a handful of twisted hair bands. I grinned and sectioned out her thick, golden hair, arranging it into three for braiding.

"Ye know, brushing your curls out will just make it frizzy. My cousin Viola has curly hair, and I learned that from her."

"Did ye do each other's hair?"

"Sometimes, but Scarlet, my mother, used to do mine for me every morning," I said softly. "I went through a stage of wanting fancy hairstyles. I made Viola compete with me over who had the most complicated style."

"What sort of thing did you have?"

"French plaits. Smooth buns with tiny plaits teased in. For about six months, we tried everything. Viola is more of a tomboy but ultra-competitive, too."

"You can do that for me," Isla decided. "Come to breakfast every day."

I sucked in a breath but focused on the task in hand.

This was...weird. But also lovely.

When I glanced up, Lochie rested a shoulder against the kitchen entrance, watching us.

I gazed right back.

"Da, can you make me toast? I can't move while Cait's doing my hair," Isla interrupted.

"I will. Caitriona?"

"Toast sounds good."

He set about it then we ate together at their small dining table, Isla crowing over a friend she'd made at school who always had pretty hair.

Too soon, breakfast was over, and I returned to my cottage to start my own day. I showered and dressed for work, sitting down to my laptop in time to see Lochie and Isla leave for school. I waved, and they waved back, Lochie linking his gaze to mine, loaded with meaning.

A strange feeling, present since I woke, buzzed in my chest.

Maybe it was an intense kind of sympathy for the little family. I wanted to help Lochie with his problem of telling Isla her background.

That was it. A simple need to fix a problem.

I rested my chin on my hands, my gaze distancing as I recalled Lochie's story. The danger his friend was in had clearly driven him to extreme action, but then again, that was his personality type. And his background with his mother fleeing his da. He'd made no reference to regretting it, and he adored his daughter beyond anyone or anything. His protective instinct drove him. It was there in every act, not just in his job.

Lochie was the perfect father for that child. His ex-wife had chosen well.

About half an hour into my working day, my phone buzzed with a text in Lochie's name. I'd changed it from Lochinvar Ross to Lochie, and the appearance brought a smile to my face.

Lochie: Thank ye for last night. I don't think I said.

Caitriona: I should be thanking you.

Lochie: How do I insert an eyeroll? Ye know what I mean.

I grinned wider.

Another message arrived.

Lochie: Will ye tell me more about your problems at work?

Caitriona: If you like. It's strange. My coat was stolen, and my lunch eaten. I'd dismissed it as an accident, but they put the lunchbox back in the fridge including the empty packets.

Lochie: Anything else?

Caitriona: My emails were hacked. I think. There were several opened that I hadn't read. Tech Support told me to change my password, but it happened again.

Lochie: Anything personal in those emails?

Caitriona: My contact with the fertility clinic I'm going to use.

I typed, deleted, then retyped the last text. There was no reason to feel strange about telling Lochie my plans. He already knew, and it was relevant to his question.

His response took a while to come in.

Lochie: Ye suspect your boss, aye? What did he do? Be explicit.

Caitriona: Overly friendly at first, then there was this weird meeting where he started talking about how well-made his kids were, and how I shouldn't leap to fertility treatment.

Putting it like that, Rupert couldn't be more of a prime suspect.

Lochie: How did he act after seeing me in your home?

Caitriona: He sent his PA to tell me I needed to work in the office more.

Another message landed, but from a social media site. I opened it.

Cait, it's Jude. I forgot to get your number, but Chelle and I are excited about dinner. See you tonight!

Ah God, I'd forgotten all about that. I readied to send a cancellation. Then again...

Jude was Rupert's nephew. I could pump him for information. I replied with my address.

Then I tapped out another message to Lochie.

Caitriona: I'm having dinner with his nephew tonight so I'll try to find out more then.

No reply came, and I lost myself in emails for a while.

By lunchtime, Lochie hadn't written back. I frowned at my phone then read over our conversation. I'd expected some words of wisdom from the man for whom protecting people was his be all and end all.

I paused on the last message. Was it the dinner with another man?

Amusement came on the back of my surprise. I'd never had a relationship before, and this short-term one presumably didn't have the same rules, but I was almost certain the huge mountain man Lochie was sulking.

Grinning, I added another message.

Caitriona: ...and his fiancée.

Lochie's almost instant response cracked me up.

Lochie: Good to know. I'll see ye after they've gone.

A knock rattled my door at seven thirty on the dot. I scurried to answer it, wiping my hands.

Jude waited the other side. Alone.

He greeted with a quick kiss to the cheek.

"Hey. Ye found me easily enough. Where's Chelle?" I ushered him in, peering at his car.

"Um, slightly awkward, but we argued about coming here, and she's at home. I didn't want to let you down so I came alone. Is this a bad idea? I can go." He pointed at the door, his nose wrinkled and his lips twisted.

With his floppy blond hair and sweet face, I used to think him kind of cute, but that ship had long sailed.

"No, no. It's fine. I'm sorry ye argued." I gestured at the table.

Jude sat, his gaze flitting over my home. "It's weird when you travel a lot. I think you forget social boundaries. I assumed Chelle would be fine but I was wrong. My bad."

"Didn't she want to come out?" I poured a glass of water from the chilled bottle I'd already brought out.

Now there was only two of us, grabbing a bottle of wine felt inappropriate.

"This is where it gets even more awkward. I made an epic mistake and told her that you and I had slept together. Eh. I always want to be honest with her, but in that, I think I should've exercised discretion."

Discomfort tightened my tummy, and I wrapped my arms around myself. "It wasn't like we dated or anything. Maybe you should've told her that there wasn't anything there?"

Jude continued his examination of my home before settling his gaze back on me. "I did. Must've done it wrong."

He probably shouldn't have come here at all, sticking with his fiancée, but it would be rude for me to say.

"We can still have a catch up," I said briskly. "I'll serve up dinner and ye can tell me about your travels."

Jude had always been good company and an excellent storyteller. I plated up dinner—spinach and ricotta cannelloni with a crisp salad—and listened while he picked through the best of his holiday stories.

By the time we were onto dessert, I'd relaxed some.

"How are you enjoying working at the university?" Jude asked.

This was my opportunity. "The work is fine, but I'm not sure I'd say I'm entirely happy."

"Is my uncle giving you a hard time? I've spent a couple of evenings with him, and he spilled a pretty big piece of news of yours. I'm sorry to tell you."

I widened my eyes. "He did? That's..."

"Vastly inappropriate and unprofessional? Yeah, it was. He's acting kind of strange about it."

"What did he say?"

Jude scrubbed over his hair, messing it. He peeked from under the strands. "Um, this is delicate. First, I should tell you that my mum won't see him anymore. He's my dad's brother, but even after Dad died, Rupert used to still get invited to family dinners. But Mum stopped and she wouldn't say why, other than he'd gone weird."

"What did he say about me?"

"That you were going to have a baby without a husband. He doesn't think it's right."

My blood boiled. "The nerve."

"I know. That's part of why I came here. I thought you needed to know and I didn't know how to broach it. We haven't seen each other in a while, but we were always good friends."

Despite my upset at his uncle, warmth filtered through from my friend's care. "I really appreciate that. You're right, ye were one of my closest friends at university."

"Right? I've thought about you from time to time and hoped you were doing okay. If you need to talk about any of this stuff, I'm still here for you."

Decency shone from him. He waited on my word.

My phone buzzed on the counter. I reached for it and stared at the screen.

"Shite."

"What is it?" Jude peered over.

I tapped out a reply.

"I'm so sorry. I'm going to have to cut our dinner short."

"Oh, sad face! But it's fine, I was about to go anyway. What's happened?"

A knock came at the door, and I leapt to open it. Lochie waited the other side, already in his jumpsuit and with the air of urgency surrounding him.

"Sorry to interrupt. I could take her to the hangar, but she's already in bed and asleep."

I squeezed his arm. Late night call-outs happened, and I was more than willing to look after Isla.

"Go. It's fine." Then I mouthed where Jude couldn't see. "I'll wait up for ye."

Lochie's gaze darkened, then he glanced over my shoulder to my guest. Whatever he saw shrank the attentive look in his eyes. "Do ye want me to wait until you've locked up?"

"No, no. I'll be fine."

He left, and I remained at the door then turned to Jude.

My friend's shocked gaze stuck on Lochie's retreating car. "Oh my God. Who was that?"

I couldn't help my chuckle. "Lochie. He's the head of the mountain rescue. I sometimes look after his daughter when he's on missions."

Jude fanned his face. "Give me a knife and fork. I want to eat up that chemistry for supper."

I rolled my eyes. "Yeah, there might be some of that." I'd never before been able to talk like this, but it was freeing. "He and I... Let's just say we're close."

"But I thought you— Never mind. Minding my own business." Jude grabbed his jacket and mock wiped his brow. "Never thought I'd see the day when you fell for a man. Right, I have to run. Next time my place?"

"Do you think Chelle will be okay with that?"

He blinked at me, already halfway out the door. "Uh, sure. I'll talk to her. Until the next time."

In a hurry, Jude was gone.

I grabbed my things, locked up, then went into Lochie's cottage. I had decisions to make on work, as Rupert's behaviour had gone from odd to unacceptable, but there was more to consider. Too much. My head practically ached with it all. I curled up on the couch and closed my eyes, letting my brain focus on one core thing. Lochie would come home and take me to his bed.

I wanted nothing more than that.

$\mathcal{L}$*ochie*

Isla's birthday dawned with bright skies and a smattering of snow fallen overnight. She burst into my bedroom at first light and leapt on my bed, a knee landing too close to delicate areas. I pulled her into a hug while she squealed with laughter.

After our near miss last week when she almost discovered Caitriona and me in bed together, Caitriona had been careful not to fall asleep. I teetered on the edge of demanding that she sleep in my arms. To acknowledge our relationship to the people closest to us. But it would mean too much to Isla if she knew we were together. She wouldn't understand when it came time to leave.

My chest ached, and I held my daughter tighter. "What's got ye all excited this morning?"

"Daddy! It's my birthday. I'm seven today," she said on a giggle.

"Naw, that cannae be right. I'm sure ye were born in the summer, maybe five years ago. Aye, that's it."

"Five? Da!" she chastised, her bright-blue eyes wide.

"Ah, maybe you're right. Let me see if I got ye anything. Into the living room."

She bounded up and out, and I followed, donning a pair of grey joggers.

At Isla's shriek, I grinned widely. Last night, Caitriona and I had decorated the room with a banner and balloons, adding to the small number of Christmas decorations Isla had made. Ah fuck, Caitriona should be here to see this. It'd been her who'd sourced it all.

Isla grabbed a balloon and batted it at me then pounced on the wrapped gift and card on the table. "Can I open it?" Then she paused. "Can I fetch Cait first? We're going to bake a cake today, so I don't want her to forget."

I breathed in through my nose, the ledge I hovered over too steep. I could say it was too early, or that Caitriona might still be sleeping, but it was no good. I wanted her here, too. "Aye, go to it."

"Yes!" She planted her feet into her boots and was out the door before I took a step, her dressing gown flapping. "Cait?" She hammered on the door.

"Happy birthday, Isla," Caitriona's warm tones resounded.

My heart swelled.

Ah Christ, I was fucked.

Then the two appeared at the door, and Caitriona's pretty gaze landed on me. I hadn't bothered with a shirt, and her attention lingered on my chest.

I rolled my shoulders so my muscles tightened, earning a gleam in Caitriona's eye.

In a matter of months, this woman had taken ownership of my brawny soul. She was far smarter than me, but I suspected she had no clue how deep the attachment between us could go. Her deal had been brave but it was also a front.

She wanted me, and I wanted her.

What a beautiful mess we'd made.

Pink-cheeked, she raised her eyebrows then turned back to my daughter who'd closed the door and kicked off her boots. "I can't believe you're seven today. Such a grown-up girl. Did ye open your present yet? Want another?"

Caitriona held up a hefty bag, and Isla clutched her balled-up hands to her mouth. She peeked at me, seeking permission. I dipped my head, and she tore into Caitriona's gift ahead of mine.

A shredding of paper later, and she extracted a pile of pretty clothes. On top, a pack of hair accessories waited. I tended to buy functional clothes for Isla, no patience for the ridiculous outfits offered for girls. Daft slogans on the front, no pockets. Her unicorn onesie had been bought on pester power and was the exception to my rule.

Caitriona's items hit a mark I'd missed.

Isla held each up in turn, cooing over the patterns and colours. Feminine yet well-made and still suitable for a child. The last item, a dress, nearly matched one I'd seen on Caitriona.

The woman in question peeked at me then raised a shoulder. "Once I started shopping, I got carried away. Scarlet came with me, and we picked out so many lovely things. I hope that's okay?"

"I love it all. Thank you." Isla hugged Caitriona tight, answering for me.

I let a soft smile be my words.

My own gift, a karaoke machine, finally received atten-tion, and I had another hug before I was dispatched to make breakfast. Isla tried on her clothes, singing into her microphone. It being the weekend, we'd planned a morning hike before Caitriona and Isla baked the promised cake.

We'd never had this—an easy, happy family birthday morning. I could barely stand the tender flare of emotions inside.

Once we were ready to head out, I drove us to a spot Caitriona chose, finding my way over the now familiar landscape though lost in a mire of brand-new feelings. Even with my sister around, Isla and I had always been a unit of two. But my daughter strode ahead, crunching through the snow, hand in hand with Caitriona, and I never wanted anything so hard as this. Always.

Christmas was in two weeks. Somehow, Caitriona would be part of our plans.

At the base of the waterfall I'd trained the team at a while ago, Caitriona showed Isla what she called the unicorn pool. They threw pebbles in, and Caitriona told stories her da had told her about the spot.

How the magical unicorns had saved a man who fell from the hidden cliffs high above.

Isla lapped it up, happier than I'd ever seen her.

Caitriona's phone buzzed. She frowned at the screen then tapped out a response while Isla scampered off, exploring.

"Everything okay?" I asked.

"It's Jude, the friend who came to dinner on Friday. He says he has something to discuss about his uncle. He's asked me to come to Inverness later to meet him."

I clamped down on a rush of dislike. The moment I'd laid eyes on the man in Caitriona's cottage, I'd had a bad feeling. I knew I was overprotective, and alongside Isla, Caitriona was right at the top of the list of people I needed to care for, but it was more than plain chest-beating jealousy or even intuition.

Jude had smiled for Caitriona but thrown a meaningful look at me, challenging and smug. All men knew this specific expression. Unmistakable, it meant a battle for the woman.

His claim evaporated when Caitriona turned back, but the contact had served its purpose.

He'd set himself against me, the wee shite.

I'd never try to control Caitriona or who she spent time with, but the urge to warn her of his intent warred with my need to maintain the arrangement she'd struck between us. For her, we were just friends who had sex. I had no rights until she gave me them.

She typed a reply. "Sorry, buddy. Not today. It'll have to wait."

Instant relief flooded me. Across the glen, Isla dragged a stick through the snow, her back to us, so I took a second to grab Caitriona by the waist and kiss her.

Her chilled lips warmed under mine.

Caitriona smiled against my mouth before throwing a glance to Isla and stepping back. "What was that for?"

"Ye put my daughter first. Thank ye."

"Always."

Her phone buzzed again in her hand. She glanced at it and grinned. "Ah, they made it. Skye said she'd come down with her kids and also her niece, Florrie. She's Isla's age. Plus Skye is good friends with the mother of one of Isla's school friends." She chewed her lip. "I was thinking after we bake the cake, we could take it to the castle and have a tea party. Skye will arrange for the other girl to come. Isla might like that. Scarlet will be there, too. I could maybe drop in the fact that she's not my birth mother. Lay the groundwork."

Acute happiness and longing constricted my throat. So

much, I couldn't speak for a moment. I held Caitriona's gaze until I was master of myself again. "Aye. I love the idea."

She watched me in return, the curiosity in her gaze mixed with something I couldn't identify.

My mountain rescue phone barked its demanding tone.

Caitriona and I both jerked.

Oh Christ, what timing.

I snapped out of my reverie and took the call. In thirty seconds, my brain had switched gear and adrenaline shot through me.

"I've had a call-out," I uttered.

"No!"

"Isla," I bellowed. "We're heading back to the car."

Caitriona's smile dropped, and she kept up with my long strides, a hand held out to catch Isla's. "I'm sorry. I can't believe this. What's happened?"

"Climbers trapped on a cliff face. Two women, both sustained injuries when the lead climber fell. One woman managed to reach her phone, and it sounds like they're half frozen and hanging from their ropes."

"God." Caitriona glanced at the weather. We'd taken our walk earlier as there was a storm coming in this afternoon. "Be safe."

"Always," I repeated her word then got us on the road.

At the cottages, beyond grateful I had Caitriona to care for Isla, I dropped them off with a request to have a slice of birthday cake saved, then headed out to the hangar. In conditions like this, we'd need a full-service call-out, and people already waited. I'd dispatched Cameron with Max as the advanced party, and rallied a crew of twelve in three cars, climbing and medical evac equipment onboard, the local ambulance service alerted to receive the casualties once we'd gotten them down.

Needing to coordinate, I threw myself into the back of the first 4x4.

The man in the seat next to me was a familiar face. Alasdair was Caitriona's father, and a helpful on-the-ground member of my crew. He'd taken time to explain to me how he lived with severe dyslexia, which meant map reading and written instruction were an issue. From the crew's perspective, it only meant awareness for whoever he buddied up with. An excellent memory gave him an advantage, though, and he knew the area and topography to inch-perfect measures.

I often gave full written debriefs to the crew but had met Alasdair once or twice to do it verbally. I liked the man a lot and respected his thoughts. His ready smile and easy manner so reminded me of Caitriona it tripped me up.

I raised my chin at him. "Alasdair, talk to me about the climbing spot."

"I told ye to call me Ally." He scratched his bearded cheek, fingertips grazing a deep scar. "Not a typical place you'd find climbers in winter. It's a long trek to ascend, and the exposed ridge is a fucker for windchill. Today was a bad day to attempt that climb."

As a rule, we made a point not to judge the people we went out to rescue. People climbed mountains because they were there. On any given weekend, tens of thousands headed to the Scottish hills. It was easy to get lost or injured, and the individuals involved rarely made the same mistake twice. But I couldn't help give him a wry smile of agreement.

We sped on, crossing a glen before ascending once more. Under the car's tyres, the snow deepened, and above us, thick clouds settled in. My radio bleeped.

Max's voice came through the line. "We're at the base of

the climb. It's fucking freezing up here. Neither of us can see another soul."

I studied the printed map. "Repeat, ye havenae located the missing party, over?"

"Copy that. There's no fucker up here but us. We can see the whole of the rock face. It's empty."

"Any signs of climbing equipment?"

"Naw. Cameron looked for footprints in the snow and couldnae find one. No ropes, crampons, nothing."

"Exactly where are ye?"

He relayed their position.

I repeated it to Alasdair and the other occupants of the car. From the initial report, the women should've been right above our advanced party.

We joined them, and an hour later reached the same conclusion.

There were no signs of the missing women at all.

"The climbers have their location wrong," one of the men suggested.

Fuck, which made it a hundred times more difficult for us.

A quick call to base brought a negative for speaking to the women directly. There was no answer to the calls that had been made back to them.

Which only meant one thing.

Our serious but focused rescue was now a hunt, and a race to save lives.

---

*H*ours on, and fresh snow spat at my cheeks, whipped by a vicious December wind. I paced back to the Jeep, mind churning, the gale trying to swipe me off my feet.

From our initial location, I'd pulled Cameron and Max back to work with me and Alasdair, segmented our crew to search parties, and called in additional members. Then we focused on a hit list of likely rock faces to try.

All to no avail.

In another hour, we'd lose the light. The worsening weather had already obscured the landscape, snowdrifts concealing landmarks.

I'd yet to see conditions as bad as this, but I knew the repercussions.

The sheer fact was if we didn't find the climbers soon, they were at risk of losing their lives, if that hadn't already happened. A heaviness settled in my heart. People died on the hill. In the RAF, I'd presided over a few recoveries of bodies, and it was a terrible thing.

I slammed myself inside the Jeep at the same moment Alasdair got in the other side. Cameron and Max joined us.

"Fuck. Fuck this wild goose chase." Max removed his helmet, scattering ice, his gaze dark with annoyance.

I felt it, too, though tried not to show it.

Alasdair sucked in a breath. "Another fail. We've ticked off the obvious list of rock faces. What now?"

I shucked off my gloves. "Cameron, check with base to see if there's any updates."

He grumbled agreement and got on the radio while I accepted a hot coffee from Alasdair. "We need that nine-nine-nine call."

Typically by now, someone in my crew would've listened to it or read the transcript, but it hadn't come through yet.

We all took a breather, then my radio blared, the voice

requesting my attention. I answered Wasp, the head of my second team.

"Snow's settled in, a foot or more in the past hour. We have to remove to lower ground before the road becomes impassable, over," he barked down the line.

"Copy that. Proceed," I replied without hesitation, my sense of alarm increasing.

The moment any crew member became at significant risk, my priorities shifted. We would fight tooth and nail to rescue a soul, but I had to keep an eye on the safety of the rescue volunteers.

Losing more people was not happening.

A minute later, and another report came in—the third team retreating from the hill.

I okayed the message then dug my still-cold fingers into my hair. "Fuck."

"We have the recording," Cameron announced.

All four of us in leaned in to listen.

A strained female voice filled the car. "We need the mountain rescue team. Send them urgently. We were climbing, and my friend fell. She's hanging from a rope. I think she's unconscious. Rocks hit my arm, and I can't move."

"English," Alasdair muttered. "I'm trying to pick up her accent."

The caller continued with the dispatcher requesting the location.

"Coire an Loch. We paddled over the water then hiked here. It was a mistake. We're exhausted. Please help!"

The caller rang off, and the four of us quietened.

"Give me your thoughts," I demanded.

"She was instant and specific with the location," Cameron offered.

"There's a chance they could've descended themselves

and not called in." Alasdair's voice filled with doubt at his own words.

I twisted my lips. It was reasonably common for a party to find their own way down the hill, but rare that they didn't call off the search once back to safety.

"It's a hoax," Max said slowly.

All three of us twisted to him.

Alasdair, his father, frowned. "Why do ye think that?"

"She said they'd paddled over then hiked. The nearest decent-sized body of water is a two-hour walk away and probably iced over around the banks. The report came in at eleven, aye? No sane person would look at the forecast today, set out before dawn with a canoe, break through ice, then hike to that climb. They would have no route back."

Wind howled and rocked the car, marking his point.

I worked the idea through my head. Like people saving themselves, hoaxes happened, but I'd never had one in all the months I'd been in charge. From the few previous cases I'd glanced over, dispatch worked it out before anyone was searching. Teenagers were the biggest culprits, and it was always male callers.

"Fuck," Cameron drawled. "The more I think it through, the more sense that makes. And that explanation works for why Base couldn't find a single climbing club with members out today. No one else took the risk. How many hikers did we see?"

"A handful at best, and none braving the higher slopes," Alasdair replied.

Unsettled, I had a decision to make, and no matter who came up with the idea, the responsibility was mine.

If those two women were clinging to a rock face and I abandoned them to their fate, that loss of life was on me. If they were even still alive.

If they even existed.

After a quick request for another crew to check the lake shore, I centred on my men. "Is there any place left to try? Any burning intuition?"

In the driver's seat, Cameron set the windscreen wipers to clean the snow then peered at the horizon. "None that is any stronger a lead than the place she named. Are ye calling it?"

I had to. There was no specific place to go, no new lead. Nothing to justify exhausting the men in my charge.

At that moment, the storm belted the heavy Jeep with an icy blast. The car shuddered, snow obliterating our view.

"Shite. We need to get out of here," Cameron muttered. "Call it, Lochinvar."

Frustration had me gritting my teeth. I had no choice. "Drive us down."

With the headlights and the powerful overhead flood-lights near useless in the white out, Cameron rolled the car along the path of our previous ascent. There was no road here, and no tracks to follow from the fresh snowfall.

I radioed in my decision, getting a relieved rally of replies from the other teams who would return to the hangar.

Slowly, we pressed on until Cameron halted, idling the engine. I raised my gaze to find him staring.

"Our tracks are gone. I cannae see to drive down. This ridge has jagged rocks edging a crevice, but it's all hidden. If I drive over it, we'll sink."

We all ducked to gaze out. The sky and land had merged to one white blur. Snow hit the windscreen faster than the wipers could clear it.

My pulse picked up speed, the guttered adrenaline of the day rekindling. Getting caught out here would mean danger for us all. We had to find a path home. I snatched up my gloves and jammed them on, then grabbed my door handle. "I'll scout ahead."

"With ye." Alasdair clipped his helmet into place and climbed out the other side.

Freezing air sucked the breath from my lungs.

Against the gale, I forced my way to the front of the car. Alasdair rounded to meet me, and we staggered through the snow. The cold ate through my layers of insulation, slicing into the small areas of exposed skin on my face.

"Shite!" I stumbled.

Alasdair caught me, steadying me until I regained my balance. Underfoot, treacherous rocks made poor footing. We'd barely driven fifty metres, yet I couldn't see our starting place.

There was no chance of finding a path.

"Back to the car," I bellowed, the breeze snatching my words.

Alasdair nodded and, clutching each other, we turned to the bright lights of the Jeep.

We closed in, stumbling. There, Max waited outside, silhouetted by the spotlights.

The force of the weather knocked me down. At my side, Alasdair dropped into the snow with a shout.

"Careful, Da." Max lurched forwards.

The bank he stood on slid under his feet. A hole opened up in the hillside, devouring the snow. And the man.

In the blink of an eye, Max vanished.

"Fuck!" I bellowed.

Alasdair rose like a man possessed and charged through the snow.

I kept up. Ice pellets clattered against our helmets. Ahead, Cameron clambered from the Jeep.

We inched over to the place Max had disappeared. Cameron had been correct—the crevice he'd worried about was right below us. Though on more solid rock, the Jeep balanced just feet from the edge.

We could all have gone over.

Instead, that fate had fallen to just one.

Alasdair leaned, an arm back for me to brace him. He peered over.

"I see him. Max, I'm coming. Dinna move," he yelled then turned to me. "I'm going to climb down."

"Hold," I blared. "Rig up."

He stalled and raised his head, resistance in the set of his jaw. I understood—if it was Isla, I'd have dived headfirst after her. I also got how close these men were, not just the immediate family members, but the whole crew would walk through fire for the others.

But we'd gone from being caught on the hill to needing a technical rescue. I had to keep a steady hand.

Cameron landed by my side, and I jerked into action.

"Max, Max, report in, over," I snapped into the radio.

"Aye, alive. Naw injured."

His response settled a small part of my fear.

"Can ye get into a harness so we can haul ye up?" I asked.

A pause came. The howl of the wind had us leaning in to the radio.

"I'm a wee bit injured."

"Fuck. I'm going down." Cameron opened his rucksack, extracting a harness and ropes. "Dinna argue. I'm more agile than both of ye. Set me up."

I radioed in the incident while a stone-faced Alasdair helped Cameron with his harness. The response from base, though expected, chilled me.

I'd sent the other teams off the hill because of the storm. No one was near to offer assistance with our extraction.

We were on our own.

In short order, I checked the Jeep's stability then approved the use of the winch. No matter how strong Cameron was, we'd need the pulling power to get both men out of the hole.

Then the young team leader lowered himself into the gaping crevice.

He slipped out of sight, easing himself down. Max's da guided him, his gaze feverish, attention stuck. I watched the winch, waiting for the call that Cameron had reached his target.

After what felt like an age, my radio barked.

"Clear, over."

I stopped the ropes and waited. Around us, the temperature plummeted, the weather only worsening. Several minutes on, Cameron's voice came back in.

"Coming up. Go slow. Max's arm's probably broken, over."

At the edge, Alasdair clenched his fists, obviously distraught.

"Easy now," I murmured to him, not that he could hear me, then I activated the winch.

By tiny winds of the cable, Max appeared in sight. His da helped him over then heaved him clear. The younger man clutched his left arm, his gait unsteady. He lowered himself to the floor and, as carefully as possible, we unclipped him then went back for Cameron.

The second lift went easier, and twenty minutes after the accident had happened, all four of us were back on solid ground.

With Alasdair supporting Max, we packed up and returned to the Jeep.

Inside, tremors rattled my bones. "Good work, everyone. Max, talk to me."

His da removed Max's helmet, examining his face.

"I'm fine. Arm's fucked. Cannae lift it."

With his expression tight in pain I knew he wouldn't admit, he gazed at each of us, and I saw the gratitude, felt it to my bones.

"We'll get ye fixed up. Here." I issued painkillers to the lad.

He swallowed them and closed his eyes.

We all took a long, deep breath.

After a minute, I regained command of my senses, working out what the fuck to do next. "Cameron, how much petrol do we have left?"

"Third of a tank."

We'd need every drop to stay warm. Already, the car had iced in. "Keep the engine on. We'll run it for bursts every hour to stay warm, and us three can take turns to clear the exhaust of snow. We'll wait it out until there's a gap in the storm."

"Not to be the prophet of doom, but this is forecast to get worse. Even when it eases, we still won't be able to drive down," Max pointed out.

He was right. "We won't. But once we can stand upright outside, we can find a flat patch of ground and set off the flares."

All three men stilled, understanding the implications.

There was no way we could get off this mountain under our own steam.

I collected my radio and willed myself calm for the next step. Not only had I endangered my team, but I'd need to bring out another crew to save us. What had started as a race for two lost souls now switched to ours.

"MRT two-one-oh to Base, over."

"Copy that, MRT two-one-oh. What is your status."

I sucked in a breath and closed my eyes. "MRT casualty rescued, all stable. Ready a heli for extraction when possible. We're going to need help getting home."

If we could find a break in the storm before our fuel ran out.

My already cold body chilled. We had emergency rations, shelter, and communications gear. There was no reason to despair.

I could worry that Isla's birthday, made so special by Caitriona, had been ruined by her da not coming home.

But it was another idea that drove tension through my tired muscles. My arising emotions for Caitriona were no small matter. I couldn't pretend they were gentle or weak. The force of them sharpened until there was only one possible outcome.

She was in my thoughts throughout today. Her profile in my vision. Her soft touch an addiction and the safe landing I craved.

I was falling in love with the lass.

No matter how I hid from it, when it came down to the wire, it was the only truth I knew.

Now I only had to survive to tell her the fact.

24

Caitriona

I paced the great hall of Castle McRae, wringing my hands and wearing lines in the flagstones.

Da, my brother, Cameron, and Lochinvar were stranded on a mountain. There had been no let-up in the weather and no end in sight for their rescue.

Max was hurt.

They were all at risk.

Fierce anxiety controlled my steps. An awful pain tore at my chest, the pressure shredding me from the inside.

"Caitriona?" Ma joined me and took my arms, stalling my movements. "Come sit for a moment. You're pale."

"I can't stop panicking."

She examined my features then led me to a chair. Hours ago, before the situation had worsened, Ma and I had put Isla to bed together in the kids' bedroom. Already cued on what I'd needed to say, I'd slipped in that Scarlet was technically my stepmother, but that family wasn't defined by blood.

The wee lass had taken it in her stride. She'd stared at me as if wanting to ask something but settled on reminding me her da would need that slice of birthday cake once he finally got home. She'd gone to sleep easily, settled by words of comfort about her father's return.

I could no longer believe them.

I'd held her hand and hid my rising fear deep inside.

Now, it poured out.

It had been too long. Dangerous evening had turned to bitter night. Survival in these conditions became perilous.

What if Lochinvar never came home?

We'd had such a wonderful day, too, despite the call-out. But as the night wore on, the more my desperation rose.

With a murmur about making tea, Ma vanished to the kitchen.

I peered around the room. My aunts, Mathilda and Taylor, sat together, talking quietly. In a corner, Maddock, home for winter break, waited in an armchair, unspeaking but here all the same. Uncle Callum had gone to the hangar, and a few others buzzed back and forth.

Scarlet returned with a steaming mug and cosied up beside me. "Here. Drink this."

"Why am I the only one freaking out?"

Ma tilted her head. "What exactly are ye worried about? Your brother?"

"All of them. That they won't make it off the mountain."

"I'm worried about Max, too, but mainly because I know he'll be a terror with his arm in a cast and nothing to do. As for the rest of it, in the past few years, your da has been caught out overnight twice. It happens, and they're equipped to withstand these conditions. It's a matter of when, not if, they'll come home. Look at Taylor. You know how precious your cousin Cameron is to her, and she's handling it. They'll be okay."

Shame stole over me. Truthfully, Max and Da had barely crossed my mind. I somehow knew they'd be safe.

I raised my fingers, staring at how they trembled. "I know. I don't understand why I'm like this."

"Don't you?" Ma took my hand in hers and chafed warmth back into it. "I don't mean to pry, but is there something going on between ye and Lochinvar?"

I swallowed around a lump in my throat, no ready answer available. I wasn't about to admit a sex-only deal to my mother, but was that the extent of it?

"There is," I said, my voice tiny. "I don't think I can describe exactly what."

"You care about him."

"I do."

Understanding poured into her soft smile. "Good."

It wasn't good. This was terrible. As a teenager, I'd stood in this very place and smiled at my cousins falling in love, or talking about their crushes. I'd put on a brave face, and in time, that had become real. Now, I hated myself.

I couldn't develop feelings for Lochinvar. What sort of tragic mess did that make me? He was leaving soon, and even if he found a way to stay, what kind of half-formed relationship could I give him?

Me, the woman who could never fall in love.

I was a joke.

Then there was the look Isla had given me. I was almost certain she'd been about to ask if I could be her ma. If she had...

God, I'd done a terrible thing.

I'd allowed her close. Encouraged her to trust and rely

on me. If she cared for me, I'd hurt her, a child, an innocent. She wouldn't get over me so easily as her father could.

My phone buzzed in my pocket. I scanned the screen.

Viola: I've just got back from tonight's concert. Oh man, it was such fun. Leo had the whole venue serenading our bairn. But I have bad news. We're not going to make it home for Christmas. Leo has gigs close together, and the travel makes it impossible. Can you come to see me? Maybe take a couple of days off this week? We're in Berlin on Thursday so it'll be easy travel. I miss you so hard!

She obviously hadn't heard about the rescue yet. How could other people be carrying on with their lives while this was going on? Except her offer trickled into my consciousness. It would be the perfect antidote from my other looming date on the horizon.

Earlier today, I'd checked my email to find a message from the fertility clinic. My request for a cancellation had come through. Finally, I had an appointment, on Thursday morning. But the excitement of it hadn't touched me, busy as I had been with Isla and then with increasing worry for her da.

Normal life couldn't progress until this was resolved.

I could barely breathe.

Across the hall, Mathilda's landline phone rang. She answered it with a finger to her ear.

I stood, grabbing Ma's arm. My heart pounded.

My aunt listened carefully, then her shoulders lowered and she exhaled. "Thank God. They're coming home. The last man has been winched onto the helicopter and they are off the mountain. They're safe."

Sighs of relief sounded around the great hall. Maddock leapt to his feet and stormed out.

I let out a small gasp tinged with pain, then sank to my

seat. Ma said something I didn't catch over the blood rushing in my ears.

This couldn't continue. The mess I'd gotten myself into would only hurt everyone involved.

It had to stop.

25

*L*ochie

I woke cold to the bone, despite my warm cottage and the solid weight of Isla sprawled against me. In the early hours, I'd finally reached the castle where Caitriona's text told me they were waiting. Caitriona had been exhausted, as had I, and we'd barely spoken.

She didn't come home with me, choosing her own bed over mine.

The incident, her hurt brother, the risk to her family, had upset her.

She'd worried for me, too. I knew it. Not from her lips, but the glances her ma sent our way. From her expression when her da embraced me hard and insisted again I call him Ally.

An ache stole over my chest. With care, I unravelled my daughter's grip on me and went to the bathroom. On the way back, an engine roared outside, and I peered from the window to see the red taillights of Caitriona's car vanishing down the road.

Well, fuck. She must have an early meeting.

I found my phone, but there was no message waiting.

Lochie: Sorry for the worry I caused ye. Call me when ye can.

Then there was nothing more to do than set about my day.

After delivering Isla to breakfast club at the school, I called Cameron. In the night, I'd had contact from the police which led me to desist from further search action now the storm had lifted.

I needed to share my thoughts with the man. He gave me the address of Braithar, the second McRae castle, and I drove over.

He received me at the door, his tired gaze echoing mine. "We're naw heading out again. Can I assume Max had it right?"

I followed him inside, taking in the splendid entrance hall with its ornate staircase.

Cameron caught my stare and raised a shoulder. "Gordain's place. I work closely with him and often stay here when the family are away. Ella, the lady of the castle, is away, too, then joining them on the tour, so the place would be empty."

"Ye dinna have your own home?"

"I havenae bothered yet. With here as an option, I'm not under my parents' feet."

For some reason, this surprised me. That Caitriona had struck out on her own while Cameron had not.

He directed me to a dining room, and we took our seats.

"The police traced the phone number," I said, not bothering with preliminaries. "It was a new number only just allocated and to an unregistered phone. They cannae trace it now."

He sucked in a breath. "Murkier and murkier."

"The police believe it was a fraudulent call. Max's intuition was spot on."

Cameron grumbled and scrubbed over his dark-blond hair. "What a waste. Twenty rescuers, one injury. The time, the fuel, the fucking heli extraction."

My own frustration rippled. "Thing is, this doesnae feel like the previous fake call-outs the service had. I read up on enough to see a difference."

"I know. I thought the same. The voice sounded so genuine."

Another man strode into the room. Max, his arm in plaster. He slung himself into a chair, his auburn hair a mess and a bruise on his cheek.

"Showed up at five AM," Cameron explained. He lifted his chin at his cousin. "Are ye going to explain the black eye now? Ye didnae do that on your fall."

"Wasn't planning on it." Max turned his attention on me, seeming none the worse for his ordeal. "I heard what ye said. That caller was acting. I'm convinced of it. They didnae hesitate in their words, repeat themselves, or stumble. It was all neat and precise." He paused for effect. "Rehearsed."

I mulled this over. "Highly likely you're right. Max, ye showed great insight and maturity last night. Ye have good instincts, far beyond a man of nineteen should have. I'm proud to have ye on my team."

Pink flushed his pale skin, but he held my gaze, accepting the compliment.

"And ye, Cameron." I glanced at the other lad. "That was a great act of bravery going after Max. I'm proud of ye, too."

He waved me off, his small head tilt showing me he appreciated what I was doing for Max. I already knew they worked well together and the training call had been a good one. Whatever other issues Max had going on, he was flourishing in the service.

"I need to prepare the write-up. I'll take your account now of the first run, Cameron, then get back to the hangar. Max, yours can wait until ye feel better."

"I'm fine. Dinna fuss over me."

We settled down to the task, Cameron supplying bacon sandwiches when we hungered. By the end of the day, I'd worked my full hours at the castle, and the break had renewed me.

Until my third text to Caitriona finally brought in an answer.

Caitriona: At my parents this evening.

I called her, but she didn't pick up.

The next day, the same occurred. I was too busy to haunt her doorstep, but it was painfully obvious she was avoiding me.

I missed her. Isla missed her.

By Wednesday night, I was done with waiting.

She returned at ten, creeping into her parking space before hotfooting it to her door. I stepped out of the shadows, my heart thundering.

"Caitriona."

She jumped, almost dropping her keys. "Lochinvar."

That slip, my full name over the nickname I'd asked her to use, cut deep. "We need to talk," I managed.

She ducked her head then blew out a deep breath, frosting in the chilled night air. "Probably, but I'm tired and I need sleep. I have an appointment in the morning, then I'm heading to the airport."

"The airport? Where are ye going?"

"Berlin. I'm taking a couple of days off work. It's been difficult there since I asked to be moved from Rupert's line management, plus the appointment is going to be intense. I need the space."

From me, too, I guessed the words she hadn't said. I raked over my hair. "What appointment is that?"

"Tests at the fertility clinic and to agree a treatment plan."

Fuck. I stared at her, all manner of responses cramming into my damn mouth. I should tell her how much I needed to hold her, or how my heart belonged to her, but all I could utter was a single, "Don't."

"Don't what? Attend the appointment I've been waiting on for months?"

"Don't leave me." I had no rationale. No reasonable thoughts. Only the crushing and instant resolve that I wanted to be part of her plans.

I'd raised a bairn I hadn't created and over the years had mulled over how much I'd missed out on the pregnancy part. The hope and worry and excitement. I'd been delivered a daughter under extreme circumstances, taking actions I had no time to decide on. Yet I hadn't moved on to considering extending my family. Hadn't been able to.

Things had started to change.

If Caitriona chose me, that made a whole new picture.

I wanted her so badly. The thoughts had been steadily increasing to a point of being real. It was still a far reach to changing the life I'd settled on, but my instincts were all there. Especially faced with her words now.

I forced my mind into order. "Tell me what's wrong between us and I'll fix it. Did I scare ye by getting stranded on the mountain? I'm sorry. Don't walk away from me because of it."

"I'm not walking away. We aren't... I mean, there's nothing to walk away from."

"There is."

I reached and took her hand. Then I placed it over my heart.

Caitriona tugged, but I held it in place.

"This is what's there. Steady, and beating for ye."

She jerked her hand from mine and stepped back. "No. Don't say that. Ye can't."

"Why not? Because I scare the life out of ye? Ye do me, too, woman. That's no reason to run."

"I'm not running."

"You're getting on a plane."

Our standoff ramped up in intensity, and I loomed over her, unable to stop the rising tension in me. It rushed, dislodging logic. Evaporating my steady temper. "Don't go."

"Don't assume there's more to us than what we agreed."

Her rebuke smacked into me so hard I saw stars.

I summoned every inch of my being and uttered the stupidest words of my life, realised too late but spoken all the same. "Wrong. I hate to tell ye this, but you're obsessed with me, lass. Hide all ye like, but that doesnae make it less true."

"Obsessed?"

"Aye. Obsessed."

My mountain rescue phone blared.

Ah fuck. Fuck!

Every damn time.

I closed my eyes for a second, my jaw locked. "I have to take this but when I get back, please talk to me. Dinna go without doing that. I'm begging ye, Caitriona."

Her gaze shuttered, hiding shock I couldn't ignore.

"I'll look after Isla," she whispered.

Not good enough.

Closing the distance between us, I pressed my lips to hers.

Caitriona gasped, and I took her mouth in a hot, desperate kiss. All while my phone blasted its alert. All while my heart splintered and cracked.

There was nothing for it but to go.

Caitriona watched me leave, strain in her features, confusion all too plain.

I'm obsessed with ye, too, I should've said. But those words only formed hours later when, on the bleak, frozen mountainside, I rehashed the conversation.

For a long while, I despised my job and everything that tore me from Caitriona's side.

A group of walkers had become lost and cold, unable to get back to their cars despite the clear night. I raised two teams and headed out into the hills.

By dawn, no lost souls had been found.

No abandoned cars located. No follow-up calls or answers to the line. Nothing but the same frustration as Sunday's hoax call.

I came home to an empty house, Isla delivered to school and a note left on my table.

Caitriona had well and truly gone.

26

*C*ait's Watcher

Where oh where did you go, my darling? I paced the spacious living room of the middle-class home, the sound of children playing upstairs irritating my senses.

I hated it. Hate. Hate.

Not at the university.

No explanation.

Not at her home.

I'd watched it for the entire day, hidden deep in the hills, half frozen in the snow, my sleeping bag stolen from its hiding place, my brain driven by despair.

At least she wasn't with the lumbering oaf of her neighbour. He'd come and gone with his brat, frowning as if the world had offended him. He'd spent a lot of time out on rescues. I chuckled at the memory of watching him storm about, ordering his troops.

Distracting him was easy. Soon enough, I'd deal with him more thoroughly.

Later.

A night in the cold hadn't fixed his attitude. Worse

storms were coming, and it was only a matter of time before he made a mistake and vanished off in one.

Cait wouldn't miss him. I'd make sure of it.

She'd have more interesting things to think about.

For the fiftieth time, I snatched my phone and went through my list of her contacts, checking their social media. She rarely posted, the fucking bitch. Didn't she know how worried I'd be?

Darkness swept over my mind.

Cait would pay for this. If I couldn't find her, then it would be by proxy. Her mother, maybe, who drove in and out of the main road into the estate, singing and not paying attention to her surroundings.

Or the little girl she seemed so fond of.

In time, she'd learn not to defy me. I should come first in all things.

I'd been too nice.

Cait would learn the hard way.

27

Lochie

My meeting of the rescue team and the lead emergency services personnel adjourned, frustration on all faces. Our police liaison officer clapped me on the shoulder and muttered polite encouragement before leaving the hangar.

We'd now had three fake call-outs, one last night and another this morning to add to Sunday's, all with different callers, different locations, and all wasting hours of our time.

The lack of a pattern made them harder to detect. In between this week, we'd had genuine rescues—providing relief that we weren't going insane—but the meeting's conclusion hadn't gone deep enough for me.

This wasnae a coincidence.

The service had been targeted, aye, but who led that service? Me. A man in hiding. I couldn't ignore that as a fluke.

The attendees filed out, and I straightened the chairs for

want of something more productive to do. I should head out to pick up Isla from the castle, but I knew the question she'd ask me and I hated denying her. She'd cried after school when I told her Caitriona wasn't home. Caitriona had told her she'd be away a few days, but Isla wanted to know when she'd return. I did, too, but with no contact, I hadn't a clue.

Or even if she'd want me.

Ever since she'd left, I'd been grouchy and entirely miserable.

Someone cleared their throat. I spun around to see a man at the door.

Ally, Caitriona's da.

He'd been in the meeting, but I thought he'd left.

"Do ye have a minute?" he asked.

I sighed but lifted my chin. "Any thoughts on the problem?"

"Aye, but not with the service."

"How's Max doing?"

"Pissed off that ye banned him from showing up until he's healed. That's naw why I'm here, though." He held my gaze, no challenge in the look, but careful consideration. "I want to talk to ye about Caitriona."

Ah fuck. She'd asked him to see me off. Exhausted, I dropped into a chair and raised a hand. "Go ahead."

"My wife told me about ye two ..." He grasped the back of a chair, and lines creased his forehead. For a moment, he said nothing, then the usually jovial man placed his words with specific care. "My daughter is my beating heart, walking around outside of my body."

I knew this, that they were close. Her da came by her home often, and her eyes lit when she saw him. I also knew the feeling with Isla.

He continued on while I inwardly sank.

"Did she tell ye anything of her background?"

"A little about her birth mother."

Some of the wind left his sails. "I'm surprised. She never talks about Kaylee. One of her relatives believes that's the reason she turned her back on relationships. The broken connection."

I had no clue what to say. As she'd pointed out, Caitriona hadn't committed anything to me beyond sex, then pushed me away once we got too close. I'd made it worse.

His stare darkened. "Do ye care for her?"

There was no point hiding it. "Far beyond reason."

"I thought as much." He leapt up, buoyant, and made his way to the exit.

"Wait. Are ye naw about to warn me or something?"

"Naw. You're not mine to counsel. Not unless Caitriona tells me otherwise. Her ma and I just needed to know which way to go in advising her."

I dug my hands into my hair, suddenly far from the imposing head of the rescue service. A lad, cap in hand and needing the word of someone more experienced.

"Ally, hold up, will ye."

He cocked his head, waiting while I pieced over my words.

"I've never loved anyone before, beyond Isla, my sister, and mother. This is nothing like that."

Ally grinned. "Good to know. It explains a lot. I willnae give ye specific advice on my daughter, but I cannae leave ye hanging. Here's some general thoughts. What do ye have to offer a woman, Lochinvar? This isn't an answer I need, but she might."

"Lochie, please," I said, miles away in my thoughts.

He tapped the doorframe and gave me another cheery grin. "Lochie. See ye on the hill."

For fifteen minutes, I stayed in my seat, pondering his words. I'd offered Caitriona nothing aside from use of my body. Christ, for all she knew, I was leaving—I'd told her we'd go at the drop of a hat, if needed.

If she wanted me, that made a new world. One where I didn't hide.

Which meant neutralising the threat.

My military training had led me to a tactic of concealing the item of value. Hiding Isla from those who would hurt her. Evasion over confrontation with an unknown force.

I'd played the odds.

Yet the greatest form of defence lay in attack. Every serviceman knew that.

Leaping up, I snatched my keys and phone. I had planning to do, starting now.

*A*fter dinner, I called Mathilda at Castle McRae to make arrangements for Isla, ensuring my daughter was happy to stay there after school tomorrow if I wasn't back in time. Then it was on to Braithar to see Cameron.

He received us, his dog at his heels.

Isla squeaked in delight and dove on the animal, scratching her ears. She'd met Ellie multiple times at the hangar and adored her. If my plan came off and we settled, I'd buy her a puppy.

Cameron's mouth lifted. "Come in, will ye?"

We entered and followed him to the lounge where Max lounged on a couch, his broken arm on his chest, and a big TV on pause.

I squinted at the picture, recognising the freeze-framed woman. "That's the lass from your phone's screensaver."

Isla peeked around me. "Her name's Elise. She's a film star. She's so pretty."

Max rolled his eyes. "Cameron has had the biggest crush on her since he was a spotty teenager. Where do ye think Ellie got her name?"

Isla let out a peal of laughter.

Max grinned. "Mention the name of her boyfriend and see how he gets."

To my entire amusement, Cameron, the cool and calm second-in-command, far more mature than his years and typically stoic, blushed.

"Shut up." He glared at Max then took up the remote to darken the television. "Do ye need me for something, Lochinvar?"

I laid off the teasing and drew him aside, leaving my daughter to play with Ellie, Max finding a ball to make a game.

"I have to go away in the morning, possibly overnight. I cannae take Isla, so Mathilda will collect her from school and have her care."

I'd landed on my feet with this job. I trusted the McRae family through and through and knew they'd look after Isla. Mathilda hadn't even hesitated.

"Ye need me to run the service," Cameron summarised.

"Got it in one. Ye have the experience to manage the teams. I'll put out the message first thing so they'll be expecting your voice on the line. We're on the lookout for hoaxes now so should be better able to handle them."

Not least for the fact that if I wasn't there, I suspected they might stop.

He slowly nodded. "I can do it."

"Aye, ye can."

"On your task, do ye need any help?" he asked.

I paused. For all he knew, I was going last-minute Christmas shopping. But his insightful expression told me he saw more than I was willing to say, likely picking up on the rising energy in me.

The offer hurt my heart. No one could help me with this, I was on my own.

I clasped his shoulder. "Naw the now, but I'm grateful for the offer. Isla? We're going. Give the dog a hug."

"Good luck." Cameron leaned on the stone entrance and watched us depart.

I'd miss this lad if we had to leave. I'd miss far more besides.

Which only made my actions that more vital to succeed.

*E*arly the next morning, I kissed my daughter goodbye at the school gate and left the McRae lands, driving south. By ten, I crossed the border to England, then kept on going. Liv was jailed in HMP Low Newton, in County Durham. Online, I'd made my request for a meeting, and to my shock, it had been approved. The appointment was in the afternoon, so I had time to kill before that.

Not literally.

Probably.

I continued on the A1 until I reached Newcastle, then parked on a busy street in the Byker district, opposite a pub.

One I knew used to be owned by Danny, Liv's eldest brother.

With no plan beyond observation, I sat in the car, staring at the place, only a couple of smokers lingering by the door to hold my attention. Rain spattered the windshield. The smokers disappeared inside the pub. After an hour, I'd had no sign of the owner and was considering the repercussions of going inside.

It would be crossing into his territory, with no backup. There was no reason for him to recognise me—I hadn't seen any of the family since I was seventeen, and Liv had sworn she'd never tell them that I had Isla, but if they'd been smart and found our marriage record, they could have tracked me down.

I'd written off the idea, as they hadn't done it already, but showing my face now could change all of that.

I'd be the prey, not the hunter.

Aye, it was a bad idea. For now, I needed to stick to reconnaissance.

I ignored my silent mobile, the lack of contact from Caitriona scouring my insides, and switched on the burner phone I used to contact my sister. I fired up my throwaway email account, not hopeful for a reply.

Two messages waited, both from Blair.

I opened them in turn and scanned the contents. She apologised for radio silence and referenced her mission— somewhere hot where everything tried to kill her.

At the end, she asked for an update on Isla.

I fast-wrote a response, then made a deliberate addition.

Lochie: We're happy, but I cannae live like this anymore. My daughter deserves better. A home. A family beyond me. I'm taking steps to go on the offensive.

Stay safe – L

I sent it and sat back, tapping a thumb on the steering wheel. With the hour or so I had free, I'd remain here until my visit to the jail, then I'd likely return for the evening watch. Once I'd caught sight of the man in question, and hopefully obtained his numberplate or other details, I'd drive north, over the border again, and head to Liv's childhood home, where I believed her mother still lived.

Decision made, I went to switch off the burner phone.

It rang in my hand, the call marked 'International' on the screen. I answered it.

"Lochie? What's your plan?" Blair's voice thundered. "Who's backing ye up?"

"Hello to ye, too. Limited plan. No support," I admitted.

"Then what the hell are ye doing?"

"I have no choice."

"The fuck ye do. Walk me through it."

It had been months since we'd last spoken, but as the model soldier, her advice was exactly what I needed.

I told her my thoughts, and my sister's distaste resounded down the line. "Back the hell up. Regroup. Ye are outgunned the moment anyone recognises ye. What resources can ye call in?"

I grumbled under my breath. By resources, she meant people. Preferably trained and armed.

If I truly meant to eliminate Liv's dangerous relatives, those should be my primary concerns. But unlike Blair, I'd never been bloodthirsty, choosing defence over assault in almost all aspects of my life.

Cameron had asked if I needed help, and I knew how readily the McRae men would stand for one another. Maybe even for me, if I asked.

"None. I have dozens of men and women at my control, a handful I'd trust with my life. None whose lives I'd be willing to risk."

"Then the mission is a bust before it even started. Dinna

half-arse it. Go home, rethink, gather intelligence. I can do the same my end now I have some downtime. There are people I know who can do this for ye. Better for your lass that we consider that option over ye slicing and dicing."

I could picture my sister's dangerous smile.

"Fuck. I thought ye were dead," I bit out.

Blair guffawed. "Can ye imagine anything denting me? Da tried and failed. I've a cast-iron hide. Dinna be soft."

We made arrangements to talk more and, by the time we'd hung up, something inside me loosened. I'd take the prison appointment, either way, but with precautions over staying safe. I needed a fully formed strategy. And people on my side.

My personal phone buzzed with an incoming message.

Cameron: Checking in. All okay?

I replied to the lad, a smile broaching my lips.

Lochie: Aye. I'm still breathing. Thank ye for caring. All okay there?

Cameron: No calls. I think Gordain's office has been broken into. Nothing's been taken, but on the floor was a paper with your name on it. A reference from your old job.

Ah fuck.

Then he knew Ross was a fake name. And so did someone else.

Lochie: Any idea who broke in?

Cameron: None. It might have been a mistake and someone left the door open.

He didn't call me on my name change, and I appreciated the fuck out of it.

A new message came in fast.

Cameron: Keep me posted. Just check in when ye can. The offer's still open for help.

I sent back a quick agreement, beyond grateful I had people who cared.

Then, heart aching, I typed out what I should've said to Caitriona.

Lochie: In case my yelling at ye wasn't clear, I'm obsessed with ye, too. Please come back to me.

28

Caitriona

An icy wind swept down Berlin's *Strasse des 17. Juni,* and Viola huddled into me, her coat's fake-fur-lined hood half-concealing her face and the padding obscuring her baby bump. At a discreet distance, her security guard strolled, scanning the other bundled-up passersby for signs of loony fans.

Not that she was likely to be recognised, particularly as her superstar husband, Leo, was at rehearsal and not with us. Either way, it was fun to be touring the city with an entourage and a warm car at our disposal for when my cousin tired.

She used her crutch today, so we were taking it slow.

Battling the elements allowed me to distance my mind from all my worries. To some extent. One aspect never faded —Lochie, and how desperately he'd kissed me before I'd left. How had I walked away?

By the only thing I couldn't let myself do—hurt him and Isla by pretending I could be all that they needed.

Yet that awful tearing feeling in my chest hadn't shifted.

"Here." Viola pointed up to the landmark ahead. "The Brandenburg Gate."

We'd made it to the gorgeous archway after a morning of exploring and brunch in a café.

"It's the symbol of reunified Germany," Viola read from her phone, then gave me a short history lesson.

My mind drifted. Yesterday had been strange. I'd attended my appointment, but after coming out, across the street I'd spotted none other than Jeremy, my friend's brother. Initially, I'd suspected him of painting my door after I'd rejected him. Wasn't he meant to be in England? He didn't look at me, but I'd hurried away, entirely spooked.

Then I'd got on a plane and had been on the go ever since.

I needed the space away to stop me feeling like I was going insane.

The gig industry worked non-stop, with Leo pulled from pillar to post. My paranoia decreased with my role in keeping Viola company, though her ma was joining us later today after finishing up work with her orchestra. I couldn't hide here forever.

A ringtone sounded. Viola dug in her pockets then examined her phone screen. "It's Leo." She took the call, linking her arm through mine as she listened. "Hang on a moment."

She peered at me. "Mind if we head over to the stadium? Leo worked out a song, and he wants to play it to us."

"Let's do it."

She grinned and stashed the phone.

It was likely that Viola was tired, and I could imagine her devoted husband worrying about her being on her feet for so long. It had crossed my mind, too.

In two minutes, we were in the chauffeur-driven car and

on our way to the gigantic arena. We'd attended Leo's gig in the same place last night, and the sold-out crowd had been wild with rock star fever.

Through security, we found our way into the vast open space, the stage slap bang in the centre.

Leo whooped and leapt from the stage to grab his wife in his arms. He held her chin and kissed her, and I looked away, smiling. He greeted me then drew us with him to the stage where he picked up a guitar.

"New song," he said into a microphone, the volume much lower than it would be tonight.

We listened, as did many of the crew members milling about.

As always, in Leo's lyrics, I picked up on phrases I could easily associate with Vi. Leo had been writing songs about her since they were teenagers, long before they became a couple.

Also long before they could realistically know they were in love.

Huh.

I listened carefully to his words.

With an upbeat tune, Leo sang about how every degree of love he felt tore into him. Shredded his insides. Broke his heart and made it new. All in stages until he'd changed so much he could never go back.

Without knowing, Leo's words described the ache in my chest.

He continued, pressing home my realisation.

My feelings had come on gradually, until the night Lochinvar had gone missing when they became unbearable. Crippled me.

I'd thought it pain at what I couldn't have, built of regret and unhappiness. But maybe it had been transformational.

Had I been entirely wrong?

Leo finished to a ripple of applause, then started another song, a swoony ballad.

Viola squeezed my fingers then picked her way across the stage, joining her man. I removed myself to a seat in the front row of the audience section and let the music and the events of the past few months wash over me.

To the backdrop of Leo's romantic tune, I pondered my life.

Fact: I definitely wasn't asexual. I loved sex with Lochie.

That was an easy assessment to make. Next, on to the feelings thing.

Aye, I had those, too. New, and bright, and all-encompassing. They scared the ever-loving hell out of me.

My natural reaction was to duck the honesty. In all other areas of my life, I demanded it, but I'd avoided strong emotion like the plague.

A person landed in the seat next to mine.

I glanced around, vaguely recognising the huge, muscled man in a black, tight t-shirt as one of Gordain's staff. A memory popped up of him removing the crazy fan from Leo's Inverness rehearsal. He'd thrown the woman over his shoulder, supplying me with a neat fantasy to try with Lochie.

"Craig." He offered a hand. "Are you a friend of Leo's missus?"

"I'm Cait, and yes, you could say that." I shook his fingers to be polite.

"Here for long?" he asked. At my answer, he swept a subtle gaze over me, pupils dilating, then proceeded to tell me a story about the tour.

In a practised move, as he spoke, Craig slipped an arm across the back of my seat.

"Want to hang with me backstage after the gig? I'll get you a pass."

Amusement bubbled inside me as, for the first time, I was about to turn down an interested man because I had someone else. Not because I wasn't interested, not because I didn't do relationships.

Gently, I removed his wayward arm and gave a shrug. "I'm just here to see my family. Sorry, but I need to make a call. Do ye mind?"

Craig gave a rueful smile but lumbered to his feet and wandered away.

With energy flickering inside me, I found my phone and called my father. "Da, this is going to sound random, but I need to ask ye something."

"Go for it," he said.

"As far back as I can remember, Aunt Georgia told me I was different because of what my birth mother did, and that I needed to be aware of it so I understood myself."

Da grumbled, but I pushed on.

"Ye know I've never been interested in boyfriends. Georgia said that I had problems depending on people. That the initial broken connection had affected me my entire life and caused so much damage. But what if she was wrong?"

Da burst in, his restraint failing. "Of course she's wrong. When I first met ye, ye were a month old and so bonnie. We never had any problem bonding. Nor did ye with your ma, brothers, cousins, and everyone else ye care about. Georgia is passing on her grief at losing Kaylee to ye. She relives it every time she sees ye, and the woman is stuck. That reflects on her, not ye."

"There could be some truth in it, though. I think I've been carrying around grief for Kaylee. Not just the fact I never knew her, but pity, too. She lost out on life and on knowing her baby. It's so terribly sad."

"It is. She was a bonnie woman. She'd have loved ye hard."

I adored my father. He said it like it was, without trying to rationalise or minimise the emotion.

My next statement nearly choked me. "I'm pretty sure that grief meant I protected my heart."

He paused. "I'm not convinced. I just assumed ye needed to find someone special. Is there something ye want to tell me?"

I laughed. "Don't pretend to be surprised, but I've been seeing Lochinvar."

"Scarlet told me. He suits ye well."

Warmth spread through my veins. Da always encouraged me to be open with how I found the world, so there was little he didn't know about me.

"Do ye really think so?"

"He's hard-working, humble, stubborn, and a great da. Do ye plan to keep him?"

"I..."

"I'll talk to your uncle about his job," Da continued. "If Lochinvar's going to stick around, he cannae remain on a temporary contract. Leave that with me."

"What if he doesn't want to stay?" I spluttered.

"Why don't ye ask him? Ah, your mother wants me. Got to go."

My father hung up, leaving me reeling.

A message appeared on my screen. My pulse sped.

Lochie: In case my yelling at ye wasn't clear, I'm obsessed with ye, too. Please come back to me.

Oh God.

Leo's second song ended, and a stage hand approached

him with questions. Viola returned to me, her expression blissful.

"Ye look happy," she said.

"I am. Or I could be. I've been doing some soul-searching."

"What did ye discover?"

"I think I'm in love with Lochie."

Viola's mouth dropped open. "Holy shite. I thought you'd say ye were falling. Come here." She hugged me, her baby bump between us.

I chuckled, buoyant, though my head still spun from the revelation. Admitting how I felt was only a tiny piece of the puzzle. "I was scared. I still am. He might leave."

"He might not."

Excitement fizzed.

Gordain strode to us, his eyebrows joined in a frown and his lips pressed together. "Your da," he pointed at me, "just told me my management of the rescue service is terrible and the entire crew will quit if I take over again."

I burst out laughing.

"I take it this is an unsubtle hint for me to extend Lochinvar's term?"

My mirth sobered. "Is that possible?"

His frown only deepened. "I've already considered it. There'll be more tours, and I cannae commit the time the mountain rescue service needs. I'm naw sure he wanted anything permanent, though, so we havenae discussed it."

I grabbed my uncle's hand. "Ask him. Please."

He tilted his head, assessing me in the same way he did a particularly rowdy crowd. Then he nodded once and took up his phone and placed a call.

"Answerphone," he said to us, then cleared his throat. "Lochinvar, I need to talk to ye. If you're willing, I'd like ye to keep the management of the mountain rescue service. Call me back and let's make it permanent."

Taking up my own phone, I tapped out a reply to Lochie myself.

Caitriona: I'll be home tomorrow. We'll talk then. You were right about everything.

I hugged myself, wading through a mire with one side happiness and the other anxious despair. All I could do now was wait.

29

*L*ochie

Across the utilitarian prison visiting room, my ex-wife advanced. Gaunt, she winced as she lowered herself to sitting.

Her gaze stuck to the table.

I'd last seen her several years ago, when she'd only been inside a short time. The difference between my energetic friend and this lass startled me, and I could only stare. Prison had ravaged Liv. I barely recognised her.

"Do ye have any money?" she asked. "You're allowed to give me twenty quid."

"Already organised with the office," I murmured. "It's good to see ye."

She bobbed her head, still not looking at me. "I'm in on my own now."

It took a second for me to work out what she meant. The mindset of being jailed was entirely alien, though I'd thought about it from time to time. "Your own cell? That's good."

Liv raised a shoulder.

"Our lass is thriving," I said fast, because I knew this would hurt.

I hadn't told Caitriona, but Liv had rejected Isla at birth, refusing to hold her. At the time, I'd hated it, but I understood, too.

Life had been a tragedy for Liv from beginning to present day. Isla was just another part of that. I'd sent pictures and updates, but Liv had never asked a single question.

It gave me greater reason to love Isla, as no one else did.

She didn't respond, so I pressed on.

"Your brothers are out of jail. I need to know if they'll come after us."

Finally, Liv raised her head. "They havenae been here. Even if they tried, I wouldnae see them."

"I need to know how much of a threat they are to Isla."

Liv frowned, then jerked a thin shoulder. "I cannae say."

"Do they write to ye? Email? Telephone?"

"No."

"What about her birth father?"

"You're her da. No one else wanted her but ye."

Exasperated, I dug my fingers into my hair. This wasn't getting me anywhere. At least I knew Liv hadn't been contacted, but that didn't help me understand if they were hunting us.

"When ye came to me, pregnant and scared, ye said they'd take the bairn. Ye put the fear of God into me over her safety."

A smile curved Liv's mouth. "I bet you've moved mountains to look after her. No man would have done more. Do ye have a wife? A mother for her?"

"No." To say I wanted a specific woman for that role would be unkind.

"Get one. Settle down and stop this panic. Ye always took things to an extreme." She stood, her hands on the table. "I'm tired. I have things to do. Are ye sure ye left that money?"

I jumped up. "I did. Wait."

She kept moving through the seats. "Dinna come back here."

A guard buzzed the door to let her out. I could do nothing but watch her go.

Outside, I retrieved my phone and keys from the prison locker. A text message waited from Caitriona. Ah Christ, even the sight of her name boosted me from the low of the visit. Then her words warmed me further. She said I was right about everything, and she'd be back tomorrow. Fuck, that couldn't come soon enough.

A missed call and voicemail also waited, from Gordain.

I listened to it as I returned to the car.

He offered me the job as head of the rescue service permanently.

Killing the call, I slid into my seat and stared into space. I'd gone from extreme worry about Liv's family to...what? Confusion, as a minimum.

Had she used my protective instincts to safeguard her bairn?

Had she even been at risk, or just playing me in the way she knew how? My mother's flight from Da when we were kids was no secret. My protector status had been prominent even at school.

Liv had loved me as a teenager. She hadn't said as much, but I knew the moment I told her I was signing up to the RAF. She went missing not long after.

Now, she still faced extensive prison time. I'd asked after her sentence, and she had years to serve.

I pieced through all I knew. I'd taken Liv in without hesitation. Married her to give the bairn my name and protection. I'd raised Isla on a military base then moved her on the moment I feared for her safety.

Had it all been for nothing?

No. I'd never regret anything to do with Isla.

If no one was chasing us... That meant so much. But I couldn't be sure of anything until I'd had those words from Liv's family.

I drove an hour north then, in a lay-by, grabbed the burner phone and readied it to send an email to Blair.

One from her loaded as I started to type.

Lochie, someone has been sniffing around your old base. Unknown male. Be aware.

Then my personal phone blared with an incoming call.

Isla's school.

My heart pounded, and I snatched the phone, answering it.

"Mr Ross," the kindly voice said. "I'm calling to check the collection arrangements for Isla today. We have a person waiting to take her home, but they aren't on your list."

I rubbed my eyes. "They should be. Mathilda McRae, aye?"

"This is a gentleman, hence the call. Ye only have Cait and Mathilda preapproved. He doesnae have the password."

My blood chilled. "Who?"

"A Mr McRae. I must admit, I dinna know this young man, and there I was thinking I knew all the McRae boys."

A warning sounded in my mind, and sickness shrank my stomach. "First name?"

The school receptionist put her hand over the receiver and asked the question.

The man's faint voice made it to me. He had a Scottish accent, but something wasn't quite right.

"He says he's Ed McRae," the woman replied.

Ice slunk into my veins. There was no one of that name on the estate. Caitriona had gone through all her relatives. No Ed or Edward came up.

"What does he look like?"

"Early twenties, fair. Excuse me? Hold up a moment." She switched to addressing the stranger.

A thump sounded. Then a yell.

Fear spiked, and I smacked the steering wheel with the flat of my hand. "Do not let her go with him. Whatever ye do, Isla cannae leave with this person."

After a moment, the woman came back on the line. Her voice quivered. "He forced the door."

"What? Go after him."

"No, no. It held. He's gone, taken off at a run. Who is he? What shall I do?"

Gone didn't mean fled. He could be checking the other exits, or for a window to smash. Fuck! "Call the police. Keep Isla safe. I'll make arrangements and call ye back."

I hung up, panicked, and searched my mind for a solution. A stranger was at my daughter's school. They'd used a fake name.

I dialled Cameron, speaking before he'd even greeted me. "I need your help. Isla's in danger."

"Tell me what to do."

I explained the situation, my fucking voice shaking. "I need ye to go with Mathilda to the school to pick up my daughter, then take her to the castle and stay with her until I get there. I'm hours away but I'm coming."

"On it. Hang on, I'm with Ally." Cameron stated the issue in short sentences then came back on the line. "Ally's calling

Mathilda now. Callum is home. He'll take her there, and we'll meet her. Leave this with us."

Relief permeated my fear, but what a time to rely on my new friends.

I'd been complacent five minutes ago, but now could only see a potential abduction attempt.

My phone buzzed as I gunned the engine, and I answered the call on loudspeaker, pulling out of the lay-by.

Gordain's voice came down the line. "Lochinvar. Did ye get my message?"

"I cannae talk now," I barked.

"Fine man, call me back and let me know if ye want the job."

Fuck. I couldn't. Not with a direct attack underway. Like stretched elastic, I snapped straight back to my original plan.

"I cannae. I need to take my daughter and leave tonight. I'll talk to ye about my replacement later."

"Lochinvar," he started.

I killed the call, all my concentration on getting home.

We had no choice now. The moment I got back and had Isla in my protection, we had to go.

30

Caitriona

    On the plane, I frayed the hem of my skirt, the flight endless and my patience at breaking point.

Someone had tried to take Isla.

Lochie, not that he'd answered my calls, must be distraught.

I flexed my fingers, interlacing them and testing my strength. My only hope was that he wouldn't have left before I got home. *Please, Lochie. Wait for me.*

We touched down, and I panicked all the way through arrivals until I got back to my car in the isolated car park. Then I sped into the pitch-black night, out into the Inverness countryside, heading home.

At the cottages, Lochie's car had gone.

No one answered the door.

"Shite." I grabbed my phone and called him, though with little hope of getting an answer.

Around, the yawning hillside and glen stared back at me. I had the acute sensation of being watched.

Then the call connected.

"Caitriona." Lochie's deep voice was pitched so low, stress plain.

"Where are ye?" I breathed.

"Castle McRae. Where are ye?"

I flew back to the car. "Be there in ten."

I drove badly, skidding on the ice that had formed under the snow. Finally, I reached the castle.

My uncle generally locked the huge entrance door overnight. Not for fear of anyone coming in, but for good practice. I stood outside and hesitated before knocking.

Almost silently, it opened.

Lochie waited on the other side. Outlined by orange light from the great hall's huge always-burning fire, he gazed down at me, his eyes dark and his expression unreadable. Then he gestured with his head for me to come inside.

I did, hugging my arms to myself for want of being able to throw myself at this man. For all I knew, he was packed and ready to leave in the morning.

I'd pushed him away. I only had myself to blame.

Lochie secured the door then made for the stairs, a glance back indicating I should follow him. We crept through the silent castle, up the first flight of stairs and to a guest room.

Lochie entered, and I trailed in after.

On a bed, Isla slept, her golden curls spread out across the pillow. I clasped my hands to my mouth to hide my sob and, without thinking, went straight to her, climbing onto the mattress. She turned into my body, and I hugged the small girl to me.

I stroked her hair and whispered to her sleeping form that I was home.

One fear diminished. She was here and okay. No one else had her. Isla was safe.

Lochie stood across the room, letting me have my moment.

At length, my frightened heart calmed, I kissed Isla's forehead then eased away.

She needed rest, and I needed to talk to her da.

With a long arm, Lochie pointed out to the hall. My relief sank, replaced by nausea, but I did as asked and left the room. Outside, I trailed him to a pair of armchairs beside a window at the end of the corridor.

The half moon was our only light, but more than enough to have him reject me here and now.

"I was so worried," I said, hushed. "Ma called me. I got on the first plane."

"I know. She told me when I arrived back here half mad with fear."

Water filled my eyes.

I loved this man. So much, I couldn't contain it all inside. I'd thought this degree of emotion impossible, and now I wished it so, because nothing could hurt as badly as losing Lochie.

"When are ye leaving?" I forced out the question through a choked throat.

Hulking, bristling Lochie only watched me, no doubt trying to find a way to let me down.

"I assumed you'd already be away," I continued. "Seeing ye here…"

"Seeing me here what?" he said on a dangerous tone. "Finish that sentence."

But I couldn't. No more words would come.

He waited a beat, then Lochie slid to his knees on the bare floor between our chairs and took hold of my arms in a fierce grip.

"Seeing me here brought ye hope? Hurts? All of the above? Tell me before I go insane."

My instinct was to duck, to hide my face, but I couldn't do that. He had to see me, to know everything. I held his glittering gaze.

"All of those things. I am terrified beyond reason with the thought of losing ye."

Across his features, satisfaction merged with other, stronger emotions. His grip on me tightened. "Why?"

"Because I've fallen in love with ye."

Lochie swayed, as if my admission had made him dizzy. Then he pulled me off my chair and against his body. "Thank fuck for that."

He kissed me, hard, and with none of his usual control. I clung to him, submitting to the outpouring of passion, trying to find a way to take over so I could show him exactly what I'd discovered.

A door opened down the hall, and light spread over the floor. My mother emerged from a bedroom. She blinked at us, and Lochie placed me on my feet, standing alongside me.

"Ye made it," she said.

Keeping Lochinvar's hand in mine, I approached her and wrapped her in a one-armed, trembling hug. "What are ye doing here?"

"Your da and I took care of Isla this evening, then we stayed over. Neither of us wanted to let her out of our sight." She pointed at the little girl's bedroom. "I'll go and sleep on the armchair in her room. There's a bedroom free next door."

Without waiting for more, Ma left us to ourselves.

Lochie gripped my hand and pulled me to the empty bedroom. He shut us in then turned to me.

I held up a hand. "If ye intend to leave tomorrow, take me with ye."

"No."

He bore down on me, but the fear I should feel at his words didn't come. "Why?"

"I always planned to leave. If a threat to Isla arose, I'd pack us up and we'd be gone. That threat happened today, so by rights, I should be away. But I'm not. I dinna want to go anywhere. We're happy here. The hours prior to that, I'd been searching for a solution so we could finally put down roots."

God. I swallowed hard and briefly closed my eyes, but I needed to hear this. To see him.

"Then after the call from the school, as I drove back, out of my mind with worry, I had a flood of reassurance from your kin. Cameron, Max, your parents. All took turns in guarding Isla. Said they would continue until the culprit was caught. Even in the middle of my worst nightmare, I had a flicker of reassurance, and it enabled me to get my head back to where I was. To the point I'd discovered about needing ye. Caitriona, so long as I have ye, this is home. Whatever the problem is, I'll stand and fight, naw run."

Emotion welled and overpoured, and my voice came out as a desperate squeak. "But ye rejected Gordain's job offer."

"I barely knew what I was saying. I'll call him tomorrow. Anything else ye want to talk about or can I strip us and bury myself inside ye? I'm going mad."

I'd already dropped my coat on a chair in Isla's room, so it was a matter of seconds to shed my jumper and bra. In that time, Lochie was on me, hands at my waist, dragging my jeans and underwear down my body. He pawed at me, taking handfuls of my backside before hastening to shed his own clothes, all while admiring me in the room's faint light.

He paused to collect his wallet from his pocket, then extracted a condom and rolled it onto his already hard dick.

Effortlessly, he picked me up, and I wound my legs about his waist, my bare breasts against his chest, his dick lodged hard underneath me. He backed me to a panelled wall, and our mouths met in a perfectly synchronised kiss.

The sense of acute alarm that had gripped me for days, weeks, maybe even months evaporated. Lochie sent my senses into overdrive. I'd never before met a man who so perfectly lit me up. His strength, his determination, his fit to me.

We were made for each other.

I never wanted to be apart from him again.

Our kiss continued, and our bodies moved together. Lochie rocked his hips against me. I reached between our bodies and adjusted my position until I brought his dick to my entrance.

Then so slowly, he filled me, sliding home.

"Fuck, Caitriona," he muttered. "Tell me again."

"I love ye."

He withdrew and drove into me. I stifled a moan, vaguely aware of being within earshot of family.

Lochinvar jacked his hips again, then ducked to kiss my throat and neck. He pinned me to the wood with his hips then was free to grope my breasts.

"Missed ye so much. Never go anywhere again," he growled.

I smothered my laugh in his shoulder, breathing him in, the masculine scent of the man who, against the odds, I loved. "Deal."

Lochie changed his strokes, upping the pace. His hand drifted down to between my legs, fingers glancing over my clit. Then abruptly, he spun around and carried me to the bed.

On my back, I gazed up at him.

Lochie's gloriously dangerous focus fixed on me, the effect thrilling. Now with the access he'd wanted, he pressed his fingers to my clit and rubbed in time with his thrusts. Then he dipped forward to lavish attention on my nipples, sucking one then the other into straining peaks.

His hands caressed my skin. His love woke my brain.

Lochie knew my body so well. In minutes, my breathing came fast, and I clamped my hand to my mouth, holding back my sounds of pleasure. Heat wound inside me, ramping up in intensity until I couldn't stand it. There was no need to draw this out, only to connect at the deepest level lovers could. Working my hips in time with his, I jerked, my orgasm easy and joyous.

Sparks ran inside my veins. Fear and doubt swept away, lost to a rush of love.

Inside, I throbbed around his dick, mindless to anything but pleasure.

Lochie buried his face in my neck, crushing my willing body underneath his huge frame. He slammed once, twice, then shuddered, his dick pulsing hard.

He held me so tight.

"My love, my only love," he murmured onto my skin. "Do ye have any idea what ye do to me? How crazy I am for ye?"

I did, because I felt it, too. Gathering him as close as I could get, I whispered the same back.

Then exhaustion took us both. Isla was safe, we were together and in each other's arms. I had nowhere else I'd ever rather be.

A chirpy Isla burst through the bedroom door early. This time, I made no attempt to hide. In Lochie's t-shirt, I reached for her and hugged her to me.

She perched on top of the blanket, beaming. "You're back!"

"I missed ye both too much to stay away," I replied.

Lochie's arm, around my shoulder, tightened.

"Did ye sleep well?" he asked his daughter.

"Aye. Scarlet's going to make me breakfast. Are ye coming down?"

I smiled at how Scottish she now sounded, and how natural it felt waking up with her da.

"In a minute," he replied softly. "Go on ahead."

"Okay." She bounced up and was gone in a flash, closing the bedroom door behind her.

Lochie rose on an elbow and gazed down at me.

"Does she know what happened yesterday?" I asked.

"No, and I dinna want her to find out."

"Agreed." I shivered. "She's safe here. My parents will watch her like a hawk."

We both watched the other for a long moment.

He brushed a thumb over my cheek. "I've made so many mistakes with ye."

"Ye haven't."

"I did. I should've told ye from the start that I liked ye."

"I probably would've run a mile. I had no idea how I felt until I left."

Lochie's careful gaze betrayed strong feelings. "How did ye realise?"

"It broke my heart to not be at your side. The pain of it eclipsed everything. I think the only way I could love was to find my other half. You're everything to me. I'm only sorry I couldn't tell ye earlier."

He ducked and kissed me. From the second our mouths touched, I lost myself in him. All I could feel was Lochie's love, coaxing my own to life. His lips persuading mine that this was good.

Not that I needed the encouragement.

I broke away to palm his cheek, then I stared him straight in the eye. "I love ye."

Lochie's gaze burned.

He leapt from the bed and strode to the door, his boxers tented with a ready erection. Flicking the lock, he turned back to me, single-minded determination and fever in his moves.

"Do ye have a condom in your purse? I dinna have any more here."

I nodded and pointed at my bag on the floor. Lochie found the foil packet and suited up.

I threw back the blanket and welcomed him onto my body. Lochie settled into the cradle of my hips then slowly pushed inside me.

Wet and so willing, I gasped at the intense pleasure of his big dick stretching me.

"Need ye," he said, his voice tight with strain.

"I need ye, too."

Digging my fingers into his hair, I brought his mouth to mine for another kiss. We moved together, slowly screwing ourselves awake and reconnecting once again.

I'd never thought this possible, but I'd landed in an acutely happy relationship, and I intended to do everything I could to show Lochie how much he meant to me.

His huge heart. His devoted ways. His protective instincts. It all added up to a rare kind of man.

The only man who could have awoken my cool heart.

He'd been right in the fact I was obsessed. That extreme emotion had kickstarted my slumbering sentiments, and I was never going back.

In no time, I was panting, scratching Lochie's powerful shoulders. He drove into me, increasing his pace, my pleasure his sole focus.

Then with a surge of passion, I splintered and came. Lights glimmered in my vision, and utter love shone from my heart.

Soon after, he stilled and groaned, his own climax reached. Then he dropped onto me, heaving in heavy breaths. He hugged me hard.

"Love ye, too. Always. More with every minute that goes by," he said into my ear.

Noise in the hall had us shuffling apart, though I wanted to stall. I had more words to say, beyond love, and into further entirely unchartered territory.

But the world waited, and after a quick shower, we were ready to head downstairs.

"Your family stood up for me yesterday," Lochie said, outside the castle's guest bedroom. "I owe them an explanation and I need to work out what to do next."

"We do," I corrected.

A smile tugged at his lips. "We? Fuck, Caitriona. So much has happened, I dinna ken which way is up. I spoke to Blair yesterday, and I went to Liv's prison. I needed to know if her family were the ones behind the hoax calls. I think now one of her brothers was the man at Isla's school."

I dusted my hands together, forcing away the shiver of fear. "We need a war council, and everyone here is going to clamour to be in it. You're part of the family. Isla, too. There's no going it alone anymore."

He stopped and kissed me, hunger in his moves despite our highly satisfying start to the day. I smiled against his lips and led him on.

At the top of the stairs, I regarded the people below in the great hall. Mathilda and Callum, my aunt and uncle, sat by the fire, talking. Da paced, Wasp, his twin brother, keeping time with him. From the dining room, Isla's laugh tinkled, echoed by my mother's.

"Hey, everyone." I waved, descending with Lochie. "After what happened yesterday, we need your help."

Da and Uncle Wasp spun around, instantly ready. Callum and Mathilda waited.

At my side, Lochie stood tall. "Cait just used the term war council. It's accurate, as I'm in the middle of a battle and need a strategy. And hands to aid me."

Every family member nodded, as ready as I was to leap to Lochie's assistance.

This was why I loved being a McRae, and now I got to share that with the man I adored.

Da stepped forward. "Get your arses down here then. There's bacon cooked and coffee on. Fuel up, give us your facts, and we'll see about that battle plan."

31

*L**ochie*

Under the rafters of the castle's great hall, several McRaes regarded me, including Gordain on a live video call. Christmas decorations sparkled around us, their jauntiness at odds with the scene playing out.

Serious expressions.

Grim energy.

Our war council had commenced.

Caitriona's ma had taken Isla upstairs to play dress-up with a box of costumes Mathilda kept for her grandchildren. Caitriona herself perched on the chair nearest to me. At my side, in the way I always wanted her to be.

That conversation couldn't come soon enough.

Cameron breathed hard, settling into a seat. The final person to arrive, he'd hammered at the locked front door, tiredness darkening his eyes. Last night, a while after I'd got back to the estate, he'd had a call-out—a genuine one—but with hours overnight spent helping a couple off the hill.

I'd scanned the details as I ate my bacon sandwich, beyond impressed with what I'd read. Cameron was a natural leader, and the careful way he now visually checked me over, then moved on to Caitriona, showed me his innate skills.

I gave him a short nod, getting a smile in exchange.

"As ye know," I began. "Yesterday, an unknown subject approached the primary school and tried to take my daughter."

Fresh alarm rippled over the family. Caitriona stiffened and reached for my hand, squeezing my fingers. I tried to summon words of reassurance, but the support and shared feelings only fuelled my resolve.

"Before we moved, Isla and I lived on a military base in England. Her mother, my ex-wife, comes from a notorious family of criminals. When Isla was born, her ma warned me that her family wanted the bairn and could hurt her. She told me I needed to take extreme measures to keep her away from them."

I swallowed and flicked a glance to the stairs. Scarlet would keep Isla out of earshot, but even so, I'd taken pains to ensure she never knew the depths of the struggles around her life.

"There's more to it than I can explain, but Liv, my ex-wife, believed they'd try to use Isla against a rival family. Or as a minimum, use her to their own ends. For seven years, I've kept her away from them, including bringing her here when Liv's two brothers were released from jail."

Over the video call, Gordain cleared his throat. "Have they made a specific threat?"

"Negative. I only know that they're out, and that someone has been sniffing around my old base in search of me. Then there's the hoax rescue calls, the break in, and the incident yesterday. I believe these things are connected, but there's a chance they're not."

I ran over how Liv had been with me, and how I'd wondered if she'd played me to take care of her daughter when she couldn't.

Sympathetic faces regarded me, no judgement or suggestions that my reactions had been overblown.

I suspected any one of the people here would've done similar.

Cameron raised a hand. "We'll have CCTV on the abduction attempt any minute. The school had to supply it to the police. They couldnae give it to us directly."

I breathed in. "Good. The description the receptionist gave me wasn't enough to identify either brother, or to rule them out."

Cait sat forward. "There's also the chance this is connected to me."

All attention fell on her.

"Why?" her father asked.

Pale, Cait chewed her lip. "Ye all know that several months ago, someone came to the estate and painted a word on my door. Around that, there have been a number of other strange incidents."

Cait listed event after event, ones I already knew about and others I didn't. With each, my anger grew.

Someone had followed her.

Hacked her emails.

Stolen from her.

Scared her.

Her cheeks flushed red. "I didn't think it was connected. The paint on my door was some guy I spurned. A man I saw recently, though I'm not convinced it was him now. The emails could've been an IT glitch. Rupert, my boss, has been acting strange, so I'm now thinking he could be behind it all."

Her father grimaced. "Targeting Lochie and Isla as well as ye?"

She dropped her face to her hands. "What if that's so? Could he be that insane that he'd hurt someone I loved because he couldn't have me? What if this is all my fault?"

"No," multiple voices reprimanded.

I drew her in and hugged her, no small thrill in me from her public claiming. She loved me. I'd never make her regret the fall. "It's not. Dinna ever take on the responsibility for someone else's behaviour."

Gordain's voice sounded again. "Then we have two possible suspects, lumping the brothers into one category as they have collective gain. One thing to consider is that the incidents could be a combination of these agents acting separately."

"True," I acknowledged.

"The rescue calls…" Max unfurled his tall frame from his seat. So far, he'd listened silently, the opposite side of the room from his twin brother. He palmed his plaster-encased arm. "I've been listening to them back to back, trying to work out if it's one person or multiple."

"Weren't two of them female?" his father asked.

"Aye, so if it is a single player, they'd be very good with putting on voices. Which is what I looked out for."

Cait peered at him. "Player, like an actor?"

His eyes flared. "Exactly. And I'm pretty certain I picked up a hint of a Birmingham accent in two of the calls."

Cait paled further, her fingertips fluttering over her lips.

"What is it?" I asked.

A thud at the heavy oak entrance resounded in the great hall.

Callum and Ally shot up and stalked over. They slid

back the iron locks and opened it, revealing a uniformed officer the other side.

Mathilda's gaze stayed on her niece. Likewise, her two brothers stared.

"Your university friend that used to visit you here was from Birmingham," Mathilda said slowly. "You brought him to see the castle. He was charming. Overly so."

"And an acting student," Max added.

The police officer eyed us, offering a joke over the amount of people converged over the incident. No one laughed. She handed an iPad to Cameron then gestured at something, stepping outside. Cameron locked the door and brought the tablet to me.

Everyone else crowded around, and I hit 'play'.

The in-colour scene showed the reception area of the school, kids' rainbow paintings lining a wall. At the desk, the receptionist glanced up, and a pair of boots appeared in the glass doorway, at the top of the screen.

She must've buzzed the person in, but the pounding of blood in my ears displaced the sound.

The door swung open. The man entered.

Young. In a woolly hat and thick coat. Only a thin sliver of his features showing.

Cait drew back as if stung.

I knew why. I'd recognised him, too.

Everyone waited on her.

"Jude," she said on a breath. "That's who tried to take Isla. My friend Jude—an acting student from Birmingham. Rupert's nephew."

32

Cait's Watcher

Bitter anger twisted my insides, shredding my righteous control.

How dare she?

Not only did she hide, not only did she turn her back on me, but she rushed back to *him*. Stayed with *him*. Kept out of sight inside that infernal castle.

They were lucky I hadn't torched the place overnight.

Lord knows I wanted to.

I strapped on my knife belt, sliding the blade into the leather sheath. The cruel-edged hunter's knife gleamed in the morning light, then sat snug in its home. In the empty cottage, I stood and collected my other, arguably more important, weapon and checked it over.

The large window, devoid of curtains, reflected back my image, and I grinned, posing. Quite the Rambo today.

But my levity was short-lived.

The anger rose and crashed over me in a wave.

I couldn't handle this any longer. I'd been so patient,

intending to take a gentler path with my courtship, but that was over.

She'd done this. Now she'd pay the price for the action she'd forced me to take.

Stowing the shotgun, I picked up my phone and cleared my throat, gazing out on the Highland glen.

Heavy clouds loomed, snow already falling in light scatters, adding to the thick drifts.

The call connected, the signal weak.

"Hello?" I said, my voice a perfectly pitched older woman. "Help. I need help. Please. I'm on Mhic Raith. The east side, just beyond Hill House. My husband has fallen, and I tried to get to our car but I'm lost. It's so cold out here."

The call handler started their same old spiel, but I hung up.

It was time to go.

With a flourish, I armed the explosive and set my trap—it was truly amazing what you could buy online—pulled on the too-tight coat, and set out to do what I should've done months ago.

Today, I'd take what was rightfully mine.

33

*C*aitriona

"He's a dead man." Lochie held up the tablet, the screen frozen on my twisted acquaintance's face.

Desperation buzzed in my veins, and I took a step away from the footage, hating the sight of my former friend smiling at the receptionist like he wasn't about to kidnap Isla.

What the hell was he doing?

Rupert must have forced him.

Or was it all his idea?

"Jude texted me several times in the past few days," I said. "All cheerful messages, checking in. I didn't reply, too busy to worry about some random friend I barely know."

The hard light in Lochie's eyes darkened. "Read out the texts."

I grabbed my phone. "Wednesday: *Dinner tomorrow? Chelle's really sorry for acting weird.* Thursday: *I guess you can't make it tonight? No biggie. What are you up to?* Friday: *Is something wrong? I had so much fun meeting up with you again. Did you enjoy it?* Then a few hours later: *Where are you, Caitriona?"*

I lowered the phone to find the focus of the room on me.

"Clear escalation. He was thinking about ye every day," Gordain remarked through the video. "He's kept his cool, though. No obvious sign of frenzy."

Lochie gave a single shake of his head. "We have our suspect."

"It can't all have been him. He's been away, travelling," I said fast, my mind twisting over everything I knew about Jude.

"Cait," Gordain said. "Ye said ye suspected his uncle. What reason would Jude have to help the man?"

"To kidnap a child? None that I know. I need to think."

Lochie held my gaze, his jaw set. "Anything ye can remember now will help. Anything he said to ye. How do ye know he was travelling?"

I blinked, going over every word that had fallen from Jude's lips. "He told me. No, wait, I saw his pictures online."

"Was he in them?"

"I don't recall. I'll check."

I searched for Jude, but no accounts existed on either place he'd befriended me. My blood froze over. "He's taken his accounts down. But wait, he has a fiancée. Chelle. She went with him."

I ran a search on her name and found her profile.

"Any exotic locations in her recent history?" Lochie asked.

I scrolled, going back months through Chelle's profile. "None. And no pictures with Jude. But I have her workplace."

I brought up the smart Manchester-located café, their phone number listed on their page. It was barely 8AM, but surely they'd be open. I pressed the number, begging silently.

A voice answered after a few rings. "Dock House. Chelle speaking. How can I help you today?"

My heartbeat stuttered. "Chelle? It's Cait McRae, we know each other from uni."

"Cait? Oh, sure. It seems like such a long time ago. How are you?"

I opened my mouth, trying to frame the odd question I had to ask.

As far as Jude had told me, they were engaged and visiting Inverness together before they bought their own place in her parents' hometown, near the Scottish borders. Over dinner, he'd smiled and told cute stories about their romance.

Without even a word from Chelle, I knew it all to be lies.

Chelle continued speaking. "It's so funny that you called. Your boyfriend came in a week or two ago and mentioned you."

"My boyfriend?"

"Jude Gaskill?"

Oh fuck.

I clasped the phone harder and set it to loudspeaker. "Chelle, listen, this is really important. Jude isn't my boyfriend. Yesterday, he tried to kidnap my real boyfriend's daughter. It's really important that you tell me what he said."

"Oh my God!" The line crackled. "He tried to kidnap a little girl?"

"Yes. The police showed us footage, and it's him. Shite, this is going to sound terrible, but I met with him recently, and he told me you two were engaged."

A rush of air marked Chelle's gasp. She took a moment

to speak, the clatter of the café diminishing as if she'd gone into an office. "Okay, okay. Shite. He bought a coffee and stayed about an hour, chatting. He was charming and funny, and he asked what I'd been up to since university. He wanted a picture with me. To show you."

"What day was this?"

She hummed, flustered, then gave me an answer—the day before he bumped into me at work.

"Did he say anything else, like where he lived or what he'd been doing?"

Her voice trembled. "He said he lived with you in the Highlands."

I took a breath, steadying myself. The shock of the revelation eased, and I could think straight.

"Thank ye, Chelle. We're going to try to find him now, but I need your direct phone number so the police can give you a call if they need to."

I indicated my head from Max to the door, and he leapt up, catching my drift. We needed that police officer back in here.

"Anything."

She rattled it off, and I scribbled on a notepad on a side table.

"Take care. Don't walk home alone tonight," I warned her. "I'm pretty sure it's me he's after, but he's dragged you into this, too."

"God. Stay safe. Text me when anything happens." She paused. "Is your little girl okay?"

Something clicked in my mind, making Isla mine. I'd been so worried about having her love me, but I already loved her so fiercely. Aye, she was mine. "She is. We have her. Thank ye again."

We hung up. Cameron filled in the police officer who then turned to me.

I counted off the points on my hand, summarising all I'd thought of during the call.

"Jude was a friend from university. He 'found' me again after several years and presented a fake life to make me comfortable with him. The travelling, the fiancée, all fantasy. I invited him for dinner and there, told him I was seeing Lochie. Then I ignored him while I was away which led him to try to hurt someone I loved. Anyone see anything different?"

Murmurs of agreement met my summary.

Gordain nodded. "Then he could've been responsible for what happened at your work. It's less clear that he sniffed around Lochinvar's old base, though if he's around, he could be the person who broke into my office and found the base's details. We know he was in England as he went to the other lass's café, but he didnae know about Lochinvar until your dinner."

Lochie stayed silent then smacked his fist into his hand. "He's here. I'm certain of it. The hoax call-outs stopped when I was away. He's watching us. Haunting us. It fits."

His mountain rescue phone rang in a shrill tone.

We all shot our gazes to it.

Max gave a devilish grin. "Right on schedule."

Lochie took the call then hung up. "An older couple lost beyond Hill House. Dispatch couldnae confirm if it's a hoax." He scanned the room, touching his gaze on all the members of the rescue service. "I believe this is now a hunt, naw a rescue. I cannae ask ye to stand up with me..."

"The fuck ye can't," Cameron barked.

"Ye must be joking," Da said at the same time.

Multiple other members of my family chimed in with their own ready acceptance to help.

Lochie breathed hard. "Fine. We're going out together."

The people gathered instantly began talking. I snagged Lochie's arm.

"I'm going to call him. If he's here, I might be able to persuade him to come down." I switched my gaze to the police officer. "Do we have enough to arrest Jude on?"

The woman lifted her chin. "I can take him to the station. A restraining order is possible, but we'll need greater evidence to prove the rest beyond false representation."

I nodded and pressed the button to call Jude, putting the phone on loudspeaker. Everyone silenced. The call rang and rang but eventually cut out.

"Next bet, Rupert. He might have more information on his nephew." I tried the new number.

Lochie glowered as I dialled.

The line connected.

"Rupert?" I said.

"Cait, well, I am shocked. I think you made yourself perfectly clear in your message at work," he replied.

"Listen—"

"No. I don't think I will. There's no need for us to discuss this further."

"Wait—"

He hung up.

Fuck. I dialled back. No answer.

The police officer took the number and made her own attempt, frowning at the engaged tone.

I stewed. "He's sulking," I said to Lochie. "Ah God. I asked to be assigned a new manager in work, and Rupert's kind of emotional. But he's still our best bet for intelligence."

I gathered my strength, knowing what I was about to say next wouldn't go down well.

"I'm going to go and see him. He lives this side of Inverness. I can be there in forty minutes."

Lochie clenched his jaw, a visible internal struggle playing out. He wanted to tell me to stay home.

"What if we're wrong?" he ground out. "What if this Rupert is just as bad? Or what if Jude is there, waiting? Ye cannae walk into his home alone."

A good point, though there had been the sound of children playing in the background to Rupert's line. The risk felt low. I gestured across the room. "I'll take Max as a bodyguard. He can't go out on the hill with a broken arm but he can throw a punch with his left. Will that do?"

Then my world ground to a slow halt as reality caught up with me.

"You're going out there to find him. Hunt him. But he's hunting ye, too," I said. "What if he tries to hurt ye? Stay here and look after Isla while my family goes out. He isn't targeting any of them."

He smiled softly. "Do ye really think I'd sit this one out? That piece of shite tried to take my daughter." He leaned in and pressed his forehead to mine. "He wants ye. There is nothing I willnae do to protect those I love. Do ye understand?"

I pulled him into the den and threw my arms around him, my powered-up indignation at Jude falling into worry for Lochie.

"I'm scared. We don't know what he might do."

"He doesnae know what I'm willing to do, either. Drive

to see Rupert. Get whatever ye can from the man. Drive home and stay safe. I'll be back with ye before ye know it."

I clung to him. "I love ye."

Lochie kissed me. "I'll come back to ye. I swear it. My heart is yours."

With a fast, hard press of his lips, he was gone.

A grumbling Max joined me on my drive up to the city. He tried to argue that his twin should take me, as they argued over everything, but he'd been shouted down.

I didn't care who was here so long as I could contribute to finding Jude. Out in the mountains, I'd be more of a hazard than a help, particularly in the snow that steadily fell. But I couldn't sit at home doing nothing.

We arrived at Rupert's home fast. I knew where he lived from his bragging about the swanky house his wife's family had bought them. Out on the road to Culloden Moor, the two-storey home was set back in its own manicured gardens.

I steamed down the track, slamming on the brakes before I leapt from the car, Max in pursuit.

The front door opened on our approach, a woman in the frame. Children scampered through the hall at her back.

She stared, her hand over her open mouth, and her focus jumped from Max to me. "Can I help you?"

"I need to speak to Rupert. Is he home?"

"Who are you?"

"Cait. I work with him. It's important."

The woman, his wife, I guessed, narrowed her eyes, but before she could speak, I added the reason for the request.

"It's about Jude."

Whatever she was about to say fizzled, and she centred herself then proffered a hand. "Follow me."

We stepped into the house. The woman led us into the kitchen.

Rupert sat at the table, glasses on, his focus on his laptop screen. At our entrance, he peered up, then his lips formed a flat line. "Cait. I thought I told you I had nothing to say to you."

"They're here to talk to you about your nephew," the woman sniped, then spun away and closed the kitchen door.

Rupert's lip curled. "Jude? What has he done?"

I strode to the table and grabbed the back of a seat, almost vibrating with energy. "I need to know where he is."

"I'm afraid I can't help you there. We asked him to leave several days ago."

"He was living here?"

Slowly, Rupert inclined his head. Interest registered in his expression. "I can tell from your faces that something has gone wrong. Tell me."

I rapidly went through what had happened from the point Jude bumped into me until yesterday, including the lies he'd told and the kidnap attempt.

Rupert pulled a face. "I tried to warn you."

"What, when?"

"In my office. I told you how important it was to take care with who parented your child. My brother was reckless. He slept around with whoever would have him, and Jude was the result. I never understood why that boy was so interested in you, though. He asked about you all the time, and there were pictures on his phone. I talked to Jill about it, and she said not to worry."

"Pictures? Wait, Jill? Ye knew, and your PA knew?"

"Jude spent a lot of time in my office. Jill noticed some...

odd behaviour, and suggested I tell you, not that she approved of you very much. She disagreed with my recruiting you to that job. She said you were too young and would only cause trouble."

I resisted the urge to smack my palm against my head. "Are ye kidding me?"

"I meant to give you a hint about Jude that day in my office, but you upped and ran." He sniffed, offended.

I sucked in a breath, my heart thudding. Mentally, I replayed the meeting with Rupert when I thought he was being a creep. Wild anger flushed heat into me. "Ye knew Jude was obsessed with me yet ye didn't think to tell me outright? Instead, ye decided to school me on choosing the father of my bairn carefully, and all the while he was escalating. So many things had happened at work, and I suspected everyone, yet it was all him. He hacked my emails, stole from me, vandalised my home. Rupert, he tried to kidnap my boyfriend's daughter. Do ye understand what's happening? What if he'd managed to walk off with her?"

Max stepped up until he loomed over Rupert. Until now, he'd been silent, but anger and menace flashed in his eyes. He held up the hand of his uninjured arm and counted off his fingers. "Where does he work? Who are his friends? Do ye know where he went? Why did ye kick him out?"

A tremble wobbled Rupert's jowls. "He works part time at a hunting lodge, or he did. I've no idea where he is, and I don't know any of his friends."

"A hunting lodge? He has access to guns?" Max's voice came out deadly calm.

My body tensed up even more. Oh no.

"I don't know. He's a strange boy. My wife told him to leave after finding him naked, lying on a woman's coat, pleasuring himself."

Nausea rose in my throat, and I stepped back. *My purple coat!*

Rupert spluttered. "I'm sure he wouldn't hurt anyone."

"He's not a boy. He's a dangerous man obsessed with my sister. Which ye knew about and failed to tell anyone." Max leaned in, every move held tight. "If anything happens because of that fucker, I, and every other member of my family, will hold ye responsible."

Then he snatched my hand and dragged me from the house.

At the car, I pulled out my keys, but my fingers shook.

Max's gaze turned fiercer still. "Get in. Call Lochinvar. They need to know about the weapons. If Jude is armed, that's a whole new game."

I dialled Lochie, my heart all but in my throat.

We'd been gone less than an hour, but anything could've happened. Jude could have planned for this exact scenario to go down.

What if his abduction attempt hadn't been a failure but a setup?

A sham, designed to lure me home?

The call dropped, unable to connect, and my fear peaked.

What had happened to the man I loved?

*L*ochie

  At the hangar, a full service of rescue crew had turned out, geared up, talking in groups, and raring to go.

Camaraderie was high. Energy hung in the air, so thick I could taste it.

The police had used the time to confirm the call was a hoax based on a fast assessment of the throwaway number and inability to trace the line. But the officer had also investigated Jude.

He had form for harassing women.

She refused to share the details, but one fact was plain: Jude Gaskill had been building up to this.

So had I. I had the skills and training, and I wouldnae rest until we'd brought him in.

There was nothing stopping us from heading out.

Yet still, I didn't issue the order to leave.

Since the request for help had come in, we'd only assembled at the base—unheard of, particularly with the tricky weather conditions, worsening by the minute. On any other given day, we'd be out on the hill, visible and on the search. Our target to respond was six minutes—down tools, set aside your meal, leap out of bed, whatever needed to be done.

But I'd stalled the men and women under my command.

It was more than a hunch that had me pull my punches.

If Jude was out there waiting for us, we wouldnae play into his hands. He'd started today's game with his hoax call, but I intended to master it.

If we didn't budge from the hangar, he'd have to make another move, or die on the mountainside.

Cameron waited by my side. "What's your bet? A show of strength or a second call?"

"A call. He's a coward."

"Same location or a new one?"

I raked over my beard. "Naw sure. He named Hill House, which suggests he has eyes on the place, or somewhere on the approach."

"We found the sleeping bag there, too. His?"

"Undoubtably. So if ye were to lie in wait nearby, would ye take high ground or low?"

Cameron pondered this, stretching his arms behind his head, his red jumpsuit a snug fit to the lad's bulky shoulders. "High ground, with sightlines to the target. Ground cover for concealment. Multiple exits on hand, too. Anyone approaching would take it slow, but we'd have to close in on the building eventually. He'd know we'd come as a group and naw one-on-one."

A good analysis. I crossed to the map with Hill House and scanned the surroundings. "Take your best shot."

Crew members watched.

Cameron pointed at a tree-lined hillside adjacent to the house, a hundred meters out. "Here, lying in wait. His ultimate objective is Caitriona. But to get to her, he has to go through all of us first. You're his biggest target as ye have what he wants. His issue is in taking out a man your size. I cannae believe he'd be so stupid to try direct combat, even if he got ye alone. Either he has a ranged weapon or he's set a trap."

His da, Wasp, grunted agreement. "Or both."

We had a team at the castle, led by Callum, and another waiting to bring Caitriona's car back onto the estate. We were mobile, ready, and there was no chance the fucker could win.

Still, I couldn't settle until this battle was over.

My phone buzzed, and silence fell on the group. I held it up. "Personal. Stand down."

They relaxed back to muttering, and I answered Caitriona.

"Where are ye?" I said without pause.

"Almost back at Castle McRae. I couldn't get through. I was so worried."

"I tried ringing ye, too. Calls aren't connecting easily. I'm sorry, sweetheart. Mobile signal is sketchy."

She exhaled. "Thank God you're okay. Max has been cursing the fact he doesn't have his rescue radio. Listen, I need to tell ye what we found out from Rupert. Jude has access to guns. He worked for a hunting lodge."

"Guns," I repeated for the benefit of the people around me. "Does Rupert know if he took any, what kind, or if he had training?"

"Max asked, but Rupert didn't know. He didn't know the name of the lodge either. Knowing Jude's form for lying, it might not be real, but better to be cautious."

I grumbled agreement. "Did the uncle give up anything else useful?"

"He knew Jude was overly interested in me. The arse-hole knew and said nothing."

"Fucker. Listen, we have a car waiting to bring ye in, a team waiting at the castle. Get there, stay safe, give Isla a hug for me."

"A team? We haven't seen them. We had to take a detour as the loch road is blocked. Two cars have been abandoned. It looked like they crashed and the snow has built around them. We're coming in over the hills instead."

My heart froze. "What route, Caitriona?"

"Over Mhic Raith. Why?"

The road that branched off to Hill House. She was a short drive from the exact place we suspected Jude to be hiding.

"Listen," I ordered. "Ye need to turn around—"

An explosion boomed, simultaneously sounding in the hangar and over the line. The men and women in the operations room gaped at each other then hustled to the hangar entrance.

I chased them. "Caitriona? Can ye hear me?"

"Aye," her voice came through faint. "Something just blew up near to us. Fuck. The snow!"

"What about it?" I gripped the phone, pushing through my crew to the door. The hangar faced side-on to Mhic Raith's jagged, mountainous peak. Hill House perched on a slope facing the other direction, but the road curved past it, winding back on itself to return to the castle.

Snow fell thick and fast. Barely any visibility beyond a couple of hundred metres.

Then, amidst the flurry, a plume of dark smoke rose from the hill.

"Caitriona! Get away from there," I demanded. "Can ye hear me?"

I repeated myself, scrutinising the faint rustling, the evidence the line still had a connection. Then it blipped out.

Frantic, I redialled.

Ally arrived in front of me, Maddock beside him. "Was that my daughter? Where are they?"

Lips numb, I forced out the words. "The loch road was closed. They took the hill route."

Everyone within earshot spun to gaze at the mountain, now invisible once more.

Caitriona was up there. Max, too.

And Jude, lying in wait.

My first long stride crunched through the snow, delivering me in the direction of the mountain, pulled by an invisible force I couldn't deny. I only knew I had to reach her. A jerk on my rucksack stalled me.

Cameron rounded me and pushed my shoulders. "Ye are not about to walk off into the storm. I know ye have more sense in your head than that." He raised an arm and hollered. "Back inside. Into your teams."

He seized my arm and hauled me along with him.

I had to lead, had to organise the people who could rescue my woman.

Focusing on that final thought alone, I strode after the crew and rallied them inside the hangar. All had kit, maps, and rescue know-how. Few were military, though. This could be a diversion or a direct attack.

"Listen up," I boomed. "Caitriona and Max McRae are on the road near Hill House. They have a car but were close to the explosion." Caitriona's final words returned. *The snow.* My panic froze over. "It's possible they could be buried if the explosion caused an avalanche. Our primary goal is now to assist them off the hill. I believe that Jude Gaskill set the explosion. He may also be armed. We know he wants Caitriona." My voice strained, and I cleared my throat. "There's a greater risk now. To all of us. If ye dinna want to go out, it willnae be a problem."

Not a single person budged.

My already thudding heart beat harder. "Right. Team leaders, on me. Everyone, prep to leave."

With the briefing over, we piled into cars and set out. Stealth and waiting it out be damned. We had strength in numbers and we all cared about the two souls in peril.

I would bring Caitriona home. There was no other option.

aitriona

"Turn off the engine."

At Max's snapped order, I jerked to shut down my car. The rumbling ceased, replaced by muffled silence.

Around, blue and dirty-white snow clumped against the glass, thick and smothering. Branches, mud, and pine needles mixed in, enclosing us in the dark.

An avalanche had crashed into us, almost taking us off the road.

Max unclipped his seat belt, and I did the same.

"Holy fuck," he muttered.

I scanned the windows for daylight. "We're buried."

"No shite, Sherlock."

I punched his uninjured arm. "We need to get out."

"Technically, you're meant to stay in the car and wait for rescue. Lochinvar knows where we are. Try calling him."

We'd been speaking before disaster had struck. God, he must be worried. I recovered my phone from where it had landed by my feet. "No signal."

Max pressed at his screen. "Same."

I tried to place the call anyway. It failed. A text message did the same.

"They know where we are. They'll come for us," Max said.

A low wave of panic tightened my stomach. "Are ye joking? I can't sit here while a maniac is loose on the estate. Fuck that, Max. There was an explosion. Something is happening right now."

Even in the dark, my brother's eyes lit, and his attempt at making a sensible decision evaporated. "Aye, fuck that. We cannae sit here."

He yanked on his door handle then barged the door, wincing in pain.

It didn't budge.

I tried mine with the same outcome, then turned the power back on to check the locks weren't engaged. Still, nothing. Our exits were jammed by the weight of the avalanche.

We were trapped.

Max scrambled between the seats to try the back doors. He kicked at them, barely even rocking the car, but to no avail. "Yeah, that isn't happening."

"I'm going to lower the windows. Maybe we can dig our way out."

"Do ye have a spade?"

"Why would I carry a spade in my car?"

"Well, we cannae use our hands." In the gloom, he raked his fingers into his hair, frustration in the move. "Besides, we risk freezing our arses off if we cannae get through."

"We'll manage. How bad can it be?"

"Hypothermia? Pretty limiting, unless you're happy being dead."

I glowered at him. At some point, my irritating little

brothers had grown up, and Max was now a man. I still couldn't see him as anything other than annoying.

He gave me a well-duh look. "What about other supplies? Spare clothes, water, energy bars, fuel?"

"No, no, and no."

"Seriously? We live in the fucking Highlands. Winter happens. Ye should carry a basic kit in case of emergencies."

"I never drive the more remote roads. The worst that's ever happened is I had to wait down by the loch after I skidded on ice and busted a tyre. Ma drove and picked me up, then Isobel towed my car."

Today, two cars had blocked that same route, causing us to change direction.

I held up a hand to stop my brother's retort. "Could that have been deliberate? The accident? It forced us to come this way."

He sat back in the seat, his gaze focused. "Then there was the explosion. Ye cannae plan an avalanche, but it would gather attention. Bring people running."

We both quietened. That sound had driven fear through me, and the sense lingered.

"What could've blown up? A car?" I asked.

"We're right below the access road to Hill House. That place is off the grid, but it has diesel-powered generators."

"Shite. There's no chance that was an accident. I'd bet any money Jude did this."

"Agreed. Which makes us sitting ducks."

Trapped and waiting.

Oh God, this had been a mistake.

"We have to get out." I hit the door in frustration. "I'm going to tunnel out. It's our only option." Even if I tore my fingers to shreds.

Max shone his phone's torchlight around the car and

peered at the ceiling. Then he reached for something I couldn't see. In a rush, he slid back a hatch cover.

Daylight flooded in.

"Why the hell didn't ye say ye had a roof light?" He examined the fastenings.

"In four years of owning this car, I have never opened that. Fuck!"

My brother smacked the hatch, opening it a paltry inch, the hinges restricting further movement. The snow on top shuddered. "Ye know, if ye took more care of your car instead of speeding everywhere, ye would've known this was here."

Argh. "I don't speed. Get out of the way, I'm going to boot it."

"The snow will cave in."

"We'll have a better chance of digging through that than by breaking the window."

Max pulled a face at me then stole my idea. With a move worthy of an acrobat, he twisted and drove a shoe into the glass.

It popped off its hinge, flying away.

Fresh air and only a scattering of snow entered the car.

"Yes!" I cheered.

Max stuck his head out then ducked back inside. "Easy. We'll land in a snow pile—it's thick around the car—but the road is visible ahead. Grab whatever ye need to take and let's get the fuck out of here."

I didn't need telling twice. Max passed over my winter jacket from the back seat, and I put it on then slung my bag across my body. Standing on the seat, I exited the car through the narrow gap and eased onto the snowy roof.

My brother boosted himself after me, and we perched side by side for a moment.

The storm had reduced in intensity, but thick clouds scattered fresh flakes, covering us. To our right, a wide snowfield abutted the mountain, the road's verge lost to the avalanche. To the left, the hill descended into a creaking forest.

Even with my shite sense of direction, I knew the path ahead would take us home. A long walk, but better than sitting in a metal box inside a snowdrift.

"If that arsehole is out here somewhere, weaponed up and fucked in the head, we need to get moving and stay out of sight," Max grumbled. "Through the forest would be the most direct route, and safest, but it's naw easy underfoot."

"We should stick to the road," I argued. "We cannae get lost, and if anyone's looking for us, that's the way they'll come."

"I'd never get lost," Max grouched, but he agreed all the same.

With his coat around him like a cape, his plaster cast too bulky to zip inside, he stood into the churned snow beside the car. His boots sank, but he was able to move.

I hopped down after him, placing my feet into his footsteps.

With care, we rounded the car, nothing of it visible aside from the roof with the hole in it.

There was nothing for it but to trudge on. My brother was hurting—not that he'd admit it, I could tell by the way he held himself—but he strode ahead. At the edge of the avalanche zone, we found the road, still snow-covered but with obvious tyre tracks. We followed it, moving as fast as we could on the treacherous ground.

A hundred meters on, we passed a junction. I lifted my hood against the chill and sucked in a lungful of frozen air.

"Is that where ye think the explosion came from?" I asked Max.

"Aye, keep moving."

Somewhere out here, the mountain rescue service was hunting Jude. Lochie had that under control, and I knew he'd succeed. All I had to do was get out of the way and stay safe. Isla was with Ma at the castle, and I so badly wanted to see the little lass.

We could be a family—I knew that's what she'd wanted to ask before I'd left the country. Her da and I never got to have the conversation about what next. He wanted to stay, and his problems might be solvable, if they even existed. My stalker could be responsible for everything that had happened. The more I thought about it, the likelier it became.

Jude was the only obstacle between me and a future I could never have imagined possible.

Uphill, a bold colour flashed between the trees. I squinted then stalled my brother.

"Did ye see that?"

He gave a short nod, a hand out as if to restrain me.

I stared, getting a tiny glimpse of the colour again. Purple, a brilliant and unusual shade, practically glowing against the stark white and grey of the mountainside. At the distance, I couldn't tell if it was on a person or hanging from a tree.

Then recognition dawned. Was that...?

"It's my coat," I spluttered. "That colour... Ma bought me a coat in that exact shade. It was stolen from work months ago."

Then the object moved, and a person came into sight. With a white balaclava covering their face, and in my damn coat, they moved purposefully.

I focused on what he carried.

The man left the cover of the trees and strode closer.

Max and I froze and slowly lifted our arms.

It was Jude, and he had a gun trained directly on my brother.

36

Jude

Glee rippled through my body, my heart lighter than it had been in years. With a dramatic flourish, I tore off my mask and beamed at Cait. "It's me."

She stared at the gun then inched in front of the man by her side—her brother, I recognised, though he'd changed from the skinny teenager I'd met once before.

I stepped closer, almost dancing in my happiness. "No, baby girl. Never fear, I won't shoot him. Not if he behaves, anyway. I'm so happy to see you out of that car. You have no idea how worried I was."

Cait swallowed, her dainty throat bobbing. "Ye caused the avalanche that buried us."

"Well, yes, I saw that through my binoculars, but I didn't mean to. I only wanted you to come running to see what the bang was all about." I spread my arms, swinging the shotgun. "Which you did! You clever things."

Both ducked when the gun swept their way, so I trained

it on the big redhead once more and cleared my throat. "There's just a few things we need to clear up, then we can get going."

"Get going where?"

All the hate and anger and bitterness melted. This couldn't have worked better if I'd planned it. Cait was here, and we were together.

I had the perfect place for her to stay. Previously, I thought we'd live in her cottage, but there were too many nosy people around. Too many distractions. In my uncle's big house, once he and his awful family were out of the way, she'd never have to be bothered by anyone else again.

"You'll see when we get there." I grinned again, raising my shoulders. Then I gestured uphill with the gun. "Now walk. I want you nice and visible on the hillside."

Cait's brother glowered at me. I stared back.

The hate returned in a rush.

"Do it now or he loses his fucking face," I snapped.

They moved slowly, and I circled behind, careful to watch my back. Below in the glen, tiny red specs of mountain rescue people milled about like headless chickens. Spider mites, waiting to be crushed.

I only cared about one of them.

The problem.

The brute who Cait had let between her legs. Stifling, crippling rage washed my good feelings away. I'd tried so hard to forgive Cait's trespass, her dalliance with that man, but I feared for both her sanity and mine.

There was only one solution, and now, I had every advantage.

I marched my true love through the snow, leading our quarry on the hunt.

In time, she'd forget him.
In time, she'd think only of me.
At last, Cait was mine.

37

*L*ochie
In concentrated sweeps, my teams moved over the hillside, searching in vain for Caitriona's vehicle. This was a trap, we all knew it, so I'd played the strategy as best I could.

Two teams rounded the mountain to approach from the other side, on skis or snow mobiles to cover the ground. Another group remained at the castle to protect Isla. The car I'd sent to meet Cait would bring backup, but we were thinly spread.

I couldn't leave her out here.

I'd chosen to walk straight into the lion's den. Cameron and I had taken the east route, and Wasp, Ally, and Maddock the west, none of us hesitating.

Cameron shot out an arm and grabbed me then pointed. Ahead, the road ended in a thick ridge of snow. I drove to the edge then stopped.

"An avalanche," I breathed.

Then I was out of the car and into the drift.

Cameron followed, scanning our surroundings. "Keep low," he warned.

"If they're under that, we need to get them out," I retorted.

He uttered agreement, and I pressed on, searching with an edge of desperation. Skiers sometimes wore avalanche beacons, giving us a guide to locating them. But Caitriona wouldn't have had anything like that.

How much time had passed since the explosion? Under the snow, every minute counted. She could be suffocating. Despair rocked me.

I wanted to yell for her, shout down the mountain until she called back. But that risked too much.

Cameron held up a hand and knelt. "Footprints."

My heart leapt, and I studied his find. "You're right. Two clear sets, aye? It has to be theirs."

"I think so. It's hard to be sure with the fresh snowfall. I dinna think they've been here long."

Then I spied a hole in the ground, its shape not one found in nature. A car window? I strode over and peered down. "Christ, it's Caitriona's car."

I was directly on top of it.

Panic and fear loaded into my system. She'd been stuck under the snow. Ah fuck.

Cameron joined me and lowered his head inside. "There's no blood and no interior damage. We know they got out. Breathe, man."

No blood. No blood.

"But they were in there. She could've died."

I wanted to fucking howl with worry, but we had to keep going. She'd got out, Max, too, so they couldn't be far. Except...

"We should've seen them on the road," I bit out. "Why the fuck weren't they on the road?"

Cameron's expression flattened. He reported the find into his radio, summoning the second team to us. "If they didn't take the obvious path home, there's a good reason. Come on. Back to the footsteps. We'll try to follow them."

We jogged back over the compressed snow, searching the ground. Partial prints broke the choppy snow layer every few metres, and we traced them past the car.

Cameron hesitated at the Jeep. "I'll drive, ye lead."

"Do it." It would be foolhardy to give up our car before we had to.

I powered on, jogging back along the way we'd come, stalling to check the faint prints were still in place. At the junction to Hill House—a route we'd passed but ignored— the footprints clustered.

They continued on up the steep road.

I gestured to the car, my throat tight.

Cameron leaned from the window. "Why would they go up there?"

"No clue."

I took a few more steps, searching the dark trees to one side and the ridge to the other. The house wasn't in view yet, but we were almost in the exact position Cameron had speculated Jude would target.

The icy weather had nothing on the chill that rippled down my spine.

"They'd only go this way for two reasons. Shelter, if desperate, and assuming there's anything of the house remaining. Or because they were made to."

With a grim nod, Cameron hopped down and joined me, and we advanced.

At the same moment, we both spotted the one thing I hadn't wanted to see.

A third pair of prints.

Until now, we'd followed two different-sized boots, huge clumping depressions that were Max's, and daintier walking boots that could only be Caitriona's.

The third was in between, and the tracks led into the forest.

"It's him. It has to be." I fought the urge to drop to my knees. "It's Jude. They've gone with him. Why the fuck would they?"

"They were forced to," Cameron said with vehemence. "Lochinvar, he has a gun. He must have or both Max and Cait would've run. We need to change tactic. I have to stop them being approached directly by the other searchers."

"He'll hurt her," I bit out.

"He could do. I need to tell the teams."

I lifted my head enough to acknowledge him then, as he spoke to the rescue crew, focused inwardly. Again, the game had changed. Jude had Caitriona, and Max, too. Even through my horror, I could perform the basic checks. We'd heard no sound of a gunshot, nor was there blood, or an unconscious Max anywhere in sight. Plus the footsteps continued. He'd directed them somewhere, but together.

That was in our favour.

My radio bleeped. "Come in," I said.

"Dinna tell me to hold back," Maddock blurted down the line. "That's my sister and my fucking twin. We're coming after ye."

We needed them, but we also needed clear heads. God knows mine was already fucked.

"Come up as far as our Jeep then proceed with extreme caution," I ordered. "I fucking mean it. Stay out of sight. We have to continue on foot—the prints lead away towards the hills. Once ye see us, dinna move a muscle. We cannae spook this guy."

A pause followed, then Wasp's voice returned. "Roger that. We'll show restraint. Stay safe, both of ye."

My safety didn't mean shite right now. I wasn't at risk, and I'd throw myself in front of Cameron if it came to it. All that mattered was getting Caitriona back.

With that in mind, I followed her trail.

38

C̵aitriona

There was a tactic I'd read about in kidnapping scenarios, where women befriended their attackers in order to maintain their safety. Something to do with creating a link at the human level and therefore making the villain less likely to hurt them.

I should flirt with Jude and go along with his make-believe world.

But I'd never been any good at pretending.

Instead, I slunk a look of hatred over my shoulder, my body frozen from our long walk through the snow. At my side, Max moved stiffly, his jaw set. Without the ability to zip up his coat, he must be bitterly cold.

At least the storm had eased. Though an icy breeze ghosted over us on the exposed slope, the snow had stopped, and the clouds lightened to the point sun broke through here and there.

The brightness on the crisp, white hill stung my eyes.

Behind, Jude chattered merrily, sounding the same as

when he'd come to dinner, telling jaunty stories of university and of things he wondered about.

He was insane.

Dangerously so.

We left the ridge and rounded a foothill, staying in full sight of the glen below, the aircraft hangar visible in the distance. With my jacket being dark blue and Max's black, we'd be nothing but dots on the hillside. Jude, however, stood out in the stolen coat.

A memory jolted then sickened me. His uncle said they'd kicked him out after finding him masturbating while lying on a woman's coat.

Mine, no doubt.

This man was seriously fucked up. Dangerous and unpredictable.

The very last thing I wanted was a confrontation with Lochie on the hill. Jude had a gun. There could only be one outcome.

Fear fizzled.

"We have to stop soon," I whispered to Max.

"I was about to say the same thing," he mouthed back.

"What?" Jude called. "I can't hear you from here. Speak up, darling."

My brother glanced at me and gave an infinitesimal nod. He widened his eyes then gestured subtly ahead. Beyond, smooth white hid the rough, rocky ground.

What was there? I hadn't noticed anything, though at a pinch, I could work out that we weren't far from the cliffs over the unicorn pool. That was a long way down. Maybe a rally point for the rescue team?

It was enough to interest Max, but I didn't want the crew to find us. If they did, Lochie would be at risk.

"Nothing to say? Never mind," Jude continued. "I have so

much to share with you. Not you, ugly brother. Shut your ears. Cait, do you remember the first time we made love?"

Queasiness clamped hold of my stomach.

"I haven't forgotten a minute of it. I wrote down every single thing you did so it couldn't get lost in the time that's passed. You and I were meant to be, right from that moment. Your soft hair, so pretty on my sheets. Your lovely, pliable body receiving mine."

Ugh. I stifled a retch.

"Fuck's sake," Max muttered.

"I heard that. I told you not to listen." Jude's tone dropped from jovial to disturbed. "Now stop. Stop right there."

We halted and turned. Deliberately, I stepped in front of my brother again, my boots catching on the dead heather under the snow.

"Don't," Max whispered.

There was no chance I'd listen. Jude wanted me. Ergo, he probably wouldn't shoot me. He'd hurt my brother, though.

Jude peered at us, unhinged, his cheeks burned red by the cold, and his eyes too bright.

I wanted to scream at him. Despite the cold, my blood boiled. The problem was, I didn't know his plan. Was it to get Lochie into sight so he could shoot him? Or was he leading me somewhere so he could trap me? If so, why had he brought Max?

Fuck.

Jude hadn't expected us to walk right into his lair. He'd caused the explosion then sat in wait. He'd intended to snipe Lochie from a hidden position.

He blathered on, and I stared at the weapon pointing at Max. I knew little about guns, but I'd seen them with the stalker who managed the deer herd on the estate. Cameron refused to shoot animals, so another person was brought in whenever a deer was hurt or a cull needed.

Jude held a shotgun, not a rifle. At a distance, it was ineffective, blasting the pellets into whatever was in range.

Did Jude know this? Was this intentional? He'd hurt more people as they came at him, but his risk of killing was low.

Unless he intended to be up close.

I backed up to my brother so my body covered more of his. On the long walk here, I'd tried to keep directly behind him, lessening the chance of Jude getting a clear shot.

"Here's good enough." Jude brushed his floppy blond hair back then pointed at Max. "You, walk up the hill."

"No," I snapped.

Jude rolled his eyes. "Yes."

"He's not leaving me."

Jude's lips turned down in the corners. "*I'm* not leaving you. He's fucking off now. Go on, red. Off you pop. Take a long walk off a short cliff."

At Jude's back, over the crest of the hill, movement caught my eye.

Max's hand subtly pressed my shoulder blade. He'd seen it, too.

Jude hadn't.

I opened my mouth, needing to distract him. "It's cold, I'm freezing, and I don't want to be out here anymore. I'm terrified because ye have a gun on my brother. Why are we here? What do ye want from me?"

The gun in Jude's hand shook. "I'm here because you want me to be. You chose me."

"What are ye talking about?"

I wanted to get him arguing and focused on me alone.

"You want me, Cait. You asked me to sleep with you and led me on. And since then—"

"I had sex with ye as an experiment, and an unsuccessful one at that."

The two figures crept ever closer.

Jude wiped his gun arm over his nose, swinging the weapon. "No. It wasn't like that. You loved me and seduced me. Then you waited for me to realise everything we had. I know it now. I worked it all out."

"You're fucking nuts," I hissed.

I slid my hand behind my back and pointed at the ground, indicating to Max that he should drop to lying. If he did, I could move in on Jude, pissing him off until I reached him and grabbed the gun.

Then he couldn't shoot anyone.

Especially not Max or the people moving slowly in.

No one I loved would die.

"What about your emails? You put messages in there for me. You want a baby. I thought at first it was because you were on your own, and you were punishing me, but then it finally made sense. You were still waiting for me, over all these years. You didn't want anyone else and you just needed me to see it. I'm going to father your babies. I'm sorry I made you wait."

Max gripped my jacket right as I took a step. He held me back, and I wrestled his hand.

"What are you doing to her? Leave her alone," Jude yelled, his voice going shrill. "Don't touch her."

"Get down," I said to my brother.

"Dinna move," Max gritted out under his breath.

I couldn't take my eyes off Jude. Even so, I flicked a tiny glance at men creeping in.

Lochie.

Cameron.

My heart ached, and I held back my reaction, my bloom of fear and love and everything in between.

In their mountain rescue red jumpsuits, and at fifty feet away, they manoeuvred over the hill to be directly behind Jude, Cameron slightly closer. Lochie made some sort of gesture. I couldn't make it out.

Max held me to his side and bent his head to my ear. "We have this, Cait. Dinna argue. When I say go, we're going to run."

Run? I couldn't run away. Yet if Max had understood Lochie, they had a plan.

I trusted Lochie. I trusted Max and Cameron.

I couldn't allow any of them to be hurt on my behalf.

Jude raised the gun and peered down the barrel pointing at us. "No talking between you or I'll shoot. I mean it. I've been patient, but our time is up. Cait, tell that man to go away."

"How were ye going to find me after all of this was done?" I asked.

Our rescuers reached forty feet.

"I mean, you've been hiding out here, watching me—"

"Waiting for you," Jude corrected.

"Ye blew up that house then...what?"

Jude frowned, still gazing down the shotgun. "Are you asking for a protestation of love? Fine. I was going to come to collect you from your home. You don't need to live there anymore. I have somewhere for us to stay together."

"Where?"

"Uncle Rupert's place. Well, we should call it our place now. There's kids' rooms already set up, so living there will be so easy. Just you and me."

Ice slid down my spine. I could only imagine what he

intended to do with Rupert and his wife. Their lovely children.

Max's hand twisted my jacket in warning.

He wanted us to just flee. But where? I resisted the urge to glance behind at the jagged white slopes. Running would risk tripping, but then at least Max wouldn't be upright and as big a target.

It would leave Lochie and Cameron to tackle Jude.

I swallowed, hating both options.

But choice was a luxury right now, and trust beat will.

"Now," Max bit out.

In unison, we turned and bolted.

After trudging slowly uphill through the snow, my legs had stiffened to the point of pain. Running hurt. Underfoot, rocks mixed with stubby dead plants, hidden under the snow. Every footfall risked injury.

Max hauled me by the arm, but I kept up, pacing with him farther up the slope, my heart pounding and breath leaving me in clouds of steam.

"Hey!" Jude called. "Wait—"

His words cut off in a shout of anguish.

I spun around, still moving. Cameron wrestled with Jude, knocking him over, both men fighting for the gun. A few feet away, Lochie moved in.

God, they had him.

I stopped altogether.

"Go, Cait," Max demanded and grabbed my hand.

A shot exploded. The sound ricocheted through the mountains, barely deadened by the snow.

"Fuck!" Max dropped to the frozen ground, taking me with him.

Half blinded, I rolled up to my knees and gaped.

Red painted the snow behind the men.

"Cameron!" Lochie bellowed.

My cousin sprawled on the ground at a horrible angle, his face twisted away. He gave a howl of utter pain.

Oh no. No!

Even from where we stood, I could make out Cameron's shredded jumpsuit, the blood leaking from his shoulder.

Jude staggered to his feet, his mouth open in shock. "You idiot," he yelped then raised the gun again.

Lochie bore down on him then snatched the barrel and yanked it from Jude's hands. With a roar, he drew it back and smacked the hilt into Jude's head.

Jude moaned and clutched his injury. He fell back, glowering at Lochie who stood over Cameron's body, protecting him.

Then without pause, Jude spun around and sprinted.

Right towards us.

Max stepped in front of me and lowered into a fighter's pose. But Jude got nowhere near. In long strides, Lochie caught him up. He snatched his collar and slammed him to the ground. Smacked a fist into his face.

It was only then I noticed the cliff edge.

I knew we were close to the unicorn pool, and therefore to the hole in the slopes above where the water fell out of sight. I vaguely remembered Lochie talking about training his crew there for when hikers inevitably didn't notice the jagged, concealed ravine and tumbled down.

This was why Max had dragged me uphill—to get away from the edge you couldn't see until ye were on top of it.

Jude cried out and spat. He kicked at Lochie who punched him again, connecting with a crack of bone.

"We need to help Cam," Max uttered.

We did, but I couldn't leave Lochie.

Except Cameron was bleeding. Maybe dying.

With a wrench, I moved towards my cousin.

"I knew you'd come," Jude shrilled. "I've been waiting for you."

"Shut the fuck up," Lochie growled.

"You tried to take Cait from me. She's mine. I love her and she loves me. I own her heart. Me. Not you."

"You're fucking nuts. Our hearts are each other's."

It was true. I only wanted Lochie and his beautiful, big heart, warm with love for me.

Jude slid a knife from under the purple jacket. A scream lodged in my throat, but I stifled it, clasping my hands to my mouth as I stalled my feet. Max dashed to Cameron, but I froze.

Lochie danced back right and Jude took a swing. Then he ducked and grabbed Jude's arm. Jude dropped his weight, pulling Lochie down.

The ground shifted under their feet. Snow slid. Rocks crumbled.

Falling, Jude raised the knife and brought it down in a shining arc. Straight into Lochie's chest.

Then both men disappeared over the edge of the waterfall.

39

Caitriona

My scream rent the air, and my muscles unlocked. I ran the short distance to the ledge overhanging the waterfall. Desperation ate at me, and I stared into the frozen abyss.

Below, on the rocks, Jude lay spreadeagled, still, and with unseeing eyes open to the drips of water spattering him.

Dead, I hoped.

Where was Lochie? I sobbed, scanning for him. If he'd hit the water, could he have survived the fall? It wasn't deep, but the jagged rocks were treacherous.

"Lochie!" I screamed.

Clumps of snow plunged into the depths, the edges of the ravine broken.

I couldn't move away. There was nothing. No sign of the huge mountain man.

I crawled, leaning too far. I had to find him. Had to.

Max landed by my side, a hand restraining my arm.

Blood. He was covered in blood. My brother jerked his gaze around.

"Where the hell did he go?"

"He fell," I croaked. "I can't see him."

"No," Max swore. "Fuck. Cameron's bleeding heavily, shot in the shoulder. We have to help them both. I've radioed, but we need to move fast."

Which logically meant helping the man we could see, not the one missing.

"I can't leave Lochie," I bit out.

"Caitriona," came a fierce but strained shout.

I gasped and peered over farther, using my brother as a support. Below, Lochie's fingers gripped the muddy rock face.

Oh God, he was alive.

He was only feet below us but at a horrible angle under the ledge. I could only see part of him, but I knew he was in a desperate position.

"He's here," I uttered. "He didn't fall."

The earth under Lochie's boots crumbled, dropping into the dark rocks below.

Max growled and hauled me back, then took up my position to spot Lochie. "We'll get ye out. How's your grip?"

"Bad. And there's this..." Lochie replied.

Max blanched at whatever he saw. He swallowed. "You're going to be fine." He drew back and forced himself to focus on me. "Ropes, Cait."

"What did he say? What's the problem?"

"Ropes, I said. Get the rucksacks."

A clatter sounded, and we both jerked.

Max grabbed my coat and hauled me upright. "I need to lower myself down to fetch him. I'll need your help. We cannae wait for the others to get here."

"But your arm."

"I can support us both until help arrives.

I pressed my trembling fingertips to my lips then nodded once. I couldn't hold Lochie's weight. If I tried, we'd both fall. If he was badly hurt...

No, I couldn't think like that. I flew downhill to where two rucksacks waited in the snow near where Cameron curled on the ground. He breathed, and his eyes were open.

But the amount of blood... His torn jumpsuit revealed the ruin of his shoulder, a pad of some material hastily applied by Max.

"You're going to be okay," I told my cousin, forcing my way through utter terror. "People are on their way, do ye hear?"

"Where's Lochie?" he forced the words.

"Over the cliff edge." I couldn't lie, and my voice broke. "We're going to climb down and get him. Ye just stay calm, okay?"

"Fucking hell. Go, dinna wait on me," Cameron ordered.

With both bags in my arms, I half ran, half stumbled back to the ledge. Max searched inside them and extracted a coiled rope and a harness.

But with his broken arm, he had no chance of climbing down or supporting Lochie.

"You'll break your neck," I said. "There's only one option. I'll go."

"No," Max argued. "I'm healed enough. I can hold my own weight. His, too."

A pained intake of breath had us both glancing around. Cameron staggered close and sat heavily, clutching his shoulder.

"Anchor," he gritted out. "Use my weight."

"Throw the rope," Lochie shouted. "It's about to go. Throw it now."

Max attached the harness and got into position where he could see Lochie. He swore viciously then unravelled a length and passed the end to me. "Dinna let go. Sit with Cameron. Have him grip onto ye," he ordered.

I followed the command. Cameron anchored me, his breathing too fast, his pain level undoubtably unreal.

The tang of his blood filled the air.

Max threw the rope.

Almost instantly, it jolted, jerking me and Cameron, burning my fingers where it tore into my skin. An anguished shout came from Lochie, and I could only stare at Max's expression. Whatever he battled, only resolute purpose showed.

Lochie would survive this. He had to. We'd get him out.

My brother hugged the cliff face, leaning as far as he could. "Grand. You're doing fine. Kick away. Aye, higher now. Another foot and I'll reach ye." He shot a look back at us. "Keep up the tension. Pull on my command."

I stiffened my muscles. Hauling Lochie's weight seemed impossible, yet we had to.

"Pull," Max hollered.

The three of us heaved. Cameron grunted in pain but pushed onto his heels, leaning back. I did the same, standing to take the strain.

"Again," Max bellowed.

We hauled, dragging the rope several inches through the snow.

"Again," Max repeated, his throat tight.

All my energy went into the rescue. My ruined hands, my boots jammed into the mountainside. Every inch of my body and soul went into saving Lochie. He was my heart, my one great love. I couldn't lose him. Wouldn't.

Max stopped us, breathing hard. "One more time, then I need ye two to hold it on your own. Cam, how are ye doing?"

"Fine," our cousin panted. "Let's get the heavy fucker up."

Max gave a laugh that was mostly pain and gave the instruction to pull. Then he carefully released his hold on the rope.

Cameron and I braced as well as we could. But blood welled on my hands, and my grip turned slippery. Likewise, Cameron was losing power, his bleeding shoulder worsening by the second.

Yet Lochie was so close. We couldn't fail him now.

Max said something low to the man on the cliff. Whatever answer came drove greater worry through my brother. He pressed his lips together and then, with a quick glance our way, lowered himself over the cliff edge.

"What the fuck is he doing?" Cameron gasped.

"No clue."

Max's upper body remained in sight, his arms gripping a rock, and his cast an encumbrance and in the way. I imagined he was somehow giving Lochie a boost, or his body to grip onto. I had no idea.

A helicopter chopped the air. Shouts came from down the slopes. The whole confrontation had taken place in minutes and turned deadly in seconds.

Hurry, I willed the others coming to help us.

"Climb over me," Max growled. "Use me to get over the lip. Swing yourself around so ye dinna drag your chest. Aye, like that."

His chest. Where Jude had stabbed him? God, it must be bad.

The granite under Max's arms cracked. More rocks tumbled. My brother yelled, his hold failing.

"Pull now," he shouted in utter desperation. "The ledge is about to go. Pull!"

I gave a howl of despair and heaved, putting every last drop of myself into it. Cameron gave up an agonised yelp of pain but backed me, still stronger than I was despite his crippling injury.

Lochie struggled to the edge, his bloodied face in sight.

Disaster struck.

Max's stronghold failed. The rocky shelf broke into pieces, falling to its peril below. Max grabbed the rope, his weight far too much for Cameron and me. We were about to lose them both to the fall.

But hands landed besides ours.

Fresh strength joined where ours failed.

Voices of the rescue team filled the air.

In a kind of dream sequence, I watched on as Maddock and Wasp hauled Max back to safety, leaving him gasping something from the ground. Then they grasped Lochie, only half in his harness, and brought him up, communicating with careful orders and stark worry etched into their features.

Behind, the helicopter landed, more shouts and voices battling for dominance.

Cameron and I collapsed, then his da joined us and took over caring for his son.

I could only stare at Lochie.

At the man I'd loved and almost lost, and still might.

Jude's knife stuck out of his chest, embedded through his jumpsuit, the red of his blood dark and insidious.

He'd stabbed him directly in the heart.

---

a too-fast beat marked the next several hours.
Thud, thud, thud.

The rescue team worked on Lochie, getting him into the helicopter, me, Cameron, and Max alongside him. They extracted us to a city hospital, which, I wasn't sure.

Thud, thud.

Surgeons worked on Lochie, removing the evil Jude had instilled in his heart. *Keep beating, keep beating for me,* I willed.

A nurse patched up my hands. Max received treatment for minor injuries and to reset his arm, broken once more from trying to hold Lochie's weight.

Cameron went under the knife to remove the shotgun pellets and close his wounds.

I needed them all to be safe and well, but I couldn't pull myself away from the waiting room, from where the doctor would find me and tell me Lochie was okay.

Nothing else mattered.

My parents called, Isla under their care. They'd told her Lochie had been hurt but that the doctors were fixing him. I spoke to her and repeated the words, telling her we'd both be home soon.

Oh God, please be true.

After hours had passed, still I'd heard nothing. Someone pressed a cup of coffee into my bandaged hands. Food was offered, but I couldn't eat. Then Ma arrived, and I burst into tears in her arms.

Thud.

"Is the family of Bram MacNeill here?" a voice called.

I jerked up from the plastic seats. "That's me."

The doctor arrived in front of me. "Mrs MacNeill? I'm Claire White, Bram's surgeon. Your husband has had quite the ordeal."

I couldn't bring myself to correct her or to fill in Ma on the name change underway.

"Is he okay?" I asked with a wavering voice.

"The injury left a bleeding wound in the right ventricle anteriorly. It was a tricky surgery."

"His..." I had no clue what any of that meant. "Is he still alive?"

The doctor smiled. "Indeed. We were fortunate that the knife didn't do more damage. The operation was a success. He should be awake and able to see you soon."

My fear crested, and I took a heaving sobbing breath, then collapsed onto my mother. She held me tight and stroked my hair while I cried. Dimly, I was aware of her asking questions of the doctor and politely bidding her farewell. Then she led me to my chair and sat me down.

On her heels in front of me, Ma raised my soaked face to hers. "He was injured but has been fixed. Broken ribs from the fall, cuts and bruises and bumps—they'll all heal. And his heart is working just fine."

"I couldn't bear it," I quavered. "If he hadn't made it..."

"I know, sweetheart. I know."

Ma held me until the police found us to take my statement. They made reference to recovering Jude's body, but I didn't want to know.

Months ago, I'd told Lochie how dangerous obsession could be. But I'd only had half the facts. The danger lay in the holder of the emotion, not in the feeling itself. I loved Lochie with every ounce of my being, was obsessed with him to the point of no return. But he was with me, too.

From now on, not a day would go by where I didn't let him know the facts of our love.

In the battle for Lochie's heart, only I could win.

40

*L*ochie

     I woke to a band of pain across my chest, my body complaining at every slight movement. Where the fuck was I? White sheets, an annoying beeping sound, tubes piercing my skin.

Caitriona, in a wide chair, her face in her hands, white bandages around her palms.

Fuck. This was a hospital.

"Caitriona?" I croaked, then I tried again.

I needn't have bothered. She heard and leapt to her feet. With joy in her moves, she took in my expression, tears welling in her eyes.

"Oh God, you're awake."

"Cameron, Max, are they okay?"

She gave a happy laugh and wiped her eyes. "Cam had surgery, like ye, but Max is lurking around, waiting to see ye."

"How long have I been out?"

"Since yesterday. They kept ye sedated so they could

monitor your heart. But your doctor said you'll make a full recovery. Do ye remember what happened?"

I examined my memories, wading through my abject fear at seeing that fucker Jude point a gun at the woman I loved. "I do. Is he dead?"

"He is. Neck broken by the fall."

"Thank fuck for that."

Caitriona's lips curled in a half smile. "I feel the same. The police have been by. I gave my statement already. Jude's uncle left a message, too, sort of apologising, so they must have gone to him. As far as I'm concerned, I don't want to waste a second thinking about him."

She flicked her gaze over me, emotion so close to the surface.

"God, Lochie," Caitriona said. "I thought I'd lost ye. When I saw ye fall..."

She sobbed and wiped away another errant tear.

Marry me, I wanted to say.

A hasty thought. If I was going to propose, it would be on one knee, naw flat on my back. I had no clue if my woman even wanted marriage, but I'd find out, and if she'd have me, I'd make her mine forever.

"I'll never leave ye. Nothing can make me. I love ye." I drew her in for a kiss. "Entirely, and forever."

The entrance of a doctor broke us apart, and after tests and prodding, I heard the story of my surgery in more detail than I liked. They'd fixed my heart up good enough for Caitriona. That's all I cared about.

The doc left, encouraging me to sleep, but I didn't need that.

I only needed to hold my woman and know that she was well.

Within an hour, the door swung open, and a nurse

entered. "Your daughter is here, Mr MacNeill. I wanted to check if ye were awake for her."

"Aye, please, bring her in."

With Scarlet and Ally behind her, Isla swung into the room like a whirlwind and flung herself at me. My stitches pulled, and something ached, but I held my daughter close.

"Are ye okay?" she asked.

"I am now you're here." I held her hard and greeted Caitriona's parents.

"Cait said you're a hero," Isla breathed.

I raised a hand to point at the man who appeared in the doorway.

"Nah, that's this young man."

Max leaned on the frame, his face scratched and his arm in a new cast.

"What the f— I mean what the hell," I corrected myself, mindful of Isla, "was that about with ye hanging off the cliff? Ye could've died."

"And risked the wrath of Cait for letting go of ye?" His typical teasing smile flickered. "Easy decision to make. I have to say, if ye didn't weigh twice what I do, that would've gone a lot easier."

I snorted, and he grinned bigger, his da shaking his head.

A rap came at the door, and my nurse reappeared. She studied the machines monitoring my heart and other vitals, and gave us all a grin. "It's good to see your family gathered around you."

My family.

They were. The McRaes, and Caitriona, had become my family. I'd found a home with them, and made a space for myself and Isla in their world. I looked between their smiling faces, Isla escorted outside by Scarlet, as comfortable with her as if she were already her grandma. Caitriona grabbing a pen to write on Max's new cast.

Aye, my family.

I'd do anything it took to keep it.

---

*A*fter a few days of good behaviour, on Christmas Day, I was allowed home. Caitriona and Isla collected me, and we drove home together.

At the door to my place, Isla skipped inside, and I stalled my woman at the door.

"Stay with us," I asked.

Or maybe ordered.

I wanted her to live with us, always, but for now, we'd start slow.

She blinked at me then swiftly nodded. "Okay."

That decided that.

It was a few days before I was back on my feet properly, and Caitriona's parents took Isla for Christmas dinner and to a party, but my strength returned fast. I planned to meet the team, to show my face and give thanks.

We had a command centre to rebuild. A debrief over the hoaxes and how it had all panned out.

One person hadn't answered my calls.

"I cannae get hold of Cameron," I explained to Caitriona.

Sitting at the dining table, in the bright winter sunlight, she chewed her lip. "He's still in hospital. He didn't want to worry ye so asked me not to say."

Still? But it had been almost a week. Max had been to see me every day. There had been a flurry of doctors and visits. How had I missed the lack of contact from my right-hand man?

"Why?"

She swallowed. "Further surgeries. The gunshot blast caused more damage than first thought."

"Will he be okay?"

"Eventually, they hope."

Her phone rang, and she frowned at the screen then took the phone into our bedroom to answer it.

I dialled Wasp. "I only just heard about Cameron. How is he? Give me the latest."

Wasp got to the point. "He's going to be out of action for a while. He cannae use his arm until his shoulder heals."

"He must be going mad. I tried calling him."

Wasp sighed. "My son isnae one to sit still. He's forced to now, and will be so for some time."

I muttered how sorry I was for him, and how I wanted to visit soon, when he allowed me. We said goodbye, and I worried my nail on the edge of the sofa.

Being forced to lie in bed for a few days had given me a fresh perspective. Like Cameron, I rarely sat still long enough to reflect on life. I worked better on instinct and going with my gut.

If the lad had a change of career coming up, a possibility if the damage to his arm was extensive, I'd find something for him that kept him active.

Then there were my problems. With the hospital recording me by my given name, rather than my assumed one, I was back on the map for being found, should someone be hunting me.

The jury was still out on Liv's family.

I didn't trust any of them. I couldn't let them near Isla. But I wasn't sure now that they'd pursued us.

My phone buzzed with an incoming text.

Blair: Home in a week. I'll visit.

My sister was coming home? And...she'd messaged my number?

My phone buzzed again.

Blair: Merry belated Christmas. I'll bring a gift for my niece.

I sent back a reply then raised my gaze to Caitriona. She joined me on the sofa.

"My sister messaged me. Until now, we've only been in contact on an untraceable phone."

"She called a phone left in your truck. I told her everything that had happened. She'd been expecting ye to contact her and assumed you'd gone rogue and were hurt."

Ah God, in all the drama, I hadn't thought to text Blair. I'd left the burner phone on, too. What a mess.

I scrubbed over my beard. "She'll be here soon, apparently."

"I can't wait to meet her."

Caitriona gazed at me, so pretty. But sadness glimmered in her eyes.

"What's wrong?" I asked carefully. "Did something happen?"

"That call... It was the fertility clinic. They were trying to get hold of me with my test results." She swallowed and looked away. "I was so worried about what they might say, except it hasn't even crossed my mind in over a week. I've been given the go-ahead to try to get pregnant, but they warned me it could take time. She said it could be expensive and I might want to consider other options, if I had any."

My aching heart thudded. "Can I be your other option?"

Caitriona swung her focus back on me, a desperation burning in her. "I want that. I want ye. But do ye even want more children?"

I reached for her and brought her into my arms, ignoring the stabbing pains that accompanied my warmest thoughts about this woman. She was hurting more. I had all the words to reassure her, but there was something I needed to do first.

Isla had a say, and I wanted her to be a part of my plan, too.

"Aye, I do. Can ye wait for a counter offer from me?" I asked quietly.

Caitriona stiffened then settled.

For a long moment, we just held each other.

Finally, she uttered a single word that I knew meant so much more.

"Yes."

---

*B*lair arrived in the middle of the night in a borrowed car and with only a military-issue backpack. I launched out of the cottage door and snatched my tanned and somehow harder sister into a hug.

We weren't a hugging family, but she let me all the same. For a moment.

"How's the heart?"

"Still ticking."

She gave a short nod and that was it, care issued and over.

I led her inside, and Caitriona joined us. I made the introductions between my sleepy sweetheart and my indomitable only living relative.

Caitriona pressed her hands together. "I'm so glad you're here. Isla is asleep, but she'll be thrilled to see ye in the morning. I made chicken stew this evening and set ye aside a portion. Shall I warm it up now? We've also made up a bed in my cottage, right next door, so ye have your own space."

Blair looked Caitriona over then grinned at me.

I knew exactly what she was thinking, how I'd found the perfect person for me. And she was right.

Blair settled in, delighting Isla the next morning.

But however much she wanted to see her niece, my sister had an objective in mind that matched my own.

Two days later, Blair and I set out on a drive to our old hometown of Torridon. Liv's family still owned a house there, and Blair's contacts had informed us that both brothers now lived there, along with Liv's mother.

With any luck, they'd all be home.

On a mission, we arrived at the remote house on the coast. Around, a splendid backdrop of sea and mountains were washed in glorious winter sunshine.

Blair was armed. Under our shirts, body armour protected us.

But this was precautionary.

My sister's research had turned up a different picture than expected. No more did they appear to run a drug importation business. As with Liv, the brothers had become addicts in prison. The older, Danny, had turned a one-eighty after completing his sentence. He now volunteered as a lay pastor, giving up his time to counsel youngsters in trouble.

I idled the car at the end of the short road. "Ye know, for years I feared seeing these people. I talked to Cait about it, and we linked it back to my childhood."

Blair sighed. "How Da's abuse made ye overprotective to the point of extreme? Aye. It's the reason I fight, too. No point dwelling on that shite, brother. Those abilities keep me safe, and they enabled ye to protect your woman. Suck it up. We're going in."

I approached the house with a new resolution that I wanted from the day.

At my knock, Danny appeared. He smiled, glancing between us. "Can I help ye? It's rare we have strangers visit here."

"Bram MacNeill," I said carefully.

Blair remained silent.

Danny's smile remained in place, then recognition flickered.

"Bram? Of course! And Blair, is it not? I wouldn't have known ye. It's been so long. Come in."

He admitted us, and we entered a quiet and tidy home.

In a comfortable arm chair, an older woman dozed. Liv's ma.

"Ma?" Danny said. "Do ye recall Bram and Blair?"

The older woman jerked awake, scanning us. "Aye! Forgive me. Welcome."

Just like that, I'd met Liv's family again. Not that they could've been more different.

Danny made tea, telling us all about his pastor work. His ma summoned the younger brother, a quiet lad on a drug's treatment programme.

When Blair raised the father's name, all family members gave the same expression of disgust.

"My ex-husband will set foot in this house over my dead body." Liv's ma folded her arms. "It's my home. My mother owned it before me. The divorce awarded it the same. I cannae regret marrying him because he gave me my bairns, but in the name of the wee man, I cannae stand the thought of Daniel senior."

Her hands shook. Danny hugged her and reassured her.

"Your daughter, Liv," I said slowly. "I saw her in jail a couple of weeks ago."

"She let ye visit?" Danny asked. "The poor lass willnae see us. In time, we'll bring her home, if she wants it."

I glanced at my sister, because this was crunch time. I could walk away without mentioning Isla, or I could take the risk and forge a connection on her behalf.

For the entirety of her short life, I'd kept her close, but no more. Isla deserved better.

"Liv has a daughter. My daughter. Her name is Isla. Would ye like to see a photograph?"

And just like that, I built a bridge.

By the time we left, I had pictures for my daughter—an idea I'd taken from Caitriona, who had an album made by her da of her birth mother's family—and a promise to one day introduce her to her ma's relatives.

I kept our address to myself, needing more time to take greater steps, but the day felt momentous.

I only had greater ones to come.

*I*n our warm car, high up on the mountain and overlooking the McRae estate, Isla sat by my side, sharing her snack of carrot sticks with me. Just the two of us today, Blair had returned to work. This morning, Caitriona had done Isla's hair in a pretty twist, and I gazed at my lass, so grown up.

I swallowed against a surge of emotion. "Are ye happy here?"

Isla whipped her head around. "Aye, Da. Don't say we're going to leave."

"I'm not, but there's something I need to tell ye. About us, and how we go on."

She listened, her eyes wide.

I reached for the album I'd made. At the front, it had pictures of Liv and her kin, then me with Isla as a bairn, and more of her growing up. I'd left pages empty at the end to add more family photos, as and when we took them, and if we ever found out more about her biological father, but the bare bones were here.

My hands shook as I passed it over, open to the first page.

"You're old enough now to know all about your background, including your birth parents." I forced out the words, calm and clear. "Your ma's name is Olivia. She was my friend, and she fell pregnant with a boyfriend but came to me to raise her bairn. I became your father, though in my heart, not in my genes."

I'd torn my soul to shreds over this, but it had been my mistake not doing it from the start, so I deserved the suffering.

Isla nodded along, flipping the pages. "Where is Olivia now?"

"In prison. Her family would like to meet ye one day. I know them from a long time ago."

"Are they nice?"

"Aye, and they'll love ye."

"Do I have to see them?"

"Naw if ye don't want to. The choice will always be yours."

She pursed her lips but didn't say anything further.

I pushed on through my rippling emotion, needing to make the point clear. She'd learned genetics at school, so I knew she had the basics. "I'm your da, and I always will be, but not genetically. Do ye understand?"

Isla stilled, then turned her huge blue eyes on me. In her hands, she'd arrived at the last pages of the book, the blank ones, our unwritten story from now on. "Can Cait be my ma?"

I'd expected half a hundred different outcomes to my statement, but never this. I stared, my throat tight and no words coming.

"Can we ask her? Please, Da. I want to stay here forever. Ye love Cait, I heard ye tell her. Please, can ye marry her?"

She'd accepted everything with barely a blink, then decided how she wanted it to be. The baby question could come later, but I knew she'd be happy.

"Aye. We can. Will ye help me with my proposal?"

Isla squealed and leapt in her seat to hug me. I held her tight, such utter relief replacing my fear that it spun my head.

Every year, as Ally had done with a young Caitriona, I'd talk Isla through her story, making sure she knew the facts and give her the chance to ask questions. The hardest part was complete, and I was a man freed from shackles of my own making.

With Isla shouting ideas, I had a new plan to arrange. One where Caitriona became mine forever. Ours. A happy family together.

41

Caitriona

In the car next to me, Isla fidgeted, messing with her seat straps and drumming her hands on her legs. We'd paid a visit to see Casey, Lochie meeting with his rescue team, and were now heading back to ours for dinner.

Our pattern of living as a family had been easily found.

At the end of December, Casey had delivered her baby, and we'd visited multiple times, taking food for them and getting baby cuddles from tiny, month-old Callie.

It made me broodier than ever, but the desperate drive I'd had as a single woman had been replaced by a softer need. I wanted a little time with Lochie and Isla first. Nearly six months ago, they'd arrived in the cottage next door, and I'd fallen in love with both of them, wholeheartedly and completely.

Lochie had asked me to wait for an important question.

Whatever he offered me, I'd say yes.

We pulled up outside of the house, and Isla undid her restraints and shot out of the car. She rounded to my side and opened my door before I could reach the handle.

"Hurry up," she demanded.

"What's the rush?" I asked.

Isla made an off noise and grabbed my hand. All afternoon, she'd been clock-watching.

An anxious thought took root in my mind.

This was it. Wasn't it?

I peered through the dark and frosty January evening. Candles glowed in the cottage.

"Oh God," I uttered.

Isla laughed and dragged me. She hammered on the cottage door then opened it and darted in.

Right to her father's side.

In a smart shirt, Lochie knelt on the floor, waiting on me. In his hand was a small box. Around, more candles glowed, casting warm light over flowers on the table and my handsome man. I'd never witnessed a scene more beautiful.

I closed the door and leaned against it, my heart hammering.

Isla beamed at us both and cleared her throat. "Da has something to ask ye. For both of us."

Tears sprang into my eyes, and I swiped them away, not wanting to miss a second.

Lochie smiled and beckoned me closer, then opened the box to expose a gold ring studded with three diamonds. Simple, beautiful, and perfect.

"Caitriona, from the first moment I saw ye, I knew ye were extraordinary. Ye took two lost souls in me and my lass and made us a home. Both of us love ye. Both of us want to keep ye. Marry me, please. Become my wife and Isla's ma. Make us the happiest family that ever lived."

"Say yes!" Isla cheered. "Please, please, please."

My heart swelled, overbrimming with more love than I

could believe existed. "God, yes! Of course I will. I love ye both, too."

I half fell into Lochie's arms, bringing Isla into the mix. She squeezed us tight then danced around the living room, ecstatic in her joy.

Lochie stared at me. He took the ring from the box and slid it onto my finger. Then he kissed me.

"Ew," Isla yelled.

I loved her so much, but right now, I only had eyes for her da, and my hunger for him grew. Later, when his—no, *our*—little lass slept, I'd show him how much this meant.

Lochie kissed me again softly, then stood and glanced out of the window.

"Right," he said to Isla. "Grab your bag."

I glanced between them. "Where are we going?"

A horn sounded outside, and Lochie grinned.

"That's your ma. Isla's having a sleepover at theirs tonight."

Oh.

My pulse picked up, and I hugged Isla on autopilot then waved to Ma from the door. She beamed but didn't come in, instead sweeping Isla into her car.

Thank heck, because I had a huge man to tackle to the floor and prove my love to.

But Lochie had his own idea. The moment he closed the door, he turned and grabbed me, and threw me over his shoulder.

I choked on a laugh, the upside-down hallway showing me where he was taking me. Then I landed on our bed and lifted my gaze to find Lochie dragging off his shirt, shedding buttons in the process.

"Whoa, someone's in a hurry." I beamed.

"Clothes off," he ordered.

I shivered at his dark tone and stripped in seconds. Then he knelt on the bed between my legs and covered my body with his. Already hard, his dick throbbed against my core.

Bare.

In the past month, we'd slept together every night, but neither of us had mentioned birth control. Or stopping using it. I knew he was giving me a chance to adjust to the idea of us becoming a family.

I was already so rich with love.

Lochie kissed me, our words lost to our lips and the passion that swept over us like a forest fire. One kiss led to more and, in a minute, we were clasping each other, want and need building to a crescendo. His bare skin grazed mine.

My core was slick and wet, ready for him.

Then Lochie slowed and pressed his forehead to my cheek. "Fiancée," he muttered.

I chuckled and sucked in a breath. "Ye like that?"

"Wife will be better. Do I get to call ye beautiful now?"

I burst out in a laugh. Months ago, I'd asked him not to, but how things had changed.

"Aye," I murmured. "Can we get married soon?"

"Whenever ye like, my beautiful lass. I need to ask ye something." He glanced down between us, to his dick so close to my entrance.

"No more condoms," I said for him. "I already have you and Isla. You've given me everything I could ever need. But if we had a baby, too…"

Unleashed, Lochie surged and filled me, the stretch so *right*. I moaned, and he notched his head to my shoulder, pausing for a second before withdrawing to thrust again.

"That will be perfect," he uttered. "You're perfect. All mine."

Those were the last words either of us said for a long while. With the house empty, we made the most of our privacy, loving each other and taking our time to show exactly how much. From our bed to the shower and back again, it was late by the time we made it to the kitchen for food.

Deliciously sore, I hugged my arms around Lochie's t-shirt that I'd claimed, and watched him warm up then serve a meal he'd made.

Tomorrow, we'd surprise Isla by getting her a puppy. One day, we'd hopefully add to our family even more.

I'd never expected him, but Lochie was truly my other half. For so long, I'd been alone, and I'd thought myself happy.

How far I'd come.

Happiness was a grumpy, growling mountain man, made for me and perfectly mine.

And I, Caitriona McRae, was well and truly obsessed.

EPILOGUE

*C*ameron

On the warm bonnet of my car, I reclined, not that I could feel the tiniest degree of relaxation. Tension and stress racked me, and I grumbled to myself, watching the sun descend from my high point on the mountain. Months had passed since I'd been shot. Multiple surgeries had removed the pellets, the last just a few weeks ago. With physiotherapy to help the nerve damage and rebuilding muscle, I'd get back to my old self, and to my job.

I needed that physical exertion like I needed air.

A fucker to achieve when I couldn't use my strength.

In the meantime, I was going out of my mind. I couldn't work. Couldn't sleep. I felt stupid for putting myself in the line of that fucker's shotgun barrel.

Lochie allowed me to help with the training and management of the mountain rescue but refused my request to go on call-outs. I missed it. The hard use of my body.

Truth of it? I was pent up, strung out, and seriously bored.

A dangerous combination of emotions for a man like me.

I worked hard to keep a calm exterior, and not to show the wildness inside me, but the battle was getting tougher. Soon enough, I'd lose it altogether.

From down in the late-spring heather, Ellie gave a *wuff,* and seconds later, my phone rang from inside the cab. I leapt down, ignoring the pain of the jolt, and collected the device.

Leo, the screen read. My favourite rock star, and husband of Viola, my cousin. I spent a lot of time with the couple and worked for Vi's da, often living in their castle while they were away on tour.

They were home now. Vi was due to give birth in a couple of weeks so they'd be around for a while. I answered the call, a grin at the ready.

"Cam, I need to ask a favour," Leo said.

"God, anything. Put me to work."

"I have a friend coming to stay on the estate. They need collecting from the airport tonight. Viola's in some pain, and I don't want to leave her. Can you help?"

"Nae problem. Give me his name and flight time, and I'll fetch him."

"Her," Leo corrected. "This is where it gets complicated. My guest is Elise. You know the film star? She acted in one of my music videos and she needs a getaway to handle some shit that's going on. I told her where better than the Highlands? I have a bothy organised for her to stay in, but there could be problems with getting her here safely."

I hummed interest, but my mind was away, spinning. Leo didn't know, but from a young teen, I'd had the biggest crush on Elise.

Notorious for many reasons.

So fucking gorgeous she had me in pieces.

In my darkest moments, recovering from my injuries, I'd let her pretty face be my distraction. I'd played her movies too many times, lost in my own thoughts and needing to climb out, and using fantasy to do so.

Even my damn dog was named for her. I reached and ruffled Ellie's fur, and she panted happily then bounded into the car.

Aye, I knew the name Elise, but I wasn't daft enough to imagine I knew anything about the real person.

Then I caught up with Leo's words. "What do you mean problems with getting her here?"

"She's being hounded by the press. If they find her and follow her back to the estate, she'll be worse off than when she started."

My sense of alertness ramped up, adrenaline flooding my underused system. "Will they chase the car?"

"I hope not. Don't get into a pursuit."

Leo filled in the rest of the details. She'd land in Inverness in just a few hours. I'd come face to face with the woman I'd imagined so many times.

I hung up, and my heart thundered.

Finally, I had a purpose. A dark night, roads I knew like the back of my hand, aye, I was the right man for the job. I just had to wind in my age-old crush before I met the lass of my dreams, then prepare to save her from those who hunted her.

* * *

*E*lise

I was being followed. Despite the subterfuge—my disguise, zero entourage, and the cheap plane ticket to a place no one should be able to find me—I sensed attention on me, hot and cloying.

Stifling where already I could barely breathe.

I stole a peek over my shoulder, using my raised hood and carry-on bag to hide the look.

Farther back in the arrivals queue, a figure stared right back at me.

Fuck. Fuck!

A photographer, I was certain. Or was I being paranoid? That was possible. I shuffled forward as the line moved, fear sweeping down my spine.

As soon as I'd got off the plane, I'd read Leo's message about his friend collecting me. Though he'd sent a picture of the man and the car license plate, tendrils of panic flooded my already mixed-up system.

Strangers pursued me. A stranger would be driving me.

I was a mess. Daylight scared me. Life fucking scared me. After everything that happened on that movie set...

No. I couldn't think about it.

This short break was meant to help, yet dread was my new best friend.

"Miss?" A voice summoned me forward to the immigration window.

I handed over my passport with trembling fingers.

The woman showed no reaction to my name or face, and only waved me through. My heartbeat picked up more.

This was my chance.

The person who'd somehow followed me on my flight was still in the queue. I didn't have any luggage beyond my bag so I was good to go.

As soon as I'd cleared the corner, I took off.

Sprinting, I rounded the barriers and jogged through the airport, my legs unsteady after the long cross-Atlantic flight. The dark night outside called me, and I burst from the exit, sucking in my first breath of cool Scottish air.

But I moved too fast. My feet hadn't stopped when they should.

I stumbled straight into the road.

Right into the path of a large off-roader.

The wide blue eyes of the driver—the man from the photo Leo had sent—were the last things I saw. Then everything went black.

The End.

Order Cameron and Elise's exciting and swoony romance, Hunted (Wild Mountain Scots, #2), here.

Want a glimpse at Cait and Lochie's happy future? Download their free sweet and steamy bonus epilogue here.

(Note: Downloading bonus material adds you to Jolie's mailing list. You can unsubscribe at any time. For the Wild Mountain Scots series, bonus epilogues will be included as in-book content to the preorder and launch day version of the books only.)

You can jump back to where it all started with the Marry the Scot series. Meet the daddies. Boxed Set Volume I. Audiobooks.

ACKNOWLEDGMENTS

Dear reader,

I'm thrilled that you picked up *Obsessed (Wild Mountain Scots, #1)*. If you're a new-to-me reader, you're in for a treat, as I have another two series of hot Scots for you to jump on into and read.

To those of you who have been long term fans, I trust you'll have enjoyed Cait's story, and her journey to a different life than the one she'd envisaged. She believed herself asexual for so long, but the correct term would be demisexual - only experiencing attraction where strong feelings exist.

I'd like to make it clear that Georgia's views – that Cait was in some way deficient because she didn't want a relationship – are horribly outdated. Cait would've been fine on her own, and an excellent mother. All forms of family, when centred around love and respect, are equal. But this wasn't her fate - Lochie was made just for her.

The set up I've used for the Scottish mountain rescue service is fictionalised, though it's true that the RAF has retired its SAR function, and elements of the role have been taken up by civilian contractors. I have endless respect for the men and women who volunteer to go out and save souls in all kinds of conditions. It's rarely glamorous helicopter rescues. Their hard work deserves recognition.

You'll be happy to hear there are at least three more books planned, for Cameron, Maddock, and Max. Onwards with the series!

Thanks go as always to my writing besties, Zoe Ashwood and Elle Thorpe, who handle my crazy rants, proofreading, and graphic design. You guys are never allowed to go anywhere (said in a spooky voice).

Liz, my PA, has taken on the unenviable task of trying to keep me organised. She does an amazing job, and I am in awe of her skills. Thank you, Liz!

The gorgeous cover was designed by Elle at Images for Authors.

Line editing by the wonderful Emmy Ellis at StudioENP.

Perfect cover photography by Regina Wamba reginawamba.com.

Fabulous cover model: Steven Christensen.

Beta readers Shellie, Sara, and Elle, you rock! Your hilarious guesswork was fun to read during the editing process.

A huge thank you goes to my ARC and Street Team members. Your reviews and posts make me so very happy. I treasure them (and often print them for my pin board).

Love and hugs to all those invested in the happiness of the McRaes and their extended family (which now includes ye).

Are you in my Fall Hard Facebook reader group? I'm often over there chatting.

You can add yourself to my newsletter too.

Jolie x

ALSO BY JOLIE VINES

Marry the Scot series

1) Storm the Castle

2) Love Most, Say Least

3) Hero

4) Picture This

5) Oh Baby

Wild Scots series

1) Hard Nox

2) Perfect Storm

3) Lion Heart

4) Fallen Snow

5) Stubborn Spark

Wild Mountain Scots series

1) Obsessed

2) Hunted

Standalones

Cocky Kilt: a Cocky Hero Club Novel

Race You: An Office-Based Enemies-to-Lovers Romance

Fight For Us: a Second-Chance Military Romantic Suspense

Visit and follow my Amazon page for all new releases amazon.
com/author/jolievines

Add yourself to my insider list to make sure you don't miss my publishing news https://www.jolievines.com/newsletter

ABOUT THE AUTHOR

JOLIE VINES is a romance novelist who lives in the UK with her husband and son.

Jolie loves her heroes to be one-woman guys. Whether they are a huge Highlander, a touch starved earl, or a brooding pilot, they will adore their heroine until the end of time.

Her favourite pastime is wrecking emotions, then making up for it by giving her imaginary friends deep and meaningful happily ever afters.

Have you found all of Jolie's Scots? Find her page on Amazon and join her ever active Fall Hard Facebook group.

SNEAK PEEK - STORM THE CASTLE (MARRY THE SCOT, #1)

Chapter One – A Wall of Man

*M*athilda

As a little girl, I'd dreamt of hearing the words 'Marry me'. Soft music playing in the background and a ring offered from my lover's eager hands. This, of course, was before my closest example of marriage became a warning rather than an inspiration.

My childish, rose-tinted vision had never involved me standing in the corner of a glittering conference, freaking out over the proposal I'd just received.

Dominic Hanswick, my father's business partner, had watched Dad leave then taken me to one side. He'd been polite and concise as he'd laid out his terms. "Marry me, Mathilda. Save my reputation. Save your sister in the process. Think about it. I'm sure you'll find it a reasonable idea." He'd offered it so easily then he'd smiled and moved away through the tables, murmuring pleasantries to colleagues.

A business deal, he'd called it.

Who said things like that?

My head already ached like I'd been in a hit-and-run, the dreadful lunch I'd had at my parents' home still forefront in my mind. Scarlet's behaviour was the only reason I wasn't laughing this off.

Shocked, I'd barely asked Dominic any questions, but now dozens came to mind. God, he wouldn't expect me to sleep with him, would he?

I needed answers, and standing around in my flat sandals wasn't getting me anywhere. My job for the evening was done—I was only at the event as a favour to Dad, meaning I could leave and return to my hotel, but this had thrown me for a loop. With a calming breath, I left the safety of my alcove and crossed the hall.

"Mr Hanswick?" I tapped the shoulder of his smart suit, and the man turned. My would-be fiancé was a businessman, a senior partner with Storm Enterprises, the conglomerate my father ran. He was smart, had the stout figure of a man used to finer things, and at forty-two, seventeen years my senior.

Overall, Dominic was not what I had in mind when I'd envisaged my groom.

"If you have a moment, I need to ask a quick question." A vast understatement. I backed away from the group, smiling at people important to my dad. The model of a dutiful daughter.

Dominic excused himself and followed. His brow crinkled. "You have my business card. Set up a meeting, and we can talk through the finer details."

Right. And yet, "You said you wanted a marriage of convenience. In name only."

He glanced around, presumably to make sure we were out of earshot. "Naturally."

"What happens if I want to date someone?" Why was that so important? I hadn't dated anyone in months.

He sighed. "The point of selecting you, Mathilda, is that you're young, single, and practical. My home is big enough for us to live separate lives: you with your sister on one side, me on the other. This arrangement works for all involved. As for other...needs you might have, sleep with whomever you choose, but I'd recommend you stick to one-night stands. At least until we near the end of the five years. And for Heaven's sake, be discreet. I've had enough scandal to last a lifetime, and a cheating wife would set me back to square one."

"I see." I nodded along like this was anything other than insane. I knew Dominic had been the subject of press attention. He'd had an affair with a high-profile, married politician, and the newspapers had made a meal over it. Dad had ranted about the effect it had on Storm Enterprise's shareholders, so I knew Dominic was losing money fast.

Getting married would fix his reputation and save his bank balance.

None of this was my problem.

Scarlet's emotional health, on the other hand, was. Her chance at having a good future.

As if sensing my reticence, the man leaned in. Even though I was in my flats, my six-foot height meant I was looking down on him. "Your sister is off the rails. You can help her. Why wouldn't you do that? Your father will let you take her in if you're married, am I correct?"

How on Earth did he know that? I gave a slow nod. From behind me came the clamour of raised voices. Dominic's attention shifted to the source of the commotion, and his eyes widened as if in recognition. He gave me a short bow. "I have to leave. Call my assistant to set up that meeting, and we can finalise the arrangements. Just don't take a time over it. It serves us both to arrange this as soon as possible."

Then he was gone.

Rotating, I spied a vacant table in a dark corner. On the way, I grabbed a glass of water from a waiter then found a chair and laid my head back. My sister, Scarlet, nearly arrested again last week, worried me to death, and clearly Dominic knew enough about the situation to determine which buttons to push. It was the solitary reason I'd have to say yes, saving her skin and, separately, his, and why I hadn't yet laughed him out of town.

Not that I would do anything quite so unladylike.

A surge of frustration filled me from even entertaining the idea. I didn't want Dominic. He'd called me practical, and I was, but what about chemistry and heat and passion? I wanted more than the lacklustre relationships I'd so far suffered in my twenty-five years on the planet. Beth, my best friend, made a robot-Mathilda voice when I was being ultra-efficient, but inside I was like everyone else: desiring that overwhelming romance. The breathless appetite-quenching satisfaction that came from sex with someone I loved.

The love stories I devoured couldn't all be wrong.

If I took the marriage deal, on whatever terms, I wouldn't have the chance to find out. Then again, who's to say I'd ever find this relationship utopia. My last boyfriend had cheated, after all. Maybe a sham marriage and one-night stands could work. Passion based on the purely physical was better than nothing.

At the entranceway, a distance across the open hall, two men emerged through the crush. Both tall, the men carried a watchful air as the event's patrons left a moat around them, and my interested gaze skipped over each as they shook off the security staff.

The dark-haired younger man had the kind of looks you could stare at for an hour and praise God for pretty people. But it was the man beside him who caught my attention. And held it. Because *holy hell.*

Not only because of his size—he was one of the tallest men I'd ever seen—but for the way people orbited around him, and how he held his powerful, large body with ease as he reached out a long arm to take a glass of what appeared to be water. He gave the waiter a polite nod, and I warmed inside.

Lifting my drink, I tried not to stare. *"Good luck with that."* I imagined my friend's stage-whisper. If only Beth could be here to ogle alongside me. She'd nab a cocktail, rest her chin on her hands, and goggle freely.

The room lights flickered over the doorway, as if showing off for the big man, and a lick of interest curled in my belly.

Power impressed me. I couldn't help the fact.

Then, like I'd switched on a neon light that said "Look over here, big guy!" the man's gaze swept over the busy space and locked onto mine. I started, but he didn't move on as would be proper. Instead, he angled his head and ran an attentive glance over me. A fair eyebrow raised, appreciation lightening his serious expression.

The babbling noise of the room ramped up, and I dragged in a breath. Heat snaked under my high-necked dress, maybe from the intensity or maybe from the humidity, and I tore my gaze away, fidgeting on the chair. *Wow.*

If I was to ever try a one-night stand, he'd be top of my list.

Then my head panged again, and I winced. My cue to

leave. From my bag, I extracted my phone to book an Uber, and on the screen, a message already waited. Beth.

Testing testing, are you still alive? Did your dad make you do a speech?

I tapped out a reply.

Luckily, no. But he did tell a bunch of his colleagues that I'd be working for him soon. I should've just come home after lunch.

I'd journeyed to London this morning to see my family, and I could've been on the first train home to the house I shared with Beth. Instead, I'd gritted my teeth through an awful lunch, politely kissed my mother goodbye, booked into a hotel, then attended Dad's product launch. They thought I was getting the late train, though I hated travelling at night, otherwise I'd be forced to stay at my family's home. The mere thought had me shuddering.

Beth shot back an answer as Uber gave me a twelve-minute wait time.

Ugh, I'm sorry, honey. Want me to come get you tonight?

It was a generous offer, and a long drive, but I was too rattled by Dominic's offer and by no means ready to talk about it. Beth would expect me to be miserable as each visit to see my family took me a week to get over. But this... I needed to sleep on it.

Readying to leave, I let my gaze seek out the big man one last time. From first appearance, he wasn't the type of guy I'd usually find interesting. Rougher, less refined than a standard city-dweller. At a black-tie event, he was wearing jeans, so I guessed he was in the wrong room at the conference centre. He was a tourist, maybe. Though the way he and his friend had entered the place felt more purposeful than happy holidaymakers.

A mountain man, I mused, sliding my phone into its pocket in my bag. Used to harder living and working with his hands. Maybe he had a shack somewhere he emerged from each morning to cut wood and fetch water from a stream. He'd go swimming in a river some days.

Naked, obviously.

I grinned at my own fantasy, the levity of it the most exciting part of my evening. But my search of the event space was fruitless. The shy-looking model-type stood with his back to the wall. The interesting one had vanished.

More disappointed than I reasonably should be, I took a final sip from my water then eased myself up from the table. But as I stood, the strap of my sandal snapped, and I stumbled. My purse swung in a wide arc, knocking straight into my glass.

Down the glass fell, cracking on the seat. It shattered and rained razor-edged pieces over my feet. "Shit!" I squawked. And there was me, proud of how little I swore.

I danced away, but in the process, wedged my ankle against the chair leg, trapping a piece of glass. It stung. With a wince, I fell back onto the seat and clutched at my foot, losing my shoe. A sliver of glass stuck out from my skin. I touched the edge and nearly fainted.

Blood welled, and my head swam.

"What's happened here?" a deep voice sounded beside me.

I peeked up. And up.

It was the man. A *wall* of man, looking down at me. Sweet Jesus, he had to be close to seven feet tall. The top of my head wouldn't even reach his chin.

I opened my mouth and managed, "Be careful, there's glass. My drink fell."

Then, with the worst timing, a flood of emotion came over me. My evening had turned absurd. My tiny, stinging injury was nothing compared to the impossible offer my father's colleague had made me. Worse, I couldn't think of another way to help my sister than to accept him.

Marry someone I didn't care for.

Add to that the embarrassment of being a klutz in front of the most impressive man I'd ever seen, my horrible headache, and nausea from my lack of food, I wanted to curl up in a ball.

That was it. My head reeled double-time, my foot panged, and my brain checked out.

Like in an old-style romance novel, I swooned, and everything went black.

Read on...

Printed in Great Britain
by Amazon